I0551790

The
Dream Diaries

BECCA C. SMITH

Published by Red Frog Publishing, a division of Red Frog Media

Visit our website at www.redfrogpublishing.com

First published in 2014

Cover by Stephan Fleet

ISBN 9780990565024

Printed in the United States of America

Dedicated to Stephan, the love of my life.

Dream Entry #1

My name is Mara Johnson and I live in Seattle, Washington (although technically Lake Forest Park) and this is my first dream diary entry. I decided to write down all of my crazy dreams because sometimes they're a little too much to take.

Sure, I have "normal" dreams like everybody else, but I also have not-so-normal dreams as well. "Psychic dreams," I suppose you'd call them. I really despise the word "psychic." I cringe anytime anyone tries to label me with it, but I guess there's no other word for it. I dream about horrible, vicious crimes and a few days later they're on the news.

And it's not like I could be some kind of superhero and warn whoever it was I saw dying. When I dream, it's like I'm actually there. Real time. So, if I'm dreaming about you, you're already dead.

And I think it's worse in Seattle, "America's killing fields." That's what the FBI profiler of the Green River Killer said about our Pacific

Northwest area. And he's not kidding. I have a nightmare at least twice a month and maybe three out of all the killers I dream about are caught each year. Or at least reported about on the news.

Sometimes it makes me wonder if the other murders I see are actually real. What if my brain creates these horrific images because it's so used to seeing the real ones? Like I'm connected to evil or something. I can't allow myself to think like that though, it'll make me crazy. As in, more crazy than I already feel. So, I'm just going to write out all my dreams here in this diary and pray no one finds it. Because if anyone did, they'd probably lock me up.

***

Mara placed her new diary on her bedside, wondering if it was such a smart idea to be writing down her nightmares. Paranoia threatened to overwhelm her. Knowing every detail of a crime would make her look guilty. How would Mara be able to explain her journal to the police if they arrested her for murder? And how archaic was it to write on actual paper! She wasn't used to writing anything at length with a pen. Her phone was practically surgically attached to her fingers. But she felt safer having her most private thoughts written down on only one source that no one could hack into. She knew how easy it was to find things in the ether of cyberspace and download it to her cell or laptop. And the things she planned on writing in her diary would definitely be hack-worthy material.

Turning off the light on her nightstand, Mara snuggled into her warm and cozy down comforter and closed her eyes. She was exhausted, but not tired, a sensation she was all too familiar with.

Having nightmares on a regular basis made the whole sleep thing a little difficult. It had been this way since she was seven and had her first "vision."

Mara's great uncle, Uncle John, had been her favorite person on the planet before he died. He wasn't actually her uncle by blood, but she was more connected to him than the woman he married, her great aunt Eleanor. Uncle John was so full of love and light! Mara always looked forward to visiting him. Both Mara's grandfathers had died when she was only a baby, so Uncle John was the closest thing she ever came to having a grandfather. John and Eleanor were in their seventies when Mara was a kid and they lived on a small island in the Puget Sound called Lopez. Her great aunt was Uncle John's second wife, since his first wife had passed away before Mara was born. Great Aunt Eleanor had been their maid.

She didn't think much of her great aunt except for the fact that her skin always reeked of alcohol. It always made Mara gag when she was forced to sit on her lap for bedtime stories. But dealing with Great Aunt Eleanor was always worth it to spend time with Uncle John. He would take Mara and her sister, Josie, on adventures around the island. One of their favorites was walking down to the beach to dig for clams, then carrying the tasty treats back home and steaming them for dinner.

Mara berated herself. She should have known her great aunt was going to kill her husband. It had been so obvious the summer before it happened, when the whole family stayed with Eleanor and John for a family reunion.

The two of them had argued the last night of Mara's stay. When her sister, Josie, tried to hold Mara back from investigating,

Mara shrugged her off and left their room to see what her great aunt and uncle were screaming about.

Mara snuck up to their bedroom door, then cracked it open to garner a better view.

In front of her seven-year-old eyes, Mara saw her great aunt leveling a pistol at Uncle John, screaming at him to stop hitting her.

He was ten feet away.

She was punching herself in the stomach, face, arms and legs: anywhere that would show a bruise.

Mara didn't understand what she was seeing at the time, but hindsight made it clear later on. Her great aunt was planning to kill Uncle John and she wanted witnesses to say it was self-defense.

As a child, though, Mara simply didn't know what was happening. Her great uncle looked scared, but at the same time, calm, as if he had dealt with this kind of behavior before.

When Uncle John glanced at the doorway and saw little Mara peeking in, he smiled and told her to go back to bed.

But Eleanor?

She whirled on her niece and stared at her as if Mara had betrayed her.

As if Mara had ruined all her plans.

Great Aunt Eleanor's look told Mara that she wanted to kill her niece.

So, Mara did the only thing she could think of: she ran into the room where her parents were sleeping. When her mother told her to go back to her own room, Mara grabbed a small throw-blanket off a chair and lay on the floor. There was no way she was going back out into that hallway.

Not with Eleanor there.

Though she didn't know it at the time, it was the first time Mara had stared into the eyes of a killer.

Something she never wanted to do again.

The next morning Mara awoke alone in the room.

Without knowing why, she stood up, opened the sliding glass door leading to the back patio, walked outside and crawled into the doghouse in the center of the courtyard.

Mara hid there, not knowing why. It was as if a voice had told her to, guiding her to the doghouse. Whispering it would be safe there.

Within moments, the slurred bellows of her great aunt reached Mara's ears. "Didn't your mother ever teach you not to play with knives?"

Little Mara froze in fear. Where was her mother? Where was her father, sister, aunts, uncles? Didn't they hear what Eleanor was screaming? Didn't they know Mara was shaking in the back of a doghouse, terrified her life was about to end?

But everyone – except Eleanor – had gone down to the beach to dig for clams, not wanting to disturb their sleeping daughter…

The legs.

That was what Mara remembered the most.

Seeing her great aunt's fat, hairy legs walk past the doghouse made Mara's skin crawl.

Eleanor kept repeating the phrase, "Never play with knives, little girl," followed by an amused cackle as she searched the grounds for little Mara.

When Eleanor was twenty feet away, Mara saw the blade of a

butcher knife grasped in her great aunt's hand.

Her heart immediately pounded in her throat.

Murdered by a seventy-year-old woman who she never really liked and stank of alcohol!

Mara's heart almost stopped altogether when Eleanor leaned down and made eye contact with her.

Her aunt had found her.

And Mara was about to die.

But she didn't.

At that exact moment, Mara's family returned to the house from the beach with a bag full of clams in each hand.

Their friendly faces and shouts of "good morning," and "hello," were enough to make Eleanor quickly hide her knife and walk back inside the house.

Mara never told anyone what had happened.

She just wanted to forget it and never think about it again. The event was so out of Mara's realm of *reality* that, after she was riding back home on the ferry, she almost forgot about the entire incident. Life made her forget. Playing with her friends, going back to school, being a kid.

It wasn't until the night Great Uncle John was murdered that it all came back to her.

And Mara had dreamt the whole thing.

Eleanor was screaming at him, blaming him for her horrible life. That she didn't have to wait to make killing him look like self-defense. That she didn't need witnesses. No one would miss him. No one would care...

Then, BAM! Eleanor shot John in the head.

That would have been bad enough, but Mara was forced to

watch as her great aunt dragged John's body into the bathroom and proceeded to chop him into pieces. There was so much blood! Mara tried desperately to wake up, but the dream wouldn't let her. She had to witness her great aunt stuff the body parts into a bag and dump them in a barrel outside, dousing the whole lot with gasoline.

When Eleanor lit the flame that would destroy the only grandfather she ever knew forever, Mara finally woke up.

In those days, Mara and her sister Josie shared a room. Mara had opened her eyes frozen in shock and fear. She couldn't call out, she couldn't move. It took her over an hour before she could squeak out a tiny yell to her mother, Claire, on the other side of the house. Her voice was so quiet Josie didn't even wake up at the sound.

But mother's instincts didn't need volume.

Mara experienced a flush of relief when she heard her mother's voice call back, "I'm coming!"

Claire stayed up all night with her daughter, trying to calm her down.

The next morning Claire phoned Eleanor and John to assuage Mara's fears about his death, and Eleanor assured her that everything was fine, that John was only away on business.

It was a story that Eleanor managed to keep up for almost six months – until the local police became involved. They found the charred pieces of John's bones, and then a very public trial followed. Eventually Eleanor went to prison for the crime.

The Lopez Butcher.

That was what the press called her.

The name always sent chills down Mara's spine.

Eleanor was a killer and Mara was related to her. By Blood! Sometimes that thought alone kept Mara awake at night.

But just ten years after the murder, most people had forgotten, to Mara's relief. Luckily, no one knew she was related to Eleanor. Her dad's name protected the family from being discovered, since Eleanor was related to Mara's mother, and it wasn't like anyone knew her mother's maiden name anyway. Mara had only told her best friend, Zia, about her family connection to The Lopez Butcher. But Mara trusted Zia to keep it secret.

Mara was grateful her relationship to The Lopez Butcher was hidden because high school was hard enough without being shunned and ridiculed because you were related to a murderer.

All Mara knew, though, was that after her dream about Uncle John being butchered, something must have opened up a part of Mara's brain. A part that could witness horrible crimes like his death, because she'd been having the nightmares ever since. Or maybe it was being related to a killer. Maybe her great aunt had dreams like Mara's and she finally acted on them by killing her husband. These were the thoughts that plagued Mara. She hated seeing what she saw. It didn't make her feel special or unique, it made her feel dirty. Like some part of her was connected to something sinister.

Mara constantly had to shove those kinds of thoughts down. Especially now, when she was trying to sleep!

Other than her dreams, though, Mara was a normal teenager. She had just turned seventeen in the summer and, now that school was starting again, her parents had bought her an old '66 Volkswagon Beetle. It was a clunker, but her father, George, declared that, since "all VW Bugs run on rubber bands and luck," he was willing and able to fix anything that might go wrong. Mara didn't want to call him "cheap," per se, but he was definitely a penny pincher. She didn't care though. Having her own car was thrilling beyond measure. It meant freedom. Sure, she only went to the movies and the mall, but now she could do it without her parents.

Her best and pretty much only friend, Zia, also received a car for her seventeenth birthday over the summer. It was a *brand new* VW Bug, so it was fun to compare the modern day version of the car with Mara's older model. Mara thought it would be weird not to take the bus with Zia. They had been regular bus-ers since the seventh grade so they were both enjoying their freedom immensely.

The first day of senior year would be starting the next day and Mara was a bit nervous. Kimiko Thompson and mean girls in general, hated her for some reason. Probably because they couldn't understand why Zia wanted to hang out with her more than them, but Mara decided long ago to simply try to keep out of their way. If she didn't have Zia, her life would be full of what she considered "Facebook Friends," which basically translated to nothing real, just acquaintances who wanted to make their Friend count high so they stooped to accepting her Friend request. In the halls of school, they completely ignored her.

Mara tried to quiet her mind so she could fall asleep. Since this was always an impossible task, she resorted to her tried and true method of shutting out her busy thoughts by repeating the words, "I'm exhausted," over and over. Eventually the tedium of that mantra made her head believe it and forced her to focus on one thing as opposed to a million.

An hour later, she finally dozed off.

***

Oh no.

Mara chastised herself for starting that damn dream journal and rehashing thoughts of her great aunt! She knew it would make her have another nightmare!

But when she saw whose house she was in, Mara knew she would have dreamed this, diary or not.

She was in the Garner's house across the street from hers.

No. No. No. No.

She couldn't bear watching something horrible happen to someone she actually recognized again. Since her great uncle John's murder, Mara thankfully had never witnessed a crime against anyone she knew personally.

Ed Garner. He was in his seventies and couldn't hurt a fly. His wife, Millie, had died a few years back from liver cancer; since then he'd pretty much become the hermit of the block. The Garners had been a staple in the neighborhood Mara's whole life and always gave out the best Halloween candy every year. Who would want to hurt a nice old man? Especially a widower!

Mara realized immediately that this dream was different from her others. Normally, she'd watch the horrific scenes take place as if she were in some kind of 3D movie, seeing what happened like a fly on the wall. This time, however, she was physically *inside* the killer's body!

Because she had never experienced this before, Mara hoped that maybe he was just a burglar. Maybe, this was the Universe altering her visions into something more tolerable. It would be terrible to watch such a nice man like Ed Garner being robbed, but at least he'd be alive. And maybe the thief would walk by a mirror and she could identify him. Mara could lie and say that she'd been up late because she was nervous about the first day of school and she saw the burglar running out of the house.

Mara had the whole scenario planned as she watched the man (yes, definitely a man, she could tell by his gloved masculine hands and large feet) walk through the upstairs hallway. She would be a hero. Maybe this would change her destiny and she'd never have to see another murder again.

The man opened the door at the end of the corridor. Inside the room Ed slept soundly in his bed.

Mara shook the fear out of her as best she could, trying to rationalize why a burglar would risk being caught by going directly to where the occupant of the house was located. Did most people keep their money and valuables in their bedrooms? Yes, that had to be it. He'd be very quiet, but he'd be able to steal all Mr. Garner's goods without even waking him.

Denial. Denial. Denial.

The word haunted her mind, Mara tried to push it out of her thoughts. She had to stay positive. Nothing had happened yet: usually her visions started right in the middle of a killing, there was no lead-up like what was happening now. Her usual nightmare dreams were vicious and short, so…

This had to be something different.

It just had to. Because if this was happening *as* Mara was dreaming it and this man was going to *at this moment* murder her neighbor, then Mara would never be able to forgive herself for not waking up and calling the police. The time it had already taken for the intruder to walk down the hallway could have been enough time to scare him off and save Mr. Garner's life.

Wake up! Mara screamed to her subconscious.

But she was locked in the intruder's head.

Mara kept trying to somehow take over this man's body. Force him to leave the house. But it didn't work that way. She was stuck as an observer.

Desperately wanting him to search the room for valuables, Mara's heart sank when he pulled out a container from inside his jacket. When he opened it, inside lay a syringe filled with a clear liquid.

Mara's instincts and years of dreams kicked in as she immediately looked at the reflection of the window, hoping that at least she could be of some good. If this man was going to murder Ed Garner, she was going to make sure she could identify him.

Disappointment flooded through her. He wore a dark ski-mask to match his dark clothing.

Mara wished and prayed she could wake up. This was too much to bear. Being made to watch something so vile was a cruelty that proved to her there was true darkness in the world.

The man took the syringe and walked softly toward Ed.

Wake up! Wake up! Mara screamed in her head again.

Nothing.

She couldn't do it.

Details.

She needed to remember the details. Anything that might catch this guy.

Mara wanted to close her eyes in her own dream, but a part of her curse was the inability to shut it off. She'd always compared it to the torture scene in the movie *A Clockwork Orange*, as if there were invisible prongs prying her eyes open.

The man reached down and injected the liquid into Ed's neck.

Ed woke up gasping.

He jumped to a sitting position, clasping his chest, trying to breathe in air. He suddenly noticed the killer standing before him and choked out, "Who are you?!" Upon realizing that the man was the person responsible for his seizing chest, Ed tried to leap to his feet, but whatever was in that syringe got the best of him. He stumbled, tangling himself in the blankets.

The killer pulled off his mask.

Mara desperately tried to see his face in any reflective surface, but there was nothing near him.

When Ed saw who the man was, he looked confused. His breathing came in short, quick gasps as he sputtered, "I… don't… know… what… lies…"

But he never finished his sentence.

His head dropped to the floor with a small thud.

Ed Garner was dead.

Normally, this was when Mara woke up.

But it didn't happen.

Her dreamscape changed and she was in the middle of a field of sunflowers. The yellows and browns were so sharp she found her dream-self squinting from brightness. It was such a stark contrast of horror versus beauty that Mara wasn't sure what to do.

"Mara," a voice sounded behind her.

She whirled around and her whole being filled with joy.

Great Uncle John stood before her. No bullet holes, no evidence of what her great aunt had done to him anywhere on his body.

Mara fell into him. The dream was so real, she could even feel the heat from his chest as he embraced her lovingly. She wanted to stay there forever. Mara didn't want to think about what she had just witnessed. Being with Great Uncle John felt safe.

He pulled away slightly to look down at her.

That was when she realized she was now in her seven-year-old body, staring up at her great uncle's kind, adoring eyes. "You're in danger, Mara."

"Is the killer coming here? Is he on some kind of spree?" Her thoughts jumped to the most terrifying scenario.

Uncle John shook his head. "You're safe tonight. But the danger is coming, Mara. Keep your eyes open."

"Is this really you?" Mara wanted it to be her grandfather of the heart. Seeing him made her feel better.

"It doesn't really make a difference, does it, whether I'm your subconscious or a guardian angel? All that matters is that you listen: watch with both sets of eyes. You'll need them to save what you love most."

Huh?

"Wake up," he whispered.

***

"Seriously, wake up!" Josie's voice caused Mara to open her eyes. Her younger sister grabbed Mara's arm and yanked her out of bed, pulling her to the window. "The cops are all over the Garner's place! What happened? There's a body bag, but they're not telling anyone what's going on, just to 'Stay in your houses.'"

Her sister's long blond hair was pulled back in a messy ponytail and her bright blue eyes were wide with expectancy. Josie was younger than Mara by two years and on days like today, it showed.

Both girls were thin like their parents, and they had their mother's delicate facial features, although Josie's nose had a bump on the bridge from where she broke it on the monkey bars when she was six.

Mara rubbed her eyes, hoping beyond hope that her dream had been simply that: a dream. But seeing the police and the flashing lights of an ambulance parked across the street only proved that what she dreamed had really happened. But it was the second dream that haunted her at that moment. Uncle John's words kept repeating in her head: *Watch with both sets of eyes. You'll need them to save what you love most.* What did that mean? *Both* sets of eyes? As far as Mara knew, humans only had one set of eyes. And what did she *love the most*? It was probably a brain fart after having to witness Ed Garner's

15

gruesome death, but still… It had been so real…

Mara swatted the thought away and focused back on her sister. "How should I know what happened?" Mara hid the truth, not wanting to talk about her vision.

"Oh please! You've been dreaming about murders for like ever and you're telling me one happens across the street and you don't see it? I know you better than that. And I know it's only impossible to wake you up when you're in one of your trance-thingies."

No, Josie wasn't going to let this one go.

Mara sighed and flopped back down on her pillow.

This, apparently, was proof that Josie was right, because she sat down next to Mara. "Spill," she ordered.

Her sister's enthusiasm irritated Mara. "It's kind of gross that you're all into knowing the details, you know."

Josie rolled her eyes. "Yeah, yeah, it's called being human, ever heard of it? Staring at car accidents, watching horror movies, any of these things ring a bell?" Then she dropped her false bravado and the reality of the situation kicked in. "It's Mr. Garner, Mara! Like the nicest fuddy-duddy on the block! Who would want to hurt him? I'm not being morbid, I'm just… I don't know… scared. Hearing about a murder is one thing, but seeing an actual real crime across the street? It's freaking me out!"

Mara could see that her sister was scared. And she should be. All this happened while the neighborhood slept peacefully. A supposedly *safe* neighborhood at that. "I couldn't see the killer's face, he was wearing a mask." She didn't want to tell Josie that she was in the murderer's body. It almost felt like she'd be admitting to the crime itself. Then she realized being stuck in his head made Mara experience first hand what it was like to kill someone. "I'm going to barf." She ran to the bathroom.

Before Mara could empty the contents of her stomach, Josie was right behind her, holding back Mara's long brown hair. For a fifteen year old, her voice was soothing. "You're going to be okay, Mara. Just get it out."

After a few dry heaves, Mara knew she wasn't going to puke.

Her sister let go of her hair and the two of them sat on the bathroom floor. Josie reached over and squeezed Mara's arm in support, then instructed, "Don't tell Mom or Dad. I just thought… if you saw the guy, maybe… but it won't do any good to come forward. The cops will just think it was you."

"Thanks," Mara groaned, her worst fears brought to light by her lovely sister.

"You know what I mean." Josie tucked a piece of Mara's hair behind her ear affectionately. "I'm sorry I barged in here and almost made you throw up. I'm an idiot."

Mara cracked a small smile, though it was forced from the surging emotions flowing through her. She sighed deeply. "It's okay. I just… it was a long night."

"Well, it's going to be a long day, too. First day as a Senior." Josie wrinkled her nose sarcastically, "And aren't you sooo excited?"

"Not in the least."

Josie stood up and helped Mara to her feet. "Well, either way, you better get ready. We have to leave in a half hour."

"We?" Mara asked with dread. It didn't take future-seeing dreams to know what was coming next.

"Yeah. Mom says you have to drive me to school this year."

Fan-tastic.

Dream Entry #2

This stupid diary was supposed to be about my horrible dreams. I didn't expect to have one the night I started writing in it! I have about five minutes before my mom yells at me to go to school, so I thought I'd jot down a few things about last night's nightmare. 1) It was the first time I've ever been inside the killer's head before. (And hopefully the last!) 2) Ed Garner seemed to know the man because he started to tell his killer something about lies. 3) How did the police know it was murder? I mean, to the untrained observer it would probably look like Mr. Garner had a heart attack in bed. Someone must have seen the killer run out of the house or something for the police to be called in. And 4) What the heck was in that syringe? Some kind of poison, obviously, but it wasn't instant. I don't think that was an accident. I think the killer wanted Ed alive for a few brief moments to confront him. I'm about as positive as I can be about that. But why? What did Mr. Garner do to this guy?

I have to think about it some more, but I think these things could be important. I think my dream or vision or whatever it was with Uncle John was important, too. It can't be coincidence that right after seeing Ed die I was suddenly with Uncle John in a field of sunflowers. He always used to call me his little sunflower. I guess it could be my subconscious trying to deal with Mr. Garner dying in front of me. I could have created Great Uncle John in my dream to comfort me. I just don't know. I'll have to percolate. But now for the details of the murder…

***

After Mara wrote down every single detail of what she saw in her dream, she heard her mother yelling at her to come down for breakfast. She quickly stuffed her diary in her three-ringed binder in case she wanted to write in it at school. Running to her bathroom mirror, Mara made sure she was presentable.

She wasn't exactly a fan of her looks, but most of the time she decided not to care. Her hair was dark brown and cut in long layers, which she usually tied back in a ponytail. Having hazel eyes made her feel somewhat different, in a good way, since her mom's were brown and Josie and her dad's were blue. She hardly wore any make-up, just some mascara to make her eyes look a little bigger, but otherwise cherry-flavored lip balm suited Mara just fine. When she was positive she was free of any zits or mascara smudges she raced out her door.

Her bedroom was on the second floor, along with her parents and Josie's rooms. The house wasn't huge, but it was comfortable and "home" to Mara. Okay, yes, most of the houses on the block

19

were built about the same, but all had their own unique personal touches, and Mara loved the familiarity of her neighborhood so much better than the cold, cookie-cutter, gated-community McMansions springing up all over town.

Squeaking on the dark brown hardwood flooring that covered the whole house, Mara's black and white Converse sneakers were almost falling apart since she wore them so much. Her steps were much quieter on the only carpeted area in the house: the stairs. And it was a good thing too since Mara had a habit of falling both up *and* down the stairs. It wasn't that she was particularly clumsy, she just was usually too wrapped up in her own thoughts to pay attention to something like walking properly.

Mara's mother, Claire, decorated the house with framed picture collages of the family's entire existence since both her pregnancies. It was kind of embarrassing how many photos there were of Mara and Josie. Her sister would joke that their mother was a stalker, but both girls knew it was because Claire simply loved them to pieces. And, apparently, she proved this by plastering their faces over every inch of empty space in their house.

At least their rooms were safe from Claire's decorating. Mara kept hers fairly clean of wall hangings, except for the small shrine of posters and trinkets above her desk dedicated to Harry Potter. She had read every book eight times, except book five, which she only read twice. In Mara's opinion, number five was a small hiccup in an otherwise perfect series. Reading was definitely her thing. It was her one escape from the real world and the dream world. The Potter series was the only set of hardcopy books she owned, since her parents bought them for her as a kid. Nowadays she had an entire library's worth of books on her phone.

"Are you two really going to dress like that on your first day?" Claire eyed her daughters with concern as Mara entered the kitchen area.

Claire had soft curves and a round face that always seemed perpetually upturned in a smile. At least to strangers. At home, Claire definitely wore the pants in the family. Mara knew she was lucky that she had such great parents, and her mother was one of the kindest people she knew, but if Mara ever did something bad, Claire could shoot out a look that sent shivers down her spine. Her mom called it the "Floyd Look" after her father who had died when Mara was a baby. Apparently, if Grandpa Floyd wanted something done, he could simply stare at you and you'd be at his beck and call. All Mara knew was that when Claire was mad, no one *smart* wanted to get in her way.

Both Mara and Josie rolled their eyes, but it was Josie who responded. "Mom, would you stop already. We're not dressing up for school. Ever. Again."

Every year Claire wanted the girls to wear their Sunday best on the first day of school. When they were very young, she was able to talk them into it. Somewhere around thirteen though, both Mara and Josie came to the conclusion that it was extremely embarrassing going to school in their "fancy clothes." Mara had been stared at and teased all day wearing her pink pastel dress and straw hat the first day of 8th grade and she vowed never to let her mother pick out her outfits again. She became a jeans and t-shirt kind of girl after that and stayed loyal ever since.

Today, Mara was sporting her favorite Hogwarts jersey and dark blue skinny jeans. Josie was dressed similarly in jeans, but her shirt displayed the Seahawks logo on the front. Not that her sister was into sports, but she was better at fitting in than Mara. Mara would even go as far as to say that her sister was somewhat popular. It was always a strange thing when people asked Mara if she was *Josie's sister*, since Mara was the oldest. It should have been the other way around, but Josie made the bigger impression on people, so they always thought of her first.

"Mom, no one is going to care about what anyone is wearing *today*." Josie nodded her head toward the window. The flashing police lights were a sudden reminder of what happened the night before.

Claire barely glanced at the window. "I don't want you girls talking to any of those reporters out there." She eyed Mara cautiously.

She was fishing. Mara knew her parents mostly tried to write her visions off as bad dreams, nothing more. It always threw a wrench into their fantasy world when one of the nightmares popped up in the news.

Mara decided to take her sister's advice from earlier and not worry their mother. "I'm not going to talk to anyone. I would have nothing to say anyway."

Relief flooded Claire's face, but she tried to hide it by changing the subject. "Your father left early so he doesn't even know… about that." She didn't want to name the crime or the victim. "I'll call him when you two leave." Claire glanced at the clock. "Speaking of which, you girls better hurry. You're going to be late for your first day."

Mara and Josie grabbed the sack lunches that their mother had left on the kitchen island and headed out the side door leading to the driveway.

The police were tape-roping off the Garner's entire house and most of the road in front of it. Behind the tape barrier stood a slew of reporters and cameramen trying to investigate what had happened. Mara wasn't sure how many details the police had revealed to the public yet, but from the loud shouting, she guessed: not much.

It still struck her as odd that cops even knew it was murder. It wasn't as if anyone could have heard anything like a gunshot. Ed Garner had been murdered with a *syringe*: something like that really could have been mistaken for a heart attack, which wouldn't attract this much news. The general public wouldn't care if a nice old man died in his sleep. And Ed lived alone: as far as Mara knew, his only son lived in Portland or something. Mr. Garner's son wouldn't have known that anything had happened to his dad for days.

It had to be that someone witnessed the killer breaking in. Or his getaway. Then called it in. It gave Mara a strange sense of hope. Someone else possibly saw who did it. They might have a chance to catch this guy!

Remembering her vision last night, Mara shuddered. She didn't want to think about the images in her dream. They were so vivid that when merely recalling them it was like she was experiencing the murder "live" all over again.

Josie's voice brought her out of her reverie, "We gotta go." Her sister gently placed a hand on Mara's arm.

Josie was being extra nice, a rarity, but Mara appreciated it. It almost made up for the fact that Mara now had to drive Josie to school. Every day. For her whole *senior* year! Lame.

23

Nodding her head, Mara unlocked her forest green VW Bug and scooted into the driver's seat. Reaching across to the passenger side, she pulled the door handle to unlock her sister's side. One thing about her '66 beetle that was odd, was the fact that there were no locking levers on the top edge of the door, which meant anyone could open it from the inside even when driving. And, unfortunately, it was just as easy to unlock it from the *outside* as well. All anyone had to do was push open the triangle-shaped vent window, reach in and pull the door handle up. Not exactly safe or burglar-proof, but from everything else about her car (i.e. no shoulder straps or head rests) Mara could see that safety apparently wasn't the priority in the sixties. Still, like all seventeen year olds, she didn't mind at all. Those things only added to the uniqueness of her vehicle.

Pulling out of the driveway, Mara drove in the opposite direction of the Garner's because of the police block-off. It was the wrong way to get to school, but it was somehow freeing to drive away from that scene. The more distance she created between herself and the crime somehow made it feel less real, like a bad TV show or movie, instead of the nightmare-murder-come-true it actually was.

It only took five minutes to arrive at school being that Mara's house was a couple of miles away. Driving up to the giant monstrosity was always a little intimidating. Forest Green High School. *Very* imaginative name: painted a deep brown color, the high school blended in with the small evergreen forest surrounding it. The campus consisted of one large compound with four main hallways and a warehouse-size gymnasium/auditorium. Everything was enclosed due to the constant rain that Seattle was famous for, which made Mara feel a little claustrophobic at times. Mara was just one of fifteen hundred students in the ninth through twelfth grade school, so it was easy to get lost in the crowd whenever she wanted. It would be quite cozy if it weren't... school.

There were two parking lots reserved for students on the east and west sides of campus. Mara preferred the west since most of the popular kids parked in the east. Being that this was her first year driving she figured it was better just to ignore them. That way she could fly under the radar and be neither tortured nor teased publicly. Her social life had improved slightly when Josie started the ninth grade last year. Her sister was well liked by her class and made the cheerleading squad, something no ninth grader had done before. When the girls in Mara's grade realized that Josie was her little sister, they upgraded her status to *ignore-completely* as opposed to their usual snide berating snarks that Mara had been used to for her freshman through junior years.

It wasn't ideal, but she'd take it.

Mara was just happy she had Zia to make her days more bearable. Zia was her best friend on the entire planet and the only friend she needed. Unfortunately, Zia was completely blind to the fact that the popular kids hated Mara and loved her. Kimiko Thompson was the worst offender, always inviting Zia to parties in front of Mara and deliberately leaving Mara out. Zia was so sweet, though. She'd politely decline and say she was hanging out with Mara. This, of course, enraged Kimiko even more, but she was careful to reserve her Mara-aimed cruelty for when Zia couldn't witness it.

Mara rarely ratted Kimiko out, she kept those incidents to

herself, though some of the things Kimiko had done would have made Zia furious. It wasn't that Mara was trying to make her enemy look better, it was that she knew if she made a big deal out of it, things could get a lot worse. A *lot*. It was easier just to let a comment here or there slide by rather than blow it up into a full-out war Mara was sure to lose. She had no doubt about that. Kimiko had an army of mean girls at her disposal. What did Mara have? A car and a tenth grade sister. Yeah, she wasn't winning any battles with that arsenal.

Still, this was a new year. Maybe the mean girls would cut her some slack. Mara doubted it, but what else could she do?

She exited her car and debated whether or not to bring in her umbrella. The sky was overcast, but it didn't look like it would rain, though Seattle weather could change abruptly throughout the day. Deciding against it, she grabbed her book bag from the back seat and walked with Josie toward the entrance.

People were already forming crowds just outside the front doors. From their animated expressions Mara could tell they had heard the news about Ed Garner. It was too close to home not to gossip about and, even though Mara was sure no one knew the details, murder was enough to spook them.

Without a good-bye, Josie left Mara's side when she saw her sophomore clique.

Alone, Mara moved past the small packs of students and walked inside Hallway D, heading to her locker. Each of the main hall throughways were at least two football fields long and they all were sandwiched between the two parking lots. Unfortunately, Mara's newly assigned locker was at the east end of the hallway, making it even more ridiculous that she'd parked on the west side of the building. Still, she consoled herself while trudging through the seemingly endless hallway, limiting exposure to Kimiko and her crew at least gave her some exercise.

After the long trek, Mara situated herself so that her back was to the east side entrance, that way hopefully no one would see her. Normally, she didn't care this much, but after last night's dream experience, she just couldn't handle any bad energy at the moment. She knew she would be oversensitive for a while, so it was best not to "poke the sleeping bear," as it were.

Opening her locker, Mara wanted to give herself a face palm. *First day, Ding Dong, you don't have any books yet.* She had been so wrapped up in everything that had happened last night and this morning and so paranoid about running into Kimiko Thompson that she didn't even connect to the obvious fact that her locker would be empty on School Day #1.

Mara stuck her bag into her locker, as if this had been her intention all along, then pulled from the bag the three-ringed notebook that held her diary and a pencil. Being able to choose the order of her classes, Mara had decided that she wanted Calculus to be her first period. She enjoyed starting the day off with math. It helped her cope with whatever the day might bring. It woke up the part of her that loved to figure things out.

Today, she just hoped it would help her forget.

"Did you *know?*" Zia's voice sounded from behind Mara.

She turned around to see her best friend wearing an expression of worry all over her face. Zia was so beautiful, Mara often wondered why Zia wanted to be her friend when she could be friends with anyone she wanted. Her dark skin was accentuated by a smattering of freckles across the bridge of her nose and her large brown eyes seemed even bigger because of her abnormally long eyelashes. With a button nose and perfectly full lips, the girl was gorgeous. Zia's tight curled hair was pulled back in a fluffy ponytail that bounced slightly when she walked. Considering Zia was five foot nine, Mara was surprised that she hadn't already started a modeling career. It wasn't like she wasn't stopped in the mall every five seconds by scouts. Okay, maybe it was once, but still.

Mara understood immediately what her friend meant. Zia knew about Mara's dreams and was the one who had convinced her to start a diary about them. Mara could keep her parents in the dark about her nightmares, because that was where they wanted to be, but she couldn't do that to Zia.

Mara nodded. "It was right across the street, what do you think?"

"Can you tell me what happened? Or do you need some time?" Zia asked thoughtfully.

Mara surveyed the area, not wanting any prying ears to listen in. The hall around her locker was pretty packed, but everyone appeared to be talking to other people and not paying them any mind. So she told Zia every scary detail and voiced all of the questions and doubts Mara had herself.

Just as she finished, though, the first period bell rang. They only had five minutes to get to class.

Mara hurriedly closed her locker and they started walking together.

Zia reeled from what Mara had told her. She shook her head in amazement. "You don't think you should tell the police?"

"Tell them what? I know every detail of the case, arrest me

now?" Mara sighed. She didn't trust people, not when it came to her dreams. If Mara didn't experience it first hand she wouldn't believe it herself either. "If I had seen his face, maybe, but telling the police that I dreamt about a guy wearing a ski mask and all in black…? They'd throw me in jail on the spot. Or the loony bin."

"I guess, but still… What if something you don't even know is important could help them? This guy could do it again, you know."

"I know you're right, but I'm sure with all their C.S.I. stuff, they already know what happened. I really couldn't see him. What help could I possibly be?" During her dream, Mara's main thought had actually been to call the police and catch this guy. But that was when it was happening. Now? So much time after the murder? She couldn't do it. At the best, everyone would think Mara was crazy or just trying to get attention. At the worst… they'd think she had something to do with it.

And what if she told them everything she saw and she was wrong?

What if Mara just had a really bad dream on the same night her neighbor was murdered?

Yeah, right. Mara knew Zia was trying to help, but she could do without the pressure.

Her friend seemed to pick up on this because she nodded, smiling supportively. "You're right. I'm just sorry you had to go through that alone."

"Yeah, me too, but it is what it is, right? At least he didn't hack the guy to pieces or something horrible like that. It was kind of humane, I guess – in a not so humane way."

Mara arrived at Calculus.

Zia gave her a quick hug. "I'll meet you after class. I have Social Studies first period, oh joy." She rolled her eyes and tried to give Mara an encouraging smile.

"Fun. Say hi to Kimiko for me," Mara said snarkily.

Zia shook her head, amused. "She's not that bad. You should give her a shot."

"A couple shots to the brain maybe." Mara was being mean, but she couldn't seem to stop herself.

Zia laughed. "I'll see you later."

Mara waved good-bye and entered her math class. Being that there were only thirty seconds until the last bell rang, the room was already full.

Mara's heart leapt in her throat when she noticed that the only empty seat in the room was next to Adam Layton. It didn't help that she had thought Adam was cute ever since he moved into their school district three years ago freshman year. He was bullied by the popular kids the day he arrived, and the guys in her school were more physical in their taunting than the girls. He'd come to class with fresh bruises and cuts, but refused to tell the school authorities who had hurt him.

Today, he looked wound-free, and really freaking cute, with his short dirty blond hair, big blue eyes, perfectly straight nose and slightly pouty lips. The fact that he was one of the smartest kids in school made him even more attractive to her.

Mara wondered how she was going to be able to concentrate on Calculus when Adam would be sitting right next to her.

She sighed. At least she wouldn't be thinking about Ed Garner.

Dream Entry #3

I'm not exactly writing about my dreams, but I'm writing to look like I'm busy so Adam won't make eye contact with me. He tried to when I first sat down and I froze. I think he was going to say hi. What's wrong with me? He probably thinks I'm a jerk like everyone else that treats him like crap. But I'm crap, too! Well, you know what I mean. I'm treated like crap, too, so we would have a lot to talk about. But the thought of talking to Adam makes my chest hurt.

I really hope I'm not about to get a panic attack. I have them every once in a while and they're so embarrassing, especially when I have them in class. One time I had one in History when the teacher called on me. I started hyperventilating so bad I thought I was going to die. Literally die. I seriously believed that Kimiko had slipped me cyanide at lunch and that she was successfully murdering me in front of everyone! Luckily, my teacher thought I was asthmatic and sent me to the school nurse, who taught me a few breathing tricks to help me calm down. I committed them to memory ever since. In fact, I'm going to start them now. Omg. Adam's calling my name. He's trying to get my attention. Write. Write. Blah, blah, blah, I'm writing, I'm writing, math notes, math notes, look busy...

***

"Mara!" Adam whispered loud enough that Mara had to respond or she was positive he'd get in trouble with the teacher. She couldn't do that to him, no matter how painfully shy she was.

Mara looked up from her notebook and made eye contact with Adam. His eyes sparkled in amusement and it made her palms sweat. Mara was positive she looked like she had swallowed Drain-O, but she tried to force a smile.

"Yes?" she whispered back, looking quickly around to see if the teacher had noticed. Nope. Up at the front of the room, Mr. Trenchard rattled on about inverse functions, oblivious to anyone else but himself. Mara just hoped it stayed that way. The last thing she needed was to get in trouble on the first day of school.

Instead of talking, Adam slipped her a small piece of paper. Mara took it quickly, not wanting the teacher to see. As if she were a spy stealing state secrets, she placed the paper in her notebook to read it.

Mara's face flushed. The note had Adam's cell number with the sentence *So we can text* written above it.

She froze. It was bad enough when she thought she'd have to write back to him, but to have his number? And to text... what? Regularly? Did he have one specific question or did he want to talk to her a lot? Mara tried to steady her hands so he wouldn't see she was shaking. Why did this make her so nervous? Texting was so much easier than talking! But if they started a texting friendship, then sooner or later Adam would want to talk to her in person. Mara wasn't sure if that was possible. Her vocal chords often betrayed her when she was anxious.

But she had to do this, had to text back an answer to Adam. She had no other choice. Yes, it made her want to puke. But in a good way. Why did she have to turn into a blathering idiot when she liked someone?

Cell phones weren't allowed in class, but everyone used theirs anyway. It was all about how discreet you could be. Students were caught everyday, but if you were really good, they'd never even know you had your phone out. Some students even tried to cheat using the Internet for tests. Come test time, though, teachers circled the aisles like sharks trying to make sure no one Google'd the answers, but clever cheaters managed to hide their phones despite the teachers' hunting tactics. Although, last year, Mara's English teacher, Ms. Rose, went through the trouble of updating Wikipedia the night before one of her tests with incorrect answers. Five students were suspended for cheating. After that, not many people risked cheating anymore, but texting to friends in class? That would never stop.

Okay. Mara watched Mr. Trenchard like a hawk as he kept lecturing. Part of her was beginning to feel the guilt and worry that she hadn't listened to a word he was saying. That was probably going to bite her in the butt later when she attempted to do her homework, but with the adrenaline racing through her she didn't seem to care at the moment. When her teacher turned his back to the class to write a problem on the dry erase board, she took her chance and pulled out her phone from her back pocket. Being a *good girl*, Mara had turned it off, so now she waited impatiently for it to turn on.

Keeping her eyes on Mr. Trenchard, Mara typed Adam's number into her cell. Luckily, her math teacher hadn't seen.

Taking a deep breath, Mara had enough common sense to turn off her ringer and she prayed Adam had done so, too. The lovely *blip* of a text message notification could mean the end of them both. This was becoming more stressful than the fact that she liked a boy. Mara was not a rule-breaker by any means. She couldn't even jaywalk on a street with no cars. Going against the grain was physically painful for her. Her desire to people-please was the strongest motivator in her life. Peer pressure was useless on her. Mara pressured herself just fine.

Since Adam didn't have her cell number she had to text first. Oh man.

What was she going to say? *What do you want? What's the meaning of this? Who are you? Why are you making me do this? We're going to get in trouble! You're really hot.*

But instead she chose: *Hey. This is Mara.*

She was so nervous about being discovered, she hit send. And immediately regretted it. *This is Mara?* Real smooth. Of course he knew it was her, he was the one that gave her his number. And who else would be texting as he literally watched her type and hit send.

Before she could panic further, Adam texted back: *I saw you on the news this morning. You were in the background about to get in your car. Did you know him?*

Great. When she was staring at Ed Garner's house, the news cameras had caught it. No, she hadn't been the focus, but if Adam Layton recognized her, other people would too.

And her heart sank a little.

Adam didn't suddenly wake up this morning and realize he liked Mara Johnson. No, he had seen her on TV in front of a house where a murder took place and wanted the scoop. If he knew about Mara's dreams, he'd probably be drooling.

And part of Mara was suddenly a little relieved. If Adam didn't like her like *that*, then there was nothing to stress about. It was kind of liberating in a way that made Mara a lot less nervous.

She texted back: *Yeah. He was really nice. Still don't know what happened.* She lied about not knowing what happened, but she wasn't about to tell Adam that she had witnessed the whole thing in her head. He'd think she was insane.

Adam texted back, but she didn't understand what he meant: *Front. He's calling on you.*

Mara tried to think of how to interpret what on earth Adam was trying to tell her. Did he mean the front of the Garner's house? But who would be calling her?

Before she could figure it out, Mara's phone was snatched out of her hand.

Dread seized her whole body. Mr. Trenchard stared down at her with a disapproving glare. "You can pick up your phone after school." Then he nodded to the dry-erase board and the newly written math problem. "And for the fifth time, would you please solve the formula. I'm sure it won't be too difficult seeing as I've been lecturing for the last ten minutes on exactly how to solve it."

How did this happen? It was humiliating.

She briefly glanced at Adam and felt mildly better. He cringed with guilt and tried to give her a supportive smile.

The whole class stared at her. Some were amused, some were sympathetic, but the majority of the class appeared relieved that Mr. Trenchard hadn't called on *them*. "I don't know it," she answered honestly.

"And *why* don't you know it, Ms. Johnson?" He was making an example out of Mara and she knew it. And she deserved it. She hadn't listened to a word he had said.

Looking at the clock, she wanted class to be almost over so she wouldn't be humiliated for long. Nope. Still forty minutes left. She decided to take her lumps and ride through the mortification. "Because I wasn't paying attention."

"And *why* weren't you paying attention? What was so important that you couldn't retain enough focus for the first class of your senior year?" He was milking this worse than Mara could imagine. She had heard stories about Mr. Trenchard from upper classmen, but she never thought that *she'd* be the one he picked on. She was too much of a goody-two-shoes for that.

Stupid Adam.

Mara had finally succumbed to the downfalls of being an idiot around a boy.

But it was Adam who spoke up for her, "Maybe because her godfather was just murdered across the street from her. It's kind of hard to concentrate on Calculus when something like that happens. Or maybe that's just me," he finished with a berating tone.

There was a gasp from the class.

Mara was too shocked to correct Adam. Ed Garner was

definitely not her godfather, but Adam's intent was clear. He was making the incident seem even more personal to Mara so that Mr. Trenchard would feel like an ass.

It worked.

He gently handed her cell back to her. "Mara, you probably shouldn't be at school today. Go home and be with your family. I'll write you a note."

Mara never knew how to talk to adults. Her parents had drilled it into her at an early age that you had to respect your elders and that they were your superiors. As a result, she'd stammer shyly a lot, pretty much doing whatever they said without argument. "Thank you, Mr. Trenchard," she managed to say.

It took a moment or two before her teacher scribbled out a note and handed it to her with a sympathetic expression. "We'll get you caught up on your school work later, just take care of yourself."

He was being so sweet that Mara started to feel bad. If she told him the truth now, she'd look like a manipulative jerk, so she muttered, "Thanks."

With one last glance at Adam, Mara left the classroom.

Now what?

She stood in the empty halls of Forest Green, note in hand, with permission to leave campus. Josie could probably walk home, but people would start to wonder why Mara's younger sister could handle what happened more than she could.

Staring down at the slip of paper, Mara sighed and went to her locker. Pulling out her bag, she headed toward the parking lot.

"Hey, wait up."

She turned around to see Adam, hurrying toward her. He was much taller than her, making him about six foot two inches, though he seemed shorter at times because he was so lanky. He carried his backpack slung over one shoulder. He smiled. "I told him that you needed your friends right now." He waved an identical note to hers. "You wanna go to Telvos?" he asked, referring to a small café a mile from school.

There went Mara's vocal chords. Like clockwork, talking to a boy she liked turned her into a mute idiot.

Adam wasn't phased at all. He seemed to know she was being shy and carefully took her bag and placed it on his free shoulder. "Come on, I'll drive."

Without saying a word, Mara followed Adam down the hallway and out to the parked cars. She hoped at some point she'd regain the ability to speak. He probably just wanted to drill her about the murder, but he had certainly gone out of his way to spend time with her. If Adam had simply wanted info, he would have left it at a texting relationship. But he wanted to take her to Telvos! Butterflies flapped madly in her tummy.

Mara had never allowed herself to think about Adam because she never thought anything would happen. Guys certainly weren't beating down her door, not when Kimiko had made it a point to alienate her. But...

Adam was even more unpopular than Mara. She always figured the ridicule would grow worse for them both if they were friends. So Mara admired Adam from afar, always feeling she had some kind of weird connection to him. She even tried to dream about him. Sometimes her gift let her visit real people's dreamscapes and not just murderers'. Mara even thought she had once, but it was impossible to tell because she never saw his face clearly.

Since Adam only moved into her school district Freshman year, Mara hadn't grown up with him. Most of the students in Forest Green had known each other since Kindergarten, so having someone new was always a treat for Mara, because here was someone who hadn't been raised to make fun of her or ignore her. On his first day, Adam managed to get into a fight with Colt Lennox (i.e., Kimiko's boyfriend) and that put him on the elite's shit-list ever since.

So Mara had successfully kept her crush hidden for three years. No wonder she was tongue-tied now. She had been drooling over this guy her entire high school existence and today of all days he decided that they were going to be friends. She was positive Adam didn't see her romantically, that he only wanted news on Ed Garner, but at the moment she didn't care. He managed to get her out of class without breaking any rules, a feat Mara *never* thought possible. At least not for her.

They arrived at Adam's car, a beat-up sedan that looked like it was built in the eighties. He smiled and his whole face lit up, which made Mara blush. "I bought it for two-hundred bucks. It didn't run for shit, but I taught myself about engines and fixed it myself."

Mara would have loved to respond, but her motor skills were still on the fritz, so she just smiled back.

Adam opened her door first, then waited until she was sitting in the passenger seat before shutting it. Then he hurried to the driver's side and slid in. "Sometimes I have to pop the clutch to start it. I don't think I fixed the starter properly, that's why I always park on a slight decline."

At some point, Mara was certain he'd kick her out for being a mute, but Adam didn't seem to mind her non-responsiveness. It was as if he knew she was too bashful to talk and was trying to put her at ease by being conversational.

And…

It was actually working.

Mara became a little more relaxed as Adam turned the key – and the car wouldn't start. He glanced over at her with a slightly embarrassed expression. "See? I just have to do this…" Adam let the car drift down the slight hill, then popped the clutch. The engine roared to life.

"I have to do that with my Bug sometimes too." *Finally! Words out of my mouth!* Mara was more relieved than Adam appeared to be at her speaking.

"We're probably the only two people in the school who drive stick-shift," Adam smiled, leaning back in his seat and stealing a glance over at Mara.

She liked it when he looked at her. It was as if he really wanted to see her reactions to anything and everything. If Mara hadn't been afraid that her face would turn fifty shades of red, she'd actually look back at Adam as well. She loved his smile and his perfectly straight teeth. Everything about him twinkled.

Mara took a deep breath and found that she was enjoying herself. "My dad taught me how to drive manual. I stalled out so many times the first time he took me out, I thought the vein in his forehead would burst." She was off-campus with the boy she'd had a crush on for ages. And she was actually talking in coherent sentences. That was a wonder all to itself!

40

"I had to teach myself," Adam shared. "My dad only believes in teaching with a belt, or a chain, or a tire iron, whatever he can get his hands on."

He said it so casually that Mara didn't understand at first what he meant.

And then she did.

But Adam was only thinking of Mara, and when he saw that he had rendered her speechless again, he shrugged with a grin. "Sorry. I don't know why I said that."

"Is it true?" It made Mara wonder at all the bruises and cuts she'd seen on Adam over the years. She had just assumed it was Colt and his gang, but now it seemed like his father may have been a culprit as well.

Adam tried to brush it off like it was no big deal. "Yeah, but don't tell anyone, okay? I've managed to convince the system that he's a changed man. That's why I get into so many fights at school. If the nurse thinks it's from fighting, she'll never know it's domestic. That way my dad stays out of trouble and I stay out of foster care. Trust me, I've lived in foster homes that make my dad look like a saint. At least he's the devil I know, you know?"

Mara didn't know. Not at all. She couldn't even begin to fathom Adam's situation. He obviously felt safer with his abusive father than going to foster care, so much so that he arranged double beatings from bullies at school just to keep himself home. It was a completely foreign concept to Mara. Her parents had never even *spanked* her or Josie. To have to live with constant thrashings your whole life must be unbearable.

And yet, here Adam was, baring his soul to a complete stranger. Why was he telling Mara something so private? Something he kept hidden from others? She could be some jerk who would tell everyone, then everything he'd been working so hard to hide would be out in the open.

Maybe that was what he secretly wanted?

No.

He wanted to share with Mara because he wanted *her* to share with *him.* But what could she really tell him? She couldn't talk about her dreams, he'd laugh at her. Here he was confessing something so personal, so intimate, so horrifying, but Mara wasn't like that. Mara had barely told anyone about her dreams over the years. Only her parents, Josie and Zia knew about her visions. That was it. She'd known Adam for three years, but this was the first time they'd ever even spoken. She couldn't trust telling him about the dreams. Not yet. She did feel, however, like she should reveal *something* about herself.

But alleviating his fear should come first, so, Mara finally answered his plea for silence. "Of course I won't tell anyone about your dad. But how can you trust me?"

Adam shrugged. "I just do. I can't explain it. I know we haven't talked before, but I feel like we've been friends the whole time we've known each other. It sounds weird, but today when I saw you on the news, I just knew it was time to talk to you. Does that make any sense?" He didn't look over at her. She could tell he was nervous as to what her response would be. Would she shut him out? Or would she understand completely?

"It makes sense. I…" She was nervous. Mara had never shared her feelings with a boy, let alone a boy that she liked! But she took his cue in braveness and said, "I always thought we had a connection, but I didn't think you liked me."

Adam appeared relieved. His smile brightened the dingy car. "Oh, I *like* you."

Mara's face flushed and she had to turn away before she turned purple.

Adam teased playfully, "I just managed to arrange for the both of us to cut class with no repercussions. I'd say that was a Win."

Mara smiled shyly and nodded in agreement.

The time for Mara to share something private had passed now that Adam had lightened the mood.

When they arrived at Telvos Café, they parked in the almost empty lot.

Once they were inside, they walked to the counter and Adam ordered them both mochas. The manager waved and called Adam by name, so she assumed he came in there often.

Finding a table in the back, the two of them sat down just as Adam's phone rang. When he saw who was calling, his expression turned dark. He stood up. "I'll be right back." Before Mara could respond, Adam answered the phone and walked toward the back of the building.

The café was small and quaint with a handful of weathered wood tables and mismatched chairs. It had a kind of eclectic vibe to it that was perfect for cracking open a good book while downing caffeinated beverages. When the barista called Adam's name, Mara walked to the counter and picked up their drinks. She almost gasped at the presentation, it was so cool. Apparently, the barista was a foam artist. The first mocha depicted a swirled image of the solar system with Saturn in the forefront. The second mocha had a 3D bear climbing out of the large mug. They were so incredible she didn't want to ruin them by drinking the coffee.

After expressing her awe to the barista, she brought back both cups to her table. Finally, taking a sip of her mocha (she chose the universe foam art because she couldn't bring herself to destroy the adorable bear), and her eyes rolled back in bliss.

This day was turning out better than she had ever expected!

Dream Entry #4

I'm writing while Adam is on the phone. He didn't look too happy at whoever was on the other end and it's been a while since he left. I hope he's okay. He just told me about his dad and that basically he's been abused his whole life.

I've never felt this way about anyone before. It's the first time that I've ever talked to a guy that I like. It's weird to experience reality and not fantasy. I doubt Adam likes me like that, but he did say he likes me. I don't want to read anything into it, though. I really want to tell him about my dreams, but I'm afraid of what his reaction would be.

I'm just starting to learn more about him so I don't want to scare him off. Maybe after we've hung out a little more I'll know if I can trust him. We went from never speaking before, to exchanging numbers and texting, to having freaking mochas at Telvos!

Still, I feel like I should share something private with him even if it isn't my dreams. I think I'll tell him about my murdering great *aunt Eleanor. I'll leave out the dream-connection part. It's scary, though, because I don't want him to think any less of me because of who I'm related to. What if he thinks being a murderer is hereditary? It could scare him off forever.*

I don't know. I'll have to think about it. But for now, I'm just going to enjoy the awesomeness that is my day right now. It's been crazy! Maybe I'm still dreaming. If I am, I don't want to wake up.

***

Mara looked up from her diary and her breath caught in her throat.

The dream just turned into a nightmare.

Kimiko Thompson and Colt Lennox walked through the door.

Mara's worst enemy and Adam's worst enemy walk into a café… It was like the start of a bad joke.

"Just ignore them," Adam whispered to Mara. She was relieved that he had come back in time to save her from "Bully Central" seeing her. He had arrived from a different direction than where he had left, though, and Mara wondered where he had gone.

Adam noticed the foam bear floating on top of his coffee and cracked a smile. "Crazy, huh? I come here for the foam art alone."

Mara nodded in agreement, but her focus was on Kimiko and Colt at the counter. "Hopefully, they'll ignore us first." She really didn't want to deal with Kimiko today. And it was just her typical bad luck that Kimiko was skipping school the same time as Mara.

Trying not to look, there was one thing that Mara had to admit: Kimiko and Colt were societally as perfect as could be. She was of Japanese decent with flawless skin, black almond eyes, button nose, full lips and a body to die for. She tossed her long, thick black hair back as if she was in a shampoo commercial, flirting constantly with Colt. Her boyfriend was attractive to most girls, but not to Mara. Colt was big, buff and bronzed. Living in rain-drenched Seattle, there wasn't much of a chance for a real tan, so UVA beds and airbrushing guns would have to do. Colt basically looked like a slightly orange living Ken doll. He pretty much had the same amount of intelligence of one as well.

So far so good. Kimiko and Colt didn't seem to notice them.

This was helped, because Adam had turned his back on the pair, covering their view of Mara as much as possible. She only saw a sliver of them, and tried not to make eye contact, but the more Mara tried, the more she looked. It was as if she couldn't stop herself. "Maybe we should go," she suggested.

Adam shook his head. "No way. We're not going to let Ken and Barbie decide where we hang out."

Mara smiled inwardly at the fact that Adam had made the same Ken doll comparison she had. One more confirmation that great minds think alike.

She took another sip of her mocha and nodded. "You're right. I just can't seem to stop staring, though."

Adam suddenly reached across the small table and touched Mara's hand. It sent a thrill through her whole body. His eyes were sparkling again, but his expression was concerned. "If they see us, I don't give a crap. Don't stress."

Mara didn't want Adam to take his hand away, but she figured her deer-in-headlights-buggy-eyes may have scared him off because he self-consciously pulled it back. She wished she could scream that she wanted more from him, or even that she could be brave enough to reach across herself. But fear won out. Instead, she nodded to her mocha. "This is really good. Thanks."

Adam shyly drank his own drink, and was about to say something, when Colt's boorish voice spoke first. "Look at the freaks skipping school."

Great.

All chances of ignoring them were destroyed as the Power Couple approached their table.

Kimiko joined in Colt's attack before Mara or Adam could respond. "We'll just have to call Ms. Peters."

Ms. Peters was the secretary in charge of truancy. You did not want to mess with her. One time she followed Trina Bilcher all the way to Ballard after someone gave her an anonymous tip that Trina planned on skipping. The woman took her job seriously. It was why Mara had never cut class in her life. Until today. But she had permission at least, so it was more of an excused absence than anything else. The only downside was that her parents didn't know about it, so getting in trouble was still on the table.

"Go ahead," Adam goaded.

Mara had nothing to fear from Ms. Peters, though. Mr. Trenchard's note was like a Golden Ticket in her pocket.

Instead of responding with another snide comeback, Colt grabbed the back of Adam's shirt and yanked him to his feet.

Even Kimiko seemed uncomfortable by this aggressive move.

Mara stood up instinctively. "Let him go!" she found herself yelling. And she wasn't a yeller. She was a hide-in-the-corner-and-hope-it-goes-away kind of girl.

Colt was at least twice as wide as Adam and he used his size to flip Adam around to face him. Adam wasn't a rail, but he was a thin guy. He had some muscle, but nothing compared to Colt's over-steroided biceps that held him in a tight grip.

But Adam didn't fight back or struggle. Instead, he stayed calm as Colt brought his head in close, using the collar of Adam's shirt. "Letting your girlfriend fight your battles for you now?"

Mara barely heard the café manager threaten to call the police as she stomped on Colt's toe as hard as her Chuck Taylor's would let her. It probably hurt her more than him, but it was enough for Colt to loosen his grip on Adam's shirt and stumble backward. Before Mara could even think better of it, she lifted her leg and kicked Colt in the groin. She struck him so hard he flew back a few feet and fell on his rump.

Colt's face turned purple and he clutched his crotch. It would have been funny if it wasn't real. But it was. Mara had just flattened the biggest jock in school. Not to mention the most popular.

Kimiko didn't say a word to Mara as she dropped to her knees to help her boyfriend, asking if he was okay.

The café manager arrived at the scene and turned to both Adam and Mara. "You two okay?"

Adam and Mara nodded, though Mara was still traumatized by what she had just done.

The manager stood over Colt and Kimiko, disgusted and furious. "You two, get out! If I ever see you in this establishment again, I'll call the cops."

Colt had regained enough of his composure to be appalled. "*She* was the one that kicked *me*!"

The manager waved a hand at his employees and the few other patrons inside the shop. "I have about ten witnesses here that saw you start this whole thing. This isn't the first time either, but it's the *last*. Trust me on that."

Mara was both relieved and shocked that what she considered dreadful behavior on her part was actually being rewarded. No one ever took her side. She'd get in trouble for something Josie did and even when her parents found out the truth, they still wouldn't take back their punishment. It was something she had grown used to as the older sibling. So having the manager not only condone what Mara had done, but throw Colt Lennox and Kimiko Thompson out for all eternity...? It made her want to buy a coffee there every day.

It surprised her even more that Kimiko wasn't even arguing. Mara had expected the same kind of attitude Colt expressed. But once things had turned physical, the girl clammed up. It made Mara wonder if Colt's temper had made its rounds on Kimiko.

Kimiko helped Colt up and supported him toward the door. Just as they were about to exit, Colt pointed at Adam with venom. "You're a dead man, freak!"

"OUT!" the manager shouted.

Colt grimaced in pain and rage. Then, like the jock idiot he was, gave one last air body-check to the manager before the door finally shut him out of the store.

When the couple was gone for good, the people in the shop all gave Mara a round of applause. Her face must have turned eight shades of red, but for once in her life she felt like a hero.

Once the clapping died down, Mara turned to Adam. He stood next to her, smiling. She wasn't certain of how to react. Mara hadn't been sure if Adam would be offended or angry that she had stepped in, but seeing Colt treat him like that…

It had brought up images in her head like in one of her dreams: grabbing, shoving, punching, strangling… It had all been so quick, Mara wasn't even able to acknowledge what she had "seen" until that moment.

She must have been tapping into Adam's memories and experiences.

Mara's gift worked like that sometimes. She'd be sitting somewhere, or talking to someone, or even listening to the radio, when she'd suddenly see images in her head. Like pulling people's memories from the sky. They could be good or bad memories, but they were always intense. It was probably because of that intensity that Mara picked up on their thoughts, but it sometimes made her feel like her head would explode from being overloaded.

The manager gently patted Mara's arm. "How would you two like a slice of triple chocolate cake?"

Um, Yum. Her face must have lit up because the manager chuckled. "Coming right up." Before he left, though, he eyed her seriously. "You did the right thing. Colt Lennox has harassed more people than I can count, but he's never been beaten by a girl I think." He smiled. Then he turned to Adam. "Hold on to this one, Adam. She's a keeper."

Mara's face flushed, then her whole body tingled as Adam wrapped his hand in hers. "I'll never let her go."

If she could pass out, she would have.

He liked her. He really liked her. At least, it seemed like he did. As insane as it sounded, Mara's insecurity was so huge that she was still having doubts, even with Adam holding her hand.

And, of course, she lost the ability to speak again.

Adam ushered Mara back to their table and pulled her seat out for her. The only thing that she didn't like about it was the fact that he had to let go of her hand to do it.

She noticed that Adam's mocha had spilled on his chair from when Colt yanked him up. All she could think about was the artistry the barista had put into that little foam bear crawling out of the cup, and it had been ruined by a jerk for no reason except to flaunt his prowess. For some reason that hurt her more than it should have. Like the little, delicate foam animal had been real and fragile and destroyed in an act of intentional violence.

The manager was already on it, though, cleaning the chair and floor himself. He brought Adam a fresh mocha, on top of which the barista had recreated the foam bear even better than before. Then the manager brought a slice of cake for each of them. It was the most decadent piece of confection Mara had ever put in her mouth. Three layers of moist milk chocolate cake with thick fudge icing in-between. She was glad she had a slice all her own because she ate the whole thing in less than five minutes. Getting into a fight brought out her appetite, she guessed.

Everyone being so supportive made Mara feel relaxed, especially since Adam was more animated than she'd ever seen him. It was as if by defending Adam, Mara had proved that she was truly his friend. She had thought he'd hate her afterward, as if she had emasculated him or something.

Mara began to realize something about herself she didn't know before. She was a fighter. She didn't plan on participating in any more of them, but it gave her a kind of confidence that when someone she cared about was in trouble she wouldn't back down. Mara always thought she would run, so it was nice to know that, when push came to shove, she wouldn't.

"Thanks, by the way," Adam said as he finished off his cake. "I've gotten so used to letting Colt beat me up that I was just waiting for it to be over."

"I figured. Because of what you said about your dad," Mara admitted.

Adam seemed pleasantly surprised at Mara's deduction. "It's weird, isn't it? Today. Us. All because I saw you on the news this morning. I've always wanted to talk to you, but I didn't know what to say. I thought texting would be easier, but then I think I gave you a heart attack asking you to do that." He laughed softly. "I'm sorry about that."

A wave of happiness washed through Mara. The combination of horrifying dreams morphing into this bliss she now felt was almost a shock to her system. Or maybe it was the extreme sugar rush combined with caffeine. Either way, Mara felt fantastic.

Mara laughed. "I thought I was going to die when Mr. Trenchard grabbed my phone."

Adam's laugh was like his smile, it made his whole being light up. "Hey, my guilt trip got us both out of school."

"I wonder if he'll find out Ed Garner is not my godfather." Mara wondered, worry creeping up on her again. "And do you think Colt and Kimiko will tell people what I did here?" That thought was even more frightening. Mara had just gone from trying to be ignored to kicking the star quarterback in the crotch! She may just have started the war she always dreaded.

"First off, there's no way Colt will tell anyone that a girl knocked him on his ass. He'll blame me anyway, so you don't have to worry about that…"

Mara stopped him there. "That's *exactly* what I'm worried about. I just made things ten times worse for you." The caffeine and sugar were rattling her nerves. "You heard him, he said you were a dead man!"

Adam reached across the table and held her hand. It was the third time he'd touched her hand today and she turned to mush whenever he did it. "I can handle Colt. And besides, I told you: I need him. I don't want my dad going to prison, and if anyone found out he's hurting me again, they'll take him away and I'd be back in the foster system." His grip tightened from the thought. "I can't do that."

Mara squeezed back supportively "Your mom's not around?" she asked delicately.

Adam shook his head. "She couldn't take Dad hitting her, so she left him a kid-sized punching bag to play with." He was trying to make light of his situation, almost fictionalizing it, probably so he didn't have to feel his emotions.

Mara understood that. She did it with her dreams all the time. If she thought of them as movies, it helped her process and cope. Everyone had to have their method of handling painful situations. It just sucked that someone as gentle as Adam had been dealt such shitty cards in life.

"I'm sorry," was all Mara could think of to say.

"Don't be. Just keep my secret. Now that you and I have found each other, leaving for foster care would be a million times worse." He smiled and pulled her hand to his lips, kissing it softly.

54

It took everything for Mara not to let her eyes roll back in her head and faint.

Adam lowered her hand back down on the table, but still held onto it. *Now that you and I have found each other.* His words repeated in her head. After all this time, the guy she'd been crushing-on truly liked her back. It made all the horrible things in her life seem trivial. She nodded her head. "You know I won't tell anyone."

"I know." And his eyes told her that he trusted her completely. "I don't want to talk about me anymore. Let's talk about you. Were you close to your neighbor?"

Mara knew this conversation was coming. Originally, she had thought it was the *only* reason Adam wanted to talk to her, but a lot had happened since then. She debated whether or not to tell him about her dreams. Mara had a feeling Adam would be okay with it, but she was enjoying herself too much to risk it. "I wasn't that close to him. He was kind of like the neighborhood's nice old man, but I never really talked to him much. I know he had a son, but I hardly ever saw him. I think he's like thirty now."

"His name is Robert," Adam revealed.

Mara tried to hide her surprise at Adam knowing Ed Garner's son's name. "You knew the Garners?"

"Not really. My mom used to clean their house. I met Robert when I tagged along to help her. They were all really nice." He comically chomped the head off the foam bear, which made Mara laugh. "Why would anyone want to kill an old guy? Especially him? Seems kind of weird. Maybe it was a suicide?" he conjectured.

"No, it was just murder," Mara spouted before she could

think about it.

"How do you know? Did you hear the police say something? Did you *see* something?" he asked curiously.

If Mara hadn't dreamt about Ed's death, she would have wanted to investigate as well. But just talking about it was causing her to re-live every gasp of desperate breath from Mr. Garner's body. She shuddered.

"No. I guess… I don't know. I could be wrong. It's just… the police were there early in the morning and Ed lived alone. If it was suicide or even natural causes I don't think all the press would be there. Someone had to have seen something and reported it to the cops," Mara voiced her theory.

"And it wasn't you?" Adam eyed her carefully.

Mara's defenses went up. "Me? No, I was sleeping."

Adam saw that her mood had changed drastically. He gently squeezed her hand. "I'm sorry. I wasn't accusing you of anything. Of course, this would be horrible for you and I'm the jerk who's making you think about it. I was just curious. I was thinking of putting my detective hat in the ring and trying to solve this one." He tipped an imaginary hat.

"Really?" Mara perked up. "Like a Hardy Boy or something?"

He nodded. "And I was hoping you'd be my Nancy Drew."

She liked the idea of the two of them spending more time together. And, if they had something they could work on there would be less time for the inevitable awkward silences. Mara didn't like thinking about what she saw happen in her dream, but *did* want to use her gift to find the killer. Maybe the two of them combined could do it. She'd have to tell Adam about her dreams, of course, but the more she learned about Adam, the more she trusted him.

"Okay, let's do it." She smiled. "The police are probably still there. We could go to my house and try and overhear some things? What do you think?"

Adam grinned. "I'm in."

Mara replied with confidence, "We'll solve this." She wasn't convinced her statement was true, but she was willing to try.

And they were off. Mara thanked the manager again and Adam drove them to her house. The police were still at the Garner's like she had figured they would be.

As Adam pulled into the driveway, her palms started to sweat: a female detective was talking to her mother on their front doorstep.

Claire's face was confused as she saw her daughter in a strange boy's car during school hours, but she waved a small "Hello" all the same.

Mara turned to Adam, slightly panicked. "We're going to have to take a rain check."

"Sure," he answered, looking at her, concerned. "She's probably asking all the neighbors if they saw anything."

Mara nodded. "Yeah. I'm more worried about explaining *you* to my mom though." She smiled nervously.

Adam smiled back. "I gotcha." Then he did something Mara never expected him to do. He kissed her. It made her eyes cross. Her first kiss. It was short, but lingered just long enough for Mara's head to spin.

"See you later?" Adam asked, not realizing the brain convulsions he had just caused.

Mara fell back to her standby status: not being able to speak, so she nodded. Exiting the car before she did or said anything stupid was her first priority. Mara waved a small good-bye as Adam pulled out of the driveway and drove out of view.

Mara walked up to her mother and the detective. Claire's eyes were wide from the shock of seeing her daughter kiss a boy she had never heard about.

"Why aren't you in school?" Claire snapped anxiously.

"My first period teacher wrote me a note. He said I should come home and be with you, since all this happened." Mara waved toward the police in front of the Garner's.

"Good idea," the detective agreed. She looked like she was in her mid-thirties, blond hair pulled back in a tight bun, tailored suit over a slightly plump body.

"Mara, this is Detective Jennifer Nicholson and she has a few questions for you." Claire gave her daughter a pointed look.

Mara gulped. "Great. Let's go inside."

Dream Entry #5

*H*e kissed me! Adam Layton really kissed me! I should be freaking out about the fact that Detective Jennifer Nicholson is standing here waiting to question me and my mom about Ed Garner's murder, but all I can think about is how amazing it was to kiss Adam. Besides, Adam was right, I have nothing to worry about. The detective is interviewing all of the neighbors to see if they heard or saw anything last night.

I was going to have to lie, but technically I wasn't really lying. I didn't actually see anything in real life. It's just that I get so paralyzed and shy when talking to adults, especially ones with authority. Look how I handled Mr. Trenchard! If Adam hadn't saved me I might have been suspended for using my cell in class. I just hope this wasn't a fluke for him and that he wasn't repulsed by my obvious lack of kissing technique. I was so shocked he was doing it that I'm not sure I was any good. I can feel my face turning red right now just thinking *about it. What if I was terrible at it? What if he never wants to see me again? What if he was grossed out by me?*

***

"Mara, the detective is asking you a question," Claire's voice interrupted Mara's tirade in her diary. She looked up at her mother, stopped writing and slid her journal back into her bag.

They sat in the living room, which had two couches: a three-seater made of brown leather and a love seat constructed of the same material. They formed an L-shape that framed a large big-screen TV mounted on the opposite wall.

Mara and Claire sat on the larger couch, while the detective sat across from them on the love seat.

"Sorry, I was just working on… something." Mara had been about to say "homework," but since she had only spent about twenty minutes in class, she knew that wouldn't fly. "What did you ask me?"

Detective Nicholson didn't seem upset at Mara's lack of attention. She smiled warmly and repeated herself. "What time did you go to bed last night?"

Mara shrugged, not really remembering, but knowing it was before the murder. "I think about ten," she answered truthfully.

"Your window is the only one facing the victim's house. Did you hear anything out of the ordinary?" Detective Nicholson asked, at the same time typing every question and answer into had a hand-held tablet.

Mara shook her head. "No. I'm not a light sleeper." Which was also true. She wished she was, maybe she could have helped

Ed.

"So you didn't *see* anything, either?" the detective prodded helpfully. "Maybe getting up for a glass of water or to go to the bathroom?"

The syringe… Mr. Garner choking… gasping for air…

Mara shuddered. "No. I was out cold."

She'd waited too long, Mara could see it in Detective Nicholson's expression. She knew Mara was hiding something. "Are you alright?" the detective asked warmly, but her eyes were calculating.

"Fine, just a little freaked," Mara answered too quickly. What was wrong with her? It was as if she herself had committed the crime and was trying to pretend she didn't know anything to the cops. She kept having to remind herself that she was innocent. That just because she saw what happened to Mr. Garner in her dream didn't make her responsible for it.

"Freaked from the murder, or from my questioning?" Detective Nicholson's jovial round face suddenly appeared cold and analyzing.

Being the mom that she was, Claire stepped in at this point. "Honestly, *both*, Detective. I think my daughter has answered all of your questions, and I don't appreciate your tone with her."

Detective Nicholson kept her eyes on Mara for a few seconds as if debating whether or not to pursue her questioning further. Then, after a moment, she smiled. "If you think of anything else, call me directly." She handed Mara her card.

Claire snatched the card from Mara's hand and stared down the detective with disapproval. "Since my daughter is seventeen, either my husband or I will be present if you want to talk to her

61

again. Is that understood, Detective?"

Go, Mom.

It didn't faze Detective Nicholson in the least, she nodded with that same smile plastered on her face that now seemed creepy instead of nice. "Thank you for your time."

"Good day, Detective." Claire was simply angry at this point and wanted her to leave.

Mara watched as her mother led the detective to the exit and shut the door behind her.

Dread filled Mara at the thought that the police might suspect her of *anything*. She doubted that she was a murder suspect, but Mara was positive Detective Jennifer Nicholson thought Mara knew more than she was telling. Which was true, but if Mara was to tell her about her dreams, she was sure the detective would think she was guilty.

Claire came back into the living room and sat next to Mara.

Right now, Mara stared at the floor and wished she could turn back time to re-answer the detective's questions. She really hated her brain. Why did she get so hung up on the memories of her dream? She should have shoved all her emotions down and just answered the questions like a typical teen. Detectives were always searching, watching, observing for any kind of clue. And Mara had just flown a red flag in her face.

As if sensing her stress, Claire put her arm around her daughter trying to comfort her. "You dreamed about Ed Garner, didn't you?"

It was now suddenly obvious to her mother that Mara had lied this morning when she pretended not to know anything about the murder.

Mara nodded slowly. She hated seeing her mother worried, but at this point Claire needed to know everything.

It took Claire a few beats before she took a deep breath and pulled Mara in for a tight hug. "Don't worry about *that woman*. They'll find who did it and forget all about you."

Mara pulled out of her mother's embrace. "Do you think I'm a suspect?"

Claire laughed, aghast. "Of course not! If anything, she just thinks you may have seen something and you're too scared to talk." She held Mara's hand. "Is that what you think? That they'll accuse you of murder?"

Mara nodded, scared.

"Oh, sweetie." Claire pulled her in for another hug, holding her tight. "That's never going to happen. I promise you that." Then she leaned out of the embrace to make eye contact with her daughter. "Who was that boy that kissed you?"

Uh, oh.

"Just a boy, Mom, jeez." Mara was embarrassed. She didn't want to talk about guys with her mother. Zia talked to her mom about anything and everything, but Mara wasn't like that with Claire. It was easier to pretend that Mara had no interest in dating than to admit she liked a boy.

"He didn't look like *just a boy*. He was pretty cute." Claire smiled – and then pinched Mara's cheek like she was five.

"Mom." Mara swatted her mom's hand away.

Claire was extremely amused, to Mara's annoyance. "You can at least tell me his name."

Mara sighed, exasperated. "Adam Layton."

Her mother's face turned concerned. "Sam Layton's boy?"

Mara shrugged. "I don't know." She had no idea if that was Adam's father's name or not.

"I hope not. Sam Layton is bad news. He used to work with Dad's friend, George Peeler, over at Tech World and he was arrested twice for hurting his wife before she left him." Claire had put on her Mom-face at this point, scared for her daughter's well being.

Mara would never tell her mother Adam's secret, but she didn't want to lie either. "Yeah, that must be his dad, then – but he doesn't hurt Adam, if that's what you're worried about. Do you really think his mother would leave her only son to a man who's violent?" Mara knew that was exactly what Adam's mom had done, but she also knew the idea would be so preposterous to her own mother that Claire would never believe a mom could do that.

Mara was right. Claire nodded, slightly relieved. "No, I guess not. It was probably just gossip anyway. How long have you two been seeing each other? Have you gone on a date yet? And why am I just learning about him today?" she drilled Mara.

"We started talking today and by the time he dropped me off, he kissed me." Mara hadn't wanted to share, but at the same time, she wanted to talk to someone.

Claire brightened. "So that was your first kiss?"

Mara groaned. "Mom. You make it sound so cheesy."

Her mother brightened even more. "I meant your first kiss with Adam, but are you saying this was your very first kiss *ever*?"

"Oh my God, Mom, you are so embarrassing." Mara wanted to run up to her room and never come out again. Then, on quick reconsideration, she figured it would be easier just to answer her quickly so she could leave. "Yes, it was my first kiss ever and I'm pretty sure I sucked at it and he'll probably never want to see me again," she confessed her fears.

"I doubt that. Everyone thinks they're terrible at first. Trust me, some people are definitely terrible, but I saw Adam's face afterwards. That boy is crazy about you." Claire grinned.

A wave of joy and relief washed through Mara. "Really? You think?"

"Oh, I *know*. I've seen that look before on many-a-man's face and you have *nothing* to worry about." Claire stood up and offered her hand to Mara, helping her daughter to her feet. "I think this calls for a celebration. I just bought some frozen cookie dough, you want to make some cookies?"

"Um, yes."

Mara followed Claire into the kitchen and twenty minutes later, they were chowing down on gooey chocolate chip cookies. After all the chocolate Mara had scarfed down that day, she was starting to feel a little sick from the sugar overload, but it was worth it. Chocolate was always worth it.

Overall, Mara felt pretty good. The detective debacle was a slight setback, but her mom was right: once the police found the real killer, they wouldn't think twice about the girl living across the street. And maybe now, if Mara and Adam could figure out who killed Mr. Garner, they could prove her innocence without a doubt.

Before she forgot about it, Mara pulled out the note from Mr. Trenchard. "He excused me for the day, but I think you and Dad might have to write a note too. I really didn't feel like I had to come home, but he was pretty insistent."

Claire wiped her hands of melted chocolate and read the note. "That was thoughtful of him. Why just you, though? You didn't know Ed Garner all that well."

"For some reason, he thought he was my godfather. I was too flustered to correct him." Mara wasn't about to reveal Adam's role in that "assumption," but she wanted her mother to know so it didn't come back to bite her in the butt. And… "Maybe you could put it in the note too? I'm just afraid that Mr. Trenchard will hate me if he finds out the truth, like I had manipulated the situation to get out of school."

Claire sighed, thinking it through. "Why would he think that Ed Garner was your godfather? That's so random. Did someone tell him that?"

Mara shrugged. "I guess so. I really don't know. I just don't want to get in trouble."

"I'll think about it." Claire tucked the note in her purse.

Mara cringed. She hated it when her mother said that. It meant she was going to discuss it with Dad, and they'd come up with some kind of plan. It was so unpredictable, it made Mara nervous. She just prayed whatever decision they came to wasn't horribly humiliating for her or wouldn't get Adam in trouble. Now Mara was sorry she'd even told her mother about the godfather thing.

Feeling a buzz in her back pocket, Mara pulled out her cell. It was a text message from Zia that simply stated: *OMG! What were you thinking?! We need to talk NOW!*

Claire asked with a sly smile, "Is it Adam?"

"No, it's Zia. From this text, I think she knows, though." Mara returned her mother's amusement. "I'm going to my room to talk to her."

With Claire's blessing, Mara walked upstairs to her room.

How on earth did Zia find out about me and Adam?

Maybe all she knew about was Adam's heroic ruse for springing them from school. It was the *What were you thinking?* part that worried Mara. What if Zia disapproved of Adam and she couldn't imagine what Mara saw in him? She didn't feel like being caught in a tug-of-war between her best friend and the guy she liked, so she figured she'd better call Zia and give her the scoop first hand.

As Mara entered her room and sat down on the bed, she dialed Zia's cell phone. Her friend picked up on the first ring. "Mara Johnson." Zia's voice sounded awed.

"Zia Quinn," Mara mimicked. "What have you heard? You're freaking me out right now." She wanted to find out which event Zia was reacting to so she could fill her in on the rest.

"Okay, first off. I am so sorry and I'll always trust your judgment from now on, I swear."

What? Mara had no idea where this was going, but she let Zia continue before chiming in.

"And second, it's not what I heard, it's what I saw. What EVERYONE saw. Girl, you're like a hero!"

"What do you mean? What did you see?" Mara had a sneaking suspicion where this was headed, and her face was already starting to turn red.

"Someone posted a video of you on YouTube! You were at Telvos and Colt Lennox and Kimiko Thompson were totally harassing you and Adam Layton – side note you have to tell me everything on that one – and then Kimiko was being so nasty to you just like you said she had before, but I always thought you were exaggerating, and then Colt grabbed Adam and looked like he was going to beat him up just for having coffee and then – YOU. You stomped his toe and kicked him in the nuts! Oh my God, Mara! You are seriously my idol. This video is going viral: it has fifty thousand views already and it's only been an hour!" Zia rambled on so fast Mara barely had time to soak in what she had heard.

The whole fight had been recorded by some customer and now everyone was watching it? She would be grounded for sure. Her dad certainly wouldn't care that kicking Colt was for the greater good, he'd just see it as violence and ground Mara for the rest of her Senior year! And if fifty thousand people had seen it, it was a good bet that a part of that number was her entire school. Colt and Kimiko were popular, as in last year's Homecoming Prince and Princess. They'd twist this so that Mara and Adam were the bad guys and Mara's life at school would be excruciating.

"Are you there?" Zia's voice sounded worried. "I'm so sorry I never believed you about Kimiko. I was such a jerk. I saw the way she looked at you. She was a downright evil queen bitch."

"I can't believe someone recorded that," Mara finally spoke into the phone.

"You should be happy they did, otherwise who knows what Colt would say had happened."

"I was hoping he wasn't going to say anything, seeing as I'm a girl. I thought he'd be too embarrassed." Mara wasn't sure what the implications of all this meant yet, but it was making her dread going to school tomorrow.

"It's the fact that you're a girl that's making this video so

68

popular. Standing up for the little guy, fighter of bullies. I love you so much right now." Zia was so excited, it made Mara smile.

"Well, I love you, too, but I doubt I could repeat that. I was just so scared for Adam I reacted before I could think about it," Mara admitted.

Zia's voice actually went up an octave at the mention of Adam. "You must spill. You've had a raging crush on him for years! What in the heck happened that you were SKIPPING class and at a freaking café with him! I thought I was your best friend. You should have texted me or something!"

Then something occurred to Mara. "Hey, why did you text me and not call me just now if you wanted to talk?"

"Because, dummy, I saw you with Adam in that video and I didn't want the phone to ring while you might be… I don't know… in the middle of something!" she laughed.

"Wow, you have more confidence in me than I do," Mara said, amused. Then she filled Zia in on every detail of how her day went. Including the kiss.

Zia sighed into the phone. "That is so f-ing romantic. I love him so much right now, too. Has he texted you yet? Has he called? What. Is. Happening?"

Zia's enthusiasm was both contagious and overwhelming.

Mara answered, "He only left my house an hour ago. I think I should give it a bit of time, don't you?"

"After the day you two had? You could call him up right now. But I know you. You should relax and gather yourself together. *Then* send him a casual text asking if he's okay," Zia advised.

"Yeah, good one. Okay, I'll do that." Mara liked that idea, though her belly did flip-flops just thinking about connecting with Adam again, even in text form.

"Okay. Well, I'm going to let you go. You know your car is still at school and so is your sister. You have about an hour before the bell rings, so you're probably going to need your mom to drop you off so you can pick them up." Zia. Always thinking of things Mara completely forgot about.

"Crap. Thanks. I better go tell my mom. But I think I'm going to pick my car up now. I don't want to see anyone yet. My sister can get a ride from someone else." The last thing Mara wanted to do was face everyone at school. Sure, *Zia* was on Team Mara, but it was highly unlikely anyone else would be, even with video proof of Colt's bad behavior.

"I'll give her a ride, but just call me later, and tell me what happens with Adam, deal?" Zia sounded excited.

Mara agreed and they said their goodbyes.

Taking a huge breath to try and calm herself, Mara flopped back on her bed, staring at the glow-in-the-dark stars on her bedroom ceiling.

What had she done?

Dream Entry #6

I didn't dream anything bad last night, thank goodness. It was a weird one, though. I was in a car with Zia and Kimiko and Zia was driving. I was in the back seat while Kimiko rode shotgun. I was so angry. We were supposed to be driving to Portland, but Zia kept making stops because Kimiko needed "to get supplies for Colt." I screamed at them, telling them we'd never get to Portland if we kept on running Kimiko's errands.

Then Kimiko turned to me, she looked really sorry, and she said, "You're right. I keep adding more pieces to a puzzle I've already solved."

Then I woke up.

It was so weird and I have no idea what it meant.

Before I went to bed though, Adam and I texted until midnight! We talked about everything from music, to books, to TV, to movies. I still can't believe all of this is happening. Going from having a crush on someone that you never in a million years thought anything would happen, to texting all night like you've known each other forever! We also talked about Mr. Garner. Adam brought up some good points. He said we should figure out who Ed Garner was and why anyone would want to hurt him. He had to have some kind of a past.

I didn't want to tell Adam that it could just be because some crazy decided that Ed reminded him of their grandpa and decided to off the guy. No one ever thinks about murder being a random decision made by a psychopath. So, we're going to investigate anything we can find on the entire Garner family.

But more importantly, I woke up this morning with my mind made up: I'm going to tell Adam today about my aunt and my dreams.

A double whammy, but if I don't tell Adam now, it'll fester and rot inside me until I explode it on him anyway. I just hope he doesn't think I'm some murdering-certifiable-looney-fake-psychic-weirdo. I like the way he talks to me, the way he looks at me. I don't want that to change. But my past and these dreams are who I am, so if he's going to really know me, then he has to know it all. Wish me luck!

***

Mara put down her pen and shoved her diary into her binder. She was still nervous about going to school. Speaking of which, Mara walked over to her desk and checked YouTube on her laptop: 100,453 views. If this kept up, she'd be on the news and her parents would find out for sure. As it was, the chances were slim that they wouldn't hear about it somehow. Seattle was a big city, but her neighborhood pocket was like a small town sometimes.

At least when it came to gossip… and local girls becoming YouTube sensations.

Ugh.

"Mara Johnson! You get down here right now!" Her father, Ben, yelled from the kitchen.

Mara knew that tone.

They knew.

She was so dead.

Already dressed and ready for school, Mara tossed her diary into her bag and left to go take her licks.

Josie joined her in the hallway. "I swear I didn't tell them."

"They were bound to find out sooner or later. I was just hoping for later." Whether her sister was lying or not, it didn't matter. Mara only had herself to blame.

"If it makes any difference. I think what you did was amazing." Josie, for once, looked at her sister with reverence. Normally, her sister acted like she could care less what her older sister said or did. It was nice to see Josie proud of her. It gave Mara a boost of confidence as she went to face the firing squad.

Ben waited for her with angry eyes. His laptop was on the kitchen island opened to YouTube. He was a tall man, well over six feet, but he seemed even taller because he was so thin and lanky. Everything about him was long: from his face, to his nose, to all his limbs. And from his expression, Mara wanted to turn around and run out the front door.

Claire stood next to him with her arms crossed, though she didn't look nearly as mad.

"Can you explain this, please?" Ben pointed to the video on his computer.

Mara was terrified of being in trouble. One of the reasons she never broke any rules was because she didn't want to deal with anyone being mad at her. The people-pleaser in her despised having anyone thinking anything bad about her. Sure, she'd learned to deal with mean girls like Kimiko, but one of the reasons she preferred being ignored was because she didn't want confrontation.

Before she could speak, Ben continued, "First off, you were skipping school with a boy I don't know, and second off…" He stopped, unable to continue.

Mara had never seen him so angry. She knew he'd be upset with her, but she had no idea he'd be rendered speechless.

Then before she could react, Ben had pulled her into a hug. He held her so tightly, Mara wasn't sure what to do. It was nice. She hugged him back, enjoying this way more than being yelled at. His voice turned from fury to deeply concerned. "Mara, that Colt boy could have killed you. I never want you doing something like that again." Her father wasn't angry, he was terrified.

Josie chimed in. "Colt wouldn't do that. There were too many witnesses."

Ben chuckled slightly, then broke free of the embrace to make eye contact with Mara. "I'm very proud of you for standing up to someone like that, and for defending your friend, but guys like Colt don't care that you're a girl. He could have really hurt you."

"I wasn't thinking, I just acted," Mara confessed.

"I never condone violence, you know that," her father stated solemnly, then added, "But I consider what you did to be defense, and you always have my permission to do that, but Mara…" he eyed Josie as well, "and you too, Josie: run, next time. Please, for

74

me. Just run. Kick him where it counts and run as far as you can until you're safe. Deal?"

Both Mara and Josie nodded.

Mara sighed in relief. That went WAY better than she thought it would. Her dad was actually proud of her. She had been certain he'd ground her for life for any kind of violence but, apparently, it was more important for his girls to be able to defend themselves.

He glanced at the video playing on his laptop. They all watched as Mara kicked Colt in the groin. Ben shook his head with a slight wince. "He definitely wasn't expecting that."

Claire had happy tears in her eyes. She grabbed Mara and held her close. "You are such a good and decent person. I'm so proud of you."

"Um, hello?" Josie joked, pointing to herself.

They all laughed.

Mara was in a mini-state-of-shock, but a good shock. At least, if school went horribly wrong today, she'd have her parents' support. That made all the difference in the world. It somehow gave her the confidence to handle anything people might throw at her. No matter what, her family loved her and would always be Team Mara.

Then her father's face turned serious again. "Now, who is this boy you were with?"

Gulp.

Luckily, the conversation didn't last long. Josie stepped in and raved about what a good guy Adam was and how hard of a time he'd had with Colt for the three years he'd moved there. Mara was relieved that her dad didn't push it, probably because he didn't really want to know the details all that much.

The girls grabbed their lunches and headed to the car. Mara was actually grateful that her sister drove with her this morning. Yesterday, it had been a chore Mara dreaded, today she could use Josie as a shield against the student body's reaction. Maybe they'd all be cool with it? Like her parents had been? She hoped so, but there was no way of telling until she got there.

The drive was quick and Mara decided to park in the east lot this time. Sure, there was a chance of running into Colt or Kimiko or both, but she wanted to be as close to her locker as possible so she wouldn't have to walk very long through the crowd of students.

When Mara stepped out of her vehicle, she received a few stares and whispered comments, but so far no craziness. She took a deep sigh of relief. Maybe this wouldn't be so bad.

With Josie by her side, Mara opened the door to Hallway D and realized just how wrong she was.

It seemed like all fifteen hundred students were piled into one hallway to get a glimpse of Mara going to her locker. People were shouting and pushing their way toward her. Even though Josie was smaller, she stood protectively in front of her sister, yelling obscenities and telling people to back off.

On the bright side, no one seemed outraged or upset with Mara. They just seemed to want to get the scoop directly from her. Some of Colt's regular punching bags were trying to give her high-fives.

It wasn't until Mara saw the bright lights of the news cameras when she knew why things had grown out of control. Her worst fear. She had made the news. This crowd wasn't just for her, it was for them. To be on TV. To have five seconds of fame talking about the heroics of girl they never talked to before today, but claiming they'd been friends with her their whole lives. The students weren't mobbing her to congratulate her, they were trying to make the News think they were her BFFs.

But that job belonged to one person.

Zia.

And she plowed through the throng of reporters and students to arrive at Mara's side. Josie appreciated the help as the two of them covered Mara with their bodies and led her back outside to the parking lot.

"This is insane!" Zia yelled over the shouting mob that followed them out of the building. "We have to get you to your car!"

"Second day of school and I still can't make it a whole day!" Mara started to worry that she'd flunk out.

The three of them piled into Mara's VW Bug and locked the doors. The car was soon surrounded by reporters, the students backed off a bit, not wanting to look bad in front of the cameras.

Then Mara heard a shout over the madness and mayhem. "I found Colt Lennox! He just walked into Hallway B!"

And just like that, the students and the reporters were gone, off to confront the bully of the video. Mara knew she wasn't safe, but at least they had been distracted.

"Thank God!" Zia was in the back seat and leaned forward.

A small knock on the car window made all three of them jump.

Mara's heart leapt into her throat when she saw Adam standing there with a smile. He spoke loudly so they could hear him through the glass. "He's not really in Hallway B, I just wanted to get rid of them for you."

Mara rolled down the window, smiling back at him. "Thank you."

"You're a genius!" Zia exclaimed. "Get in here."

Mara was about to unlock her door, but Josie was too quick. Her sister shoved her door open and waved Adam to the passenger side. "You sit in front, I'll get in the back."

Before the press or any stray students could figure out Adam's ruse, he hurried inside and they were off.

"I'm Zia, by the way," Zia introduced herself with a knowing smile.

"I'm Josie... Mara's sister." Josie acted shyly, which was unusual for her. The way her little sister had been raving about Adam's character to their dad this morning, Mara thought she'd be talking up a storm. But Josie just sat back, trying to look cool and casual instead.

Adam turned his body so he could see Zia and Josie and smiled warmly. "I know who you guys are. This school isn't that big." Then he suddenly seemed embarrassed, which was really adorable to all three of the girls. "And... you were just being polite. Sorry. I'm an idiot."

"You have nothing to apologize for after what you just did." Zia was highly impressed. "I should have thought of that."

"You were too busy trying to protect her. I honestly didn't know if it would do the trick, but it was worth a shot. If that hadn't worked I would've had to body check a few of those reporters. And as you can tell from my skinny stature, that probably wouldn't have worked out too well," he laughed.

And the girls laughed with him. In the rear view mirror Zia

gave an enormous widening of the eyes, which was BFF code for, "I really like him!"

The rest of the car ride (all five minutes of it) was getting to know you chit-chat on Zia and Adam's part, although Mara was fascinated to hear about him as well. It was amazing how little people knew about each other, even though they'd seen each other every day since Kindergarten. At least with Adam it had only been three years but, still, three years was a long time and Mara knew almost nothing about him.

They had all made a group decision to go back to Mara and Josie's house. They figured that the four of them would be high targets on the reporters' radar, so it was safer if they all stayed home for the day. At least, that was what they were hoping their parents would buy.

Opening the front door, they ran into Claire, who was on her way out. "Oh thank goodness!" she exclaimed when she saw the four of them. "I just saw you on the news, running from those locusts. I was coming to get you."

Mara sighed in relief. She had been afraid her mom would want her to face her fears and go back to school, but the news footage must have looked scary enough for her mother to drop everything to come and pick her up.

Claire ushered them inside. "Come in, come in. I have cookies." She always knew the way to a teenager's heart.

Her mother made sure Adam walked in first so she could give Mara the excited-Mom look, followed by Josie and Zia high-fiving Claire to show their support as well. If Mara knew she'd get this much excitement out of her family and friends she would have started dating a long time ago.

Adam was out of his element: he was shy and a little intimidated to be welcomed so kindly. It broke Mara's heart that the guy wasn't used to common decency. His life was mind-boggling to her. Not having family and friends that love you unconditionally was something Mara never wanted to think of. She was just happy she could show Adam that there actually were nice people in the world.

The rest of the afternoon was more fun than Mara had had in a long time. Everyone got along with Adam as well as Mara did. He even put his arm around her, and held her hand throughout the day, which sent shivers up Mara's spine every time he did it. She kept remembering their kiss… she just wanted to drag him upstairs to be alone with him.

When three o'clock rolled around, she finally received her wish. Claire offered to take Zia back to school so she could pick up her car. Mara's mother also wanted to talk directly to the principal to make sure there would be no reporters on campus so her daughters could go to school without having to worry about their safety. Josie went with them so she could go over to her friend Molly's house.

Within minutes, Adam and Mara were all alone in the house, which showed how much Claire trusted her daughter. She had always thought that her mom would never let her be alone with a boy but, apparently, Claire knew her daughter well. Mara wasn't ready for anything beyond kissing and she knew Adam would respect that.

"Let me see your room," Adam suggested innocently, then realized the implications because his face turned red. "I mean, we don't have to… I…"

Mara saved his embarrassment. "Come on, it's upstairs." She boldly grabbed his hand and led him up the steps to her bedroom.

Adam surveyed the space like it was a museum. It made Mara view everything over-critically, hoping nothing he saw would make him think less of her. But from the expression on his face, he loved every detail.

"I would kill to have a room like this," he said, walking over to her desk and pulling down the first Harry Potter book. He placed the book back where he found it and his eyes looked almost haunted, as if imagining her life was as hard as it had been for Mara to imagine his was. "You've had a good life, huh?"

"Yeah, pretty decent." Mara didn't want to gush about how her parents were amazing and her sister was as much of a best friend to her as Zia. She didn't want to sound like she was bragging, rubbing it in, so she decided not to elaborate.

Adam reached out for her with his hand and Mara took it gladly. The familiar tingles raced through her body and before she could stop herself, she leaned in to kiss him. Adam must have been feeling the same way because he returned the kiss with fervor. Mara was so instantly dizzy from the sensation that her body almost went numb from an overload of emotion. She felt so connected to Adam it physically made her chest ache. She was more confident now. If he hadn't pulled away, she would have been lost forever in the perfect moment.

"Whoa," he said breathlessly. "If we don't stop now, I don't think I'll be able to."

Mara nodded, breathless herself. "Yeah, agreed." She took a few deep breaths to calm her racing heart and Adam did the same.

His relieved smile made her toes tingle. "I've never met anyone like you," he whispered, his forehead touching hers, still holding her hands.

Being that close and not kissing was both agonizing and comforting. Mara's feelings were so intense she'd lost the ability to speak again.

Adam leaned back enough to kiss her forehead. "This is crazy."

Mara found her voice as she peered into his eyes. "Good crazy or bad crazy?"

"You know which crazy." He kissed her again.

Mara's mind went blank it was so overwhelming. His lips were soft yet forceful. There was almost a desperation to the kiss, as if they'd never be able to separate.

"I'm home!" Claire called from downstairs. "You two want dinner?"

They broke from their embrace, out of breath again, but both smiling from the rush.

Mara yelled down to her mother. "No, thanks! Maybe in an hour or two."

"Suit yourself!" Claire answered back.

Still feeling the intensity of the moment she had with Adam, Mara realized that kissing the right person was like a drug, a high she knew she'd never have with any real narcotic. She was just grateful she didn't have an addictive personality, otherwise Adam would have been in trouble.

He shook his head, then his whole body as if he had to physically force himself into the present moment. "I have to sit." Adam ran his hand through his messy hair and he plopped down on Mara's desk chair. "That was intense."

Mara sat on the edge of her bed so that their knees were touching. She found she was growing more and more confident as she reached over and laced her fingers through Adam's. "That's the understatement of the year."

His grin made her belly do flip-flops. It was as if they had some inside joke that only the two of them shared.

It was in that moment that Mara knew she wanted to tell him everything. She took a deep breath.

Adam leaned forward, concerned. "What is it? Are you alright?"

"I'm fine, but I have to tell you something and you might think differently of me afterwards. But I swear I'm not a psycho or some weird New-Agey wannabe."

Adam took her hands again so they were both leaned into each other as they sat. "I'm confused."

"I know you were young," Mara started cautiously, "but do you remember the Lopez Butcher? It was about ten years ago, but it was pretty public."

Adam's expression turned into curiosity. "Yeah. Barely though. Wasn't she some grandma who chopped up her husband?"

Mara nodded, then spoke before she chickened out, "She was my Great Aunt. As in, my grandmother's sister. As in, I'm related to her. By blood."

Adam stared at her thoughtfully. He wasn't saying a word. It made her palms sweat. Was he freaked? Was he repulsed?

Finally he said, "You know I would never judge you for something like that, right? Look who my dad is. Do you think less of me because he beats me? I mean, I'm *directly* related to him.

Maybe I'll turn out the same way?" His voice quavered slightly.

Mara understood then that they had more in common than she even knew. She was always terrified that she would become like her aunt because she was related to her, just as Adam was equally terrified that he'd turn out like his father.

It was who they were.

Mara never wanted to admit it, but her fear of becoming like her aunt scared her beyond imagining. She knew, logically, that she could never be like Eleanor. Still, irrationally, the fear was always there, lingering in the back of her thoughts. And her dreams... Mara had always wondered if her aunt had had dreams like hers – if, maybe, she'd ignored them her whole life until, finally, she had acted on them. What if Mara would do the same thing? Tired of the nightmares, tired of the violence that she finally gave in?

She voiced her thoughts aloud, "Are you scared you'll turn out like him?"

Adam averted his eyes for a moment, then turned to look at Mara. "Sometimes. When I get angry, it's like I'm afraid I'll snap. I just... I don't know."

Mara squeezed his hands tight. "I get scared, too. I don't want to be like her, but I'm afraid I won't be able to control it."

Adam looked at her quizzically.

"But why? It's not like you have homicidal thoughts, do you?" There wasn't a hint of judgment in Adam's tone. It was as if he would be okay if she answered "yes."

"Not exactly, but I do dream some pretty nasty stuff." Mara took a deep breath, then continued forward, "I know every detail of what happened to Ed Garner because I was there. In my dream. I dream about murders that actually happen." Mara spit it out before she could talk herself out of it.

Adam didn't look like he disbelieved her, it was more like he was taken aback and didn't know what to do with the information. "I see," was all he said.

"I can't predict the future or anything. If I'm dreaming of someone getting killed, it's happening at the exact same time. It's like I'm a camera in the room," she tried to explain.

Adam pulled his hands away gently. It shouldn't have crushed her, but it did. She desperately wanted him to understand but, judging by the look on his face, she wasn't sure if he wanted to.

"Maybe your mind makes you dream of horrible things because that's just who you are?" Adam posed it as a question not a statement.

Mara wasn't offended. She knew what he meant. "It started when my great aunt murdered my uncle. He was the only grandfather figure I ever knew and I loved him more than I even liked her. I hate that I'm related to her. I wish I had been related to Uncle John, then I could just be heartbroken that he died and was killed by his crazy wife. But I'm related to *her* and there's nothing I can do about that. But I saw the whole thing. Every detail. All wrapped up in a horrible nightmare I re-live almost every day." When Adam didn't respond either way, she added, "Anyway, it must have opened up some part of my brain that connected to crimes like that because I've been dreaming of killings ever since. The news is my proof that I didn't make it up, I guess."

Adam appeared stunned, as in: wide-eyed shock. He slowly started to nod his head. "So you *saw* what happened to Mr.

Garner?"

Mara nodded, not sure if she had ruined everything by telling him.

"Can you tell me what you saw?" he asked cautiously.

"I'm not sure if I should…" Mara doubted herself by the second.

Adam's hands were back in hers and his expression was serious. "I believe you." His grip tightened supportively. "Tell me, please. I want to know."

Mara told him the whole dream from start to finish. He watched her the whole time as if he were tuned into an intense horror film.

Afterward, he shook his head. "I can't believe you have to go through that." He moved to sit next to Mara on the bed. He brushed his hand against her cheek. "You are an amazing person." Adam leaned down and kissed her gently.

It almost made her want to cry. She had been so scared he was going to run as far from her as possible. Mara could still see it would take a while for Adam to truly process what she had told him, but the important part was that he believed her. He didn't think she was some attention-hungry schmuck that pretended to be psychic.

He pulled back and slowly smiled. "You still want to solve this thing? Or is it going to be too hard to re-live it?"

Mara collapsed into Adam and her heart soared when he held her. "I want to help catch this guy before he kills again."

Adam leaned back while still holding her so they could see each other. "We will. I promise."

Mara rested her head back on his chest. She was never more

content in her entire life.

"We should go over to their house. Maybe we could find something the police missed," Adam suggested suddenly.

The thought sent a shudder of fear down Mara's body. "But there are reporters still out there. I think the police aren't even done yet, are they?" She could hear the terror in her own voice.

Adam gently caressed her arms to calm her. "No one will ever know we were there. I've snuck in and out of foster homes my whole life. I know how to get into a house undetected. But if you saw the whole murder, you'll know where to look for clues. Maybe the killer dropped something? Or maybe you'll remember something when you're there. We should try, don't you think?"

Mara saw the logic, but breaking the law was a thought so terrifying she didn't even know how to fathom it. "I don't think I can do that."

Adam leaned down and kissed her softly, then pulled away. "Trust me. We need to do this."

She did trust him.

She didn't want to do it.

But a part of her did. To see where it happened. Maybe she could help for once. She knew every step the killer had taken. Every place he stopped. It would be difficult, but maybe they could find something that would help the police. Slowly, she nodded. "We have to be quick, though. I don't want to get caught."

Adam grinned and kissed her again. "We won't get caught, I promise."

"Well, my mom thinks we're coming down to dinner in…" Mara glanced at her alarm clock, "in less than an hour. So we have to be there and back in thirty."

Adam stood up and walked to the window. "Let's do it."

Mara joined him by his side. "I'm on the second floor. We can't jump."

"Oh ye of little faith. I've snuck out of a three-story place before. We can do this."

To Mara's surprise, it was a lot easier to break out of her room than she thought it would be. Then again, she wasn't the kind of girl who would ever dream of sneaking out, so she'd never thought about it before. But if she had had a rebellious streak, gaining access to freedom would have been relatively easy. There was a small awning underneath Mara's window and the jump was only seven or eight feet. Mara didn't land too gracefully, but neither one of them were hurt.

The night sky was overcast so it was darker than normal, so that was helpful in avoiding the two news vans that were parked just outside the police tape line. Mara wondered why the press was still even there. She knew that in the morning the place would be a circus again, especially if her YouTube numbers kept climbing. The neighborhood was turning into a media circus.

Mara was impressed at the way Adam led her across the street to the Garner's. He really *did* know how to avoid detection, finding every bush, tree or parked car to hide behind. It was as if they were escaping from prison and Mara was afraid a giant searchlight would suddenly focus on her and they'd both be caught.

But within seconds the two of them were standing at the back of Ed Garner's house.

Adam and Mara stayed hidden within the shadow of the

two-story home. It was easy since there was a small outcropping of trees surrounding Ed's backyard.

Although doing this was way out of Mara's comfort-zone, part of her loved the adrenaline that was pumping through her. There was a full-out battle going on inside her head. One side wanted to run back to the safety of her own home – and the other needed to walk in the shoes of the killer. It was the second thought that gave Mara pause. Was it morbid to want to retrace the murderer's steps? But if there was something she missed… Something she hadn't wanted to see because she had so desperately tried to wake-up. It was worth putting up with the raging war inside her head.

And in the end, it looked like being daring and reckless won out because she followed Adam through the window he had just opened.

Placing her feet on the ground of the Garner's first floor, Mara's head began to spin. If Adam hadn't caught her arm she would have dropped to the floor.

"You okay?" Adam asked, concerned.

Mara shook her head to steady herself. "Yeah." She took a deep breath before the dizzy spell could turn into a full-blown panic attack. The last thing she needed was to pass out or have a lack-of-air breathing fit. "I get panicky. Sorry."

Adam pulled her in and held her tightly. "Do you want to leave? We can leave. This was stupid."

Mara gently withdrew from the hug. "No. I want to see where it happened. I have to help find this guy."

Adam paused, thinking, then he slowly nodded. "Let's just make it quick."

"Yeah, good idea." Mara calmed herself with one more deep breath, then lurched ahead, leading the way.

Walking up the stairs, Mara could see the hallway from her dreams. It was almost like visiting a movie set, her vision had been so clear that night. Once she began moving down the same hallway the killer used, Mara's forehead instantly beaded sweat. At this point Mara was certain that an anxiety fit was imminent, but she kept it in check by doing her breathing exercises.

Moving forward helped as well. Sometimes when Mara's nervousness reached the point of an attack, pacing would bring her back down to normal. She was so self-involved in her own delicate inner-balance, though, that Mara wasn't paying any attention to Adam. Turning to look at him, she noticed his eyes were everywhere, looking for clues while Mara was still stuck in her own head: on the tan painted walls, the hanging pictures and art, the floor, the ceiling, the caution tape on the open doorway… at Ed's open bedroom door roped off with police tape at the end of the corridor.

"You see anything?" she asked.

"I really don't know what I'm looking for," he admitted. "The police probably went through the place pretty thoroughly. But you saw what he saw, so… anything?"

Mara didn't want to confess that she hadn't really been focusing on finding any clues, so she shrugged. "Nothing so far."

Turning away from Adam, Mara finally arrived at the bedroom door. They easily ducked under the tape and entered the crime scene.

Everything was exactly as Mara remembered it, except for the bed. It was stripped of all blankets, sheets and pillows.

It was real.

This was really happening.

Mara almost fell over again from a dizzy spell. Adam caught her again and began to help her sit in an easy chair by the window.

"No. I don't want to sit. I'm fine." Mara yanked away from Adam.

And suddenly Mara was in utter shock.

It was as if she had been asleep and woke up in Ed's room.

How did she get here? What had she been thinking? Mara had never re-visited a murder scene from one of her dreams, not even her great uncle's...

"What are we doing here?" she asked in disgusted horror.

Adam's eyes were confused and possibly hurt, Mara couldn't tell for certain. But his answer echoed her own thoughts. "I was just thinking the same thing."

"We should leave... now." Mara didn't want to look for clues. Who did she think she was? Some kind of detective? Part of her knew she had only agreed to come there because it meant doing something daring with Adam. But this... Seeing where Ed Garner died of being injected by poison...

As if in answer to her declaration of needing to exit, the front door opened downstairs.

A familiar voice yelled from below. "Is anybody in here?!"

Detective Jennifer Nicholson.

Mara almost passed out right there.

Adam was horrified.

They both knew they couldn't be caught.

Detective Nicholson already suspected Mara knew more that she was letting on. If the detective found Mara hanging out at

91

the crime scene?

Was it possible to puke and faint at the same time?

Adam whispered, terrified, "If she finds me here, they'll take me away from my dad for sure."

Why did we come here? She asked herself again.

Mara couldn't seem to fathom how this ever sounded like a good idea.

The sound of footsteps on the stairwell.

Adam rushed to the window and slid it open slowly so as not to make a sound.

Mara knew what he intended. They were on the second floor. The only way down was the staircase past Detective Nicholson.

If they were going to escape, they'd have to climb out the second-story window.

Adam whispered directly in Mara's ear. "Crawl out and hang from the sill, then jump. With your height it'll be about a seven foot drop then grass beneath you. We should be fine."

Mara didn't argue. She had no choice.

She climbed out the window, her heart racing and palms sweating. Mara couldn't think about the fact that she was jumping down from the second level. If she did, she'd freeze and Detective Nicholson would catch them for sure. So she went into what she called "zombie-mode." Whenever something was too stressful or scary for Mara to handle, it was as if a switch flipped in her head and all her emotions went away, like being a zombie. She was able to function perfectly, but it was almost as if she were a living robot.

"Hello?! Is anyone here?!" Detective Nicholson's voice was closer than before, in the hallway now.

Mara stretched her arms and dropped the remaining seven feet. The grass broke her fall. She moved out of the way for Adam to drop down next to her.

And they were off.

Mara didn't look back.

She simply booked it to her house.

It wasn't until Mara ran inside her house that she realized her mother had thought she was upstairs.

"What on earth?" Claire jumped at her daughter's sudden entrance into the kitchen.

It was then that Mara turned to make sure Adam was still with her. She had been in such a hurry to escape, she hadn't looked behind.

To her relief, Adam walked in casually behind her. She could tell he was hiding the fact that he was out of breath, trying to play it cool in front of Mara's mother.

"When did you two leave?" Claire seemed more perplexed at herself for not noticing them leaving in the first place.

Mara played into her mother's confusion. "We went outside for some air about twenty minutes ago, but that police detective showed up at the Garner's so we ran inside." It was close enough to the truth that Mara hoped her mother would buy it.

She did.

"That woman. I still haven't decided if I should make a formal complaint at how she treated you."

"She's just doing her job." Mara didn't know why she was defending the detective, but at the moment she was simply relieved her mother believed her story.

Claire walked over to the window by the front door to take a peek. Mara and Adam joined her.

Mara saw Detective Nicholson exiting the house, shouting orders at two officers who were parked outside. Since Mara hadn't seen the cop car before she entered the Garner's, she assumed it was the vehicle that brought the detective to the house.

By the anger and frustration Mara could clearly see in Detective Nicholson's face, it was obvious the detective knew someone had been inside the house.

Mara just prayed Detective Nicholson wouldn't find out it was her.

Moving away from the window, Mara tried to shake the overwhelming sense of dread flushing through her.

Dream Entry #7

*I*t's about ten o'clock and I can't sleep so I decided to write in this thing. I should only be writing about my dreams in here, but I find that everything in my life somehow revolves around my dreams anyway, so I might as well document it all.

Adam went home around seven, after dinner, and we didn't get a chance to be alone again before he left. I'm kind of freaking out. I still can't believe we went over to the Garner's. I didn't even find anything useful. I seriously panicked. I feel like such an idiot.

And what does Adam feel? What if the more time he has to think about what we did, the less he wants to see me? What if he blames me for wanting to go over there? He could have been caught by the police and sent to a foster home. It had been such a danger for him. Why did he even risk it?

And I told him about my aunt! And my dreams! He probably thinks I'm a psychopath. I had just thought that our connection *was so insanely crazy that he'd think that me sharing was the most amazing thing ever and we'd live happily ever after. It's not as if he rejected me, though. He left with a smile and even gave me a kiss on the cheek. (Not the mouth, since my parents were there!) I'm just afraid that he will hate me tomorrow, or worse, be repulsed. I better prepare myself. After everything we went through today, I just don't want to have one of my dreams tonight.*

That would really suck.

***

Mara was dreaming.

It was a strange sensation, *being aware* in a dream. It could be fun at times, creating your own universe, flying if you wanted to, defeating bad guys and being a hero. But those things only happened when Mara was inside her own head, living her own dreams.

Right now she was in someone else's head.

Mara could always tell.

Most people couldn't see the difference, but Mara could.

When she was inside someone else's dreams, things were different, and usually worse, mainly because Mara had trouble controlling someone else's dreamscape. She could only manipulate her own dreams with ease. So she was at the mercy of the dreamer's brain.

It was also impossible to tell *whose* dream she was in. It could be anyone really. Her mom, Zia, Josie, a stranger, or even a killer…

Mara hated being in someone else's head. It was always

96

difficult to escape, since she had little to no control, but she didn't want to be inside someone else's dream tonight, so she decided to try.

Mara concentrated on making herself fly.

Nothing.

She tried creating a door so that she could escape through and ditch this place.

Still nothing.

Internally shrugging, now that it was fairly certain she couldn't leave just yet, Mara settled in to see what would happen next.

She was on a suburban street with rundown houses and overgrown trees lining the sidewalks. The roots from the maples grew into the road itself, forming bumps and cracks on the pavement.

It was empty, as if everyone on the block had deserted the neighborhood for good.

Since she was probably going to be stuck there for a while, she decided to take a look around.

Not wanting to go into any of the houses for fear of things going terribly wrong, Mara walked down the empty street. It was actually rather pleasant. The houses may have been shabby, but they looked well lived in, almost cozy. And the trees may have been unruly, but they towered over the homes as if they were guarding them from the world.

The farther Mara walked, though, the more dilapidated the houses became. As the homes grew more decrepit so did the plants and foliage. It was like entering into an apocalyptic future, humanity forgotten in time and weeds.

Her instincts kicked in and she turned around to walk back to the more cozy part of the dream – but it was gone, replaced by blackened houses with ivy and moss growing wild on their walls.

Dark swollen clouds appeared out of nowhere. It began to rain. A slight drizzle at first, then a torrential downpour. Mara stayed dry, though, as if she were walking inside a waterproof bubble that protected her from the storm.

There was still no one to be seen. Mara began to wonder if she was being watched by the dreamer. Was the dreamer trying to mess with her? To see where she would go and what she would do? The funny thing was that, whoever's dream this was, tomorrow they'd wake up and remember the strange girl in their dream who walked in the rain and didn't get wet. And if they knew Mara, they'd wonder why they dreamt about Mara Johnson. This would not be the first time it had happened. She lost count of how many times Zia had started to tell her about a dream that Mara had been in – only to have Mara tell her the rest of it, to Zia's utter amazement.

People would be so jealous that Mara could remember and control her dreams. But it wasn't always a good thing. Sometimes, it could go very bad.

In the distance she could see hundreds of balloons hovering a few feet off the ground. Each balloon was carrying some kind of item that Mara could not quite make out. The rain suddenly stopped, but the sky remained dark and dismal. The contrast between the bright- colored balloons and the blackened sky was jarring.

The closer she walked toward the floating objects, the more frightened she became. She still couldn't tell what the balloons were carrying, though, and her gut started screaming at her to run the other way.

Curiosity won out in the end. She kept moving toward the mass of hovering colors, like a moth attracted to the flame. She simply had to see what was dangling from the seemingly innocent parade of balloons.

After what seemed like hours of walking, Mara was finally close enough to see what hung inches from the ground.

Body parts.

Bloody and mangled.

Arms, legs, heads, torsos, hands, feet…

Some unrecognizable, some too clear and sharp.

She covered her mouth with her hand, needing to scream, but holding back, not wanting to alert the dreamer.

Mara was in a killer's head.

The balloons flaunted the body parts around like trophies. These were his prizes, forever stored to playback and dream about at will.

She wondered if this was the same killer who murdered Ed Garner. Maybe she was connected to him now. Maybe her mind didn't want to see out of his eyes because he was killing a new victim. Maybe being in his dreamscape was a kindness, so she wouldn't have to watch him hurt anyone else.

Soon, the balloons were all around her, floating with child-like innocence while tied to nightmares.

Mara ran back the way she had come, but there was no end to the suspended body parts. She tried not to touch the bloody stumps, but they brushed up against her, leaving blood on her clothes.

On her pure white dress.

She suddenly noticed she was wearing a long, flowing white dress with spaghetti straps. It was streaked with the red from the forest of death closing in on her.

Mara ran and ran with no end to the balloons and their cargo.

Until, all at once, she was inside a basement.

It was cold and empty, all cement floors and walls. Only one small rectangular window gave any light to the space, sunlight pouring through the glass.

It lit up a wooden table leaned up against the wall.

Mara walked over to the table.

An entire body lay in pieces, forming a bloody pile on top of the darkened wood. She saw the back of the head, long hair wet with blood, covering the face of a woman. Wrapped around her jagged neck was a locket with a rose engraved on its surface.

Mara woke with a start, sweating and shaking profusely. Terror raced through her to the point where she couldn't move. She must have been inside the head of the man that killed Ed Garner. It had to be. How else could she explain what she saw? Her body was frozen on her bed. It was as if the killer stood over her. Even though, logically, Mara knew it wasn't true, her senses told her differently. It was like that sometimes. She had grown so used to her visions that they hadn't affected her like this in a long time. Even Mr. Garner's had been more of a movie rather than reality.

But this…

This was more intimate, a glimpse into the killer's personal thoughts. It was paralyzing.

Mara tried taking deep breaths to calm herself, but her breathing was shaky and she couldn't seem to relax.

It was just a dream. It was just a dream. It was just a dream. She kept repeating this mantra in her head.

She knew that wasn't true.

So she switched tactics.

Learn from the dream.

What could this dream tell her about who killed Ed?

The houses. Were they real? Did they exist somewhere?

Mara knew that the balloons weren't real, but had they been body parts of all the killer's previous victims? Or because this was *his* dream, was this just his fantasy about killing so many people and how he'd want to display them for the world to see? It wasn't as if he chopped up Ed Garner. He had poisoned him. So was this what he really wanted to do with Ed? What he had done to others?

The woman. The basement. The wooden table.

That was real.

Mara couldn't explain how she knew that, but she was certain of it. The body, a woman's body, was his first victim. It was separate from the grotesque balloon-parade of severed limbs.

If she could find the basement, she could find the killer. Better yet, the *cops* could find the killer. Mara really didn't want to have a run-in with a murderer.

Thinking it through helped her calm down a bit. Her heart slowed to a normal pace, she stopped sweating. Once her legs unlocked, Mara slid out of bed and walked to her bathroom. Splashing water on her face brought her back to the here and now. Shaking off the horrors of what she just witnessed, she climbed into bed and stared at the glowing stars plastered on her ceiling.

Mara stayed like that for the remaining four hours until her alarm sounded. She reached over and turned it off. Even though she hadn't slept for the remainder of the night, Mara felt rested. Lying in her bed and staring put her in a meditative state that was sometimes more relaxing than sleep itself. Especially when it came to her nightmares.

Quickly dressing, Mara hurried downstairs and ate a bowl of cereal before any of her family arrived in the kitchen. One-by-one, in a straggling order, Claire, Ben and Josie made their way downstairs. Overall, as everyone ate, talk was light and moods were good.

Claire assured Mara and Josie that she had taken care of any security problems they may have at school. The Principal didn't want the press there any more than Claire did, so they devised a plan that involved Mara parking in the Staff's lot and going in through the janitor's entrance. That was just fine with Mara. She wanted to avoid everyone at all costs anyway, so having a super-sneaky scheme made her extremely happy.

Mara phoned Zia and cued her into the plan. They set up a rendezvous point in Hallway D and Zia promised she'd bring Adam along as well. Mara's personal goon squad to protect her.

Grabbing their things, Mara and Josie hopped in the car and arrived at school in no time. It was almost surreal, parking with the teachers, but when Mr. Trenchard saw Mara, he came to her side immediately.

"Stay with me and I'll keep everyone away," he said with confidence. He was a big man and in good shape for a forty-something year old. "You've had quite a few days, haven't you?" His tone was worried.

Mara's shyness only expounded on itself at having a casual conversation with a teacher. She answered softly, "Thanks for walking me to class, Mr. Trenchard." It was all she could think to say, but it was enough.

Mr. Trenchard looked even more protective, if that was possible, and made sure he was slightly ahead of the sisters as they entered Hallway D.

There weren't that many students lingering about: they were all staking out the two student parking lots waiting for Mara to arrive. Apparently so was the press, because Mara could see camera lights on both ends of the hallway.

Zia and Adam were in the hall, though, waiting for them. They both said hello to Mr. Trenchard and, like Mara, obviously felt too awkward to talk frankly in front of him.

Mara was more relieved than she cared to admit when Adam's hand tangled around hers. At least he seemed okay about their romp inside Ed Garner's house yesterday. And, more importantly, didn't seem put off by Mara's being related to the Lopez Butcher or her crazy dreams. Only time would tell, but for the time being he seemed to be cool with all of the above.

Mr. Trenchard opened the door to his classroom and let the rest of them in, not even questioning the fact that Josie and Zia weren't in his first period. As if reading their minds, he said, "I'll let you four talk alone."

Mara felt a surge of affection for her Calculus teacher. He knew enough about body language and awkward teen behavior to know that they couldn't talk freely with him there.

Congregating at the back of the classroom, Zia gave Mara a hug, causing Adam to let go of her hand.

"Okay, well, better than yesterday, right?" Zia tried to sound positive.

"We'll see how the rest of the day goes, but as long as you guys are here, I'll be okay." Mara wished she could keep Zia, Adam and Josie in her pocket all day.

Zia gave her one last hug. "I'll keep an eye on Kimiko. See how people treat her. We'll figure this thing out."

Josie mock-saluted Mara, then added, "We'll meet you at the door after class."

"Thanks," Mara smiled.

It made the situation not seem as dire having the three of them watching her back. Her nightmare from last night still left her rattled, as well as her near miss with Detective Nicholson, but Mara knew that the main event for today would be avoiding attention from her recent YouTube fame. She still didn't know how the other students were interpreting the video. Mara was certain there would be Colt and Kimiko fans that would be against Mara no matter what. She just wanted them to stay away from her.

After Zia and Josie left, Adam pulled Mara in for a tight embrace. She almost wanted to cry in relief. He kissed the top of her head. "I'm sorry about yesterday," he said as he pulled back within her arms.

"We *both* decided to go over there. I'm just glad we didn't get caught." Mara looked down, worried at his reaction. "I probably shouldn't have told you about my aunt and my dreams. You must think I'm a freak."

Adam's hands held her face gently and his eyes were more intense than she'd ever seen them. "Don't say that. Don't ever say that. You were sharing something really important and private. I hope you didn't think I didn't believe you. Because I do. I *really* do."

His words made Mara feel like she could face anything that came her way today. She reached up and kissed Adam. "That's all I needed to hear."

"I just wish we would have had more time to talk alone yesterday. But we ran in and your mom was there, then your dad, then your sister and then I had to go home. I didn't have a chance to talk to you and I didn't want to text you, it seemed too impersonal." Adam touched her cheek. "I've just never heard anyone talk about stuff like that out loud, you know, that wasn't in a movie or TV show or something." He paused, then kissed her so that her whole face tingled. Adam pulled away gently. "I think your dreams are really cool, by the way. You're even more amazing than I already thought you were."

Mara wasn't good with compliments, so instead of answering verbally she leaned into his chest until he embraced her once more.

Adam continued, "As for your aunt, 'F' her. I'm related to a mom who abandoned me and a dad who beats me. We're nothing like them. Never forget that."

Mara nodded into his chest.

The rest of the class started filing in soon after, but no one was too aggressive in their gawking.

And the fact that Adam was in five out of her six classes should make life a lot easier as well. Before she had just stared at him from afar, now they could sit together and actually talk.

It suddenly hit her and before she could stop herself she muttered. "Are we boyfriend and girlfriend?" After she said it, she immediately regretted it. What kind of question was that? And right before class started? And they only just talked to one another for the first time two days ago! And a whole lot of other things that made her regret that she opened her mouth.

But Adam smiled sweetly. "Of course." Then he sat down next to her and let that settle in her exploding psyche.

She couldn't control the grin that was plastered on her face. Her first boyfriend. It made her stomach churn with excitement. It was hard to see the good in her life at times, but Mara finally felt like she was coming out ahead.

She sat back and this time paid attention to every word Mr. Trenchard said, but in the back of her mind she dreamed of Adam.

The rest of the day went as smoothly as it could. There were a couple of close calls with reporters, but Zia had been resourceful by managing to distract them long enough for Mara and Adam to get to class unscathed.

Overall, it was as normal as could be expected. Kimiko and Colt were a no-show, probably taking the week off to let things die down. That was the thing about the Internet. One day you were the hottest thing and the next day no one even remembers you. The amount of views had petered out around two-hundred thousand, and Mara just wanted it to stay that way. No need to alert "The View." She'd be happier still if the whole video just went away for good. On the plus side, most people surprisingly sided with Mara, probably because she was the one who showed up for school. It wouldn't surprise her if everyone flipped sides once the Homecoming couple returned. But as long as everyone left her alone, Mara could deal.

Since Adam had walked to school, Mara drove him home with her and Josie. The two of them had decided they were going to work on the Garner case together, so as soon as Josie went to her room, Adam and Mara opened up her laptop and began their investigation.

Adam sat behind her on the edge of the bed, while Mara sat at her desk.

He looked over her shoulder at the computer screen. "Where do we start?"

"I was thinking we just Google Ed and his wife, Millie. See what comes up," Mara admitted lamely. She hadn't really thought of a plan of action yet.

"I think the police would have thought of that," Adam teased.

"Alright, Mr. Smarty-Pants, what were you thinking?" Mara smiled.

"Well, we already went over there and didn't find anything, or at least we jumped out of a two-story window before we *could* find anything," Adam wrapped his finger in her hair playfully.

Mara offered, "What about the library? They were old, maybe one of them was in some newspaper or something. Or… oh! What about that family history website! We could find out everything we can about their family, from news articles to arrest records. Let's do that." Mara liked the idea of researching.

"You're so cute when you're excited." Adam pulled her closer and then lowered Mara to the bed. He leaned down and kissed her.

If Mara's eyes had been open, they would have been crossed. Feeling his lips pressed against hers, made her forget all about Ed Garner.

They'd research later.

"Mara! Are you up there?!" Claire's voice sounded from downstairs.

Adam pulled away with a grin and it took everything Mara had not to kiss him again, but she answered her mother. "Yeah! Adam and I are doing homework!"

He tickled her. She held back her laughter and swatted his hand.

"I want you two to do your homework downstairs where I can see you!" Claire yelled back.

After the disappearing act of the night before, Claire's trust level in Mara had gone down considerably.

Mara and Adam looked at each other and sighed.

Dream Entry #8

It's been a few days. I know I'm terrible at this diary stuff. I've just been so wrapped up in Adam that I haven't had a chance to sit down and write. We've been trying to investigate the murder, but we keep getting distracted by each other's lips. So far it's just been kissing, neither one of us is ready to go any further, (or, at least, I'm not ready). He is completely respectful of my boundaries, though. It's getting harder and harder to stop, but I want the moment to be perfect, and I'm pretty sure he does too. He's so freaking sweet it makes my head burst! I wish I would have gotten to know him earlier, even if we didn't end up together as a couple. Okay, that's bull. It would have killed me to just be friends! The point is, he's really amazing and I've never been happier.

Detective Nicholson stopped by yesterday and nearly gave me a heart attack, but after a few more questions, none of them very pressing, she left without my mom having to threaten her. The way the detective looks at me though… I think she knows it was me that broke into the Garner's. She just doesn't know why and, the way her brain works, I'm probably still on her suspect list. It was also obvious that the cops are clueless as to who killed Ed Garner. It's making me more determined to help. I tried my Internet search for anything about the Garners, but other than a family history of boring with a side of boring, I didn't find anything. But yesterday's visit from the Detective must have set my mind reeling because last night I had a dream that I think may crack this whole case!

In the dream, I went back to that weird basement in the killer's head. I ignored the disassembled body on the wooden table, (mainly because it was too terrifying to look at for long) and focused on the window. It was about six feet high, so I had to stand on my tip-toes to see out: it was the same neighborhood that I had walked down in my dream, minus the balloons from Hell. It looked normal. I searched for anything, any clue that would tell me where this was because I am sure this is where the killer lives.

And I did it! I saw a street sign on the corner: 6th and Crotonal Avenue. I'm going to tell Adam today; maybe we can do some re-con. I don't want to run into the killer himself, so we'll definitely keep our distance. No matter what, though, I have to see if this place actually exists! I know it does. I've certainly had enough proof over my lifetime to know that my dreams are real, but it always surprises me whenever I see it first hand. It's nice having reinforcement, though. Adam and I can be ninjas. We did jump out a window and escape before getting caught by the police! We'll just peek through the window and see what we see. I'm a little scared, but I have to do this. I'll write later to tell what happened!

***

"Mara! You're going to be late!" Ben shouted from downstairs.

Mara shoved her diary into her bag and ran downstairs. No way was she going to tell her parents about her plans. They'd probably keel over and die if they found out. Yes, Mara knew it was a reckless move, but she was compelled to go. Part of her wasn't sure if it was because she actually wanted to solve this murder – or if it was just a good excuse to do something exciting with Adam. Probably a bit of both. She promised herself that if she sensed even an ounce of danger or the killer himself, she'd grab Adam, call the police and get the heck out of there. She didn't want to risk his life anymore than she wanted to risk her own.

It was a bold move, but Mara was ready for it.

Now, she just had to worry about school.

After a whirlwind breakfast comprised of stuffing a piece of toast down her throat and drinking a chocolate malt Instant Breakfast, Mara and Josie boogied fast in the VW Bug and arrived at Forest Green in record time. It was Friday and, just as Mara had hoped, the media had lost interest in her YouTube video. She figured it was safe to park in the student lot since no one seemed to be lurking around to bother her one way or the other.

Exiting her Bug, Mara noticed a small crowd at the far end of the lot. It wasn't a crowd of reporters, just other kids from school.

Josie craned her neck to see what the cause of the pack was, then she shook her head. "It's them. Let's get inside."

No need to explain who *them* were. Kimiko and Colt. They had yet to show their faces the entire week, but they had finally decided that today was a good time to make an appearance – no cameras, no one watching – as a united front no less.

111

Mara was almost nostalgic for the slew of reporters. She had more confidence that the press would take her side rather than the student body. Years of neglect and hostility from her peers didn't inspire in her any belief that they'd support her. And from the looks of that crowd, it appeared as if they were fawning all over the Power Couple.

Turning away from the small pack of nothing-good, Mara and Josie hurried inside Hallway D. Grabbing her books for the whole day and stuffing them in her bag seemed like a good tactical move; that way Mara wouldn't have to come back to her locker where Colt or Kimiko may lay in wait for her. She knew she was being paranoid, but she had floored the guy by kicking his privates. It wasn't something Mara thought Colt would forgive too soon.

She was about to make a run for Calculus when she heard Colt's voice from behind her. "Mara?"

Her blood turned cold.

Here it was.

He was going to punch her in the face, or ridicule her publicly.

Just get it over with, Mara sighed deeply and turned to face him.

Instead of the angry, scary face she thought she'd see, Colt's expression was actually one of... remorse. It threw her whole psyche off so much that it rendered her speechless.

"You were right to defend yourself. I'm really sorry," Colt said loud enough for everyone to hear.

She couldn't tell if he meant it, or if he wanted everyone to believe that he did. Either way, Mara would take it: fake apologies worked the same as real ones in her book if it meant he wasn't going to make her life hell for the rest of the school year.

So Mara played along. "I shouldn't have kicked you… there… but, thanks."

After a strange, agonizing silence, Colt's smile grew even larger. "Okay, well, I'll see you around."

Kimiko averted her eyes as she left with Colt.

Josie was the first to speak, "That was so weird."

"Yeah," Mara agreed, "but it's a lot better than being tortured."

Her sister shook her head. "I don't know about that. I'd keep my guard up if I were you. Kimiko didn't even look at you. They could be plotting something."

Mara didn't like the sound of that. "Like what?"

"I don't know. But I smell a trap," Josie observed with confidence.

That was the last thing Mara wanted to think about. "Well, I'm going to enjoy the peace as long as I can." Mara decided it was better not to be paranoid. She had enough to worry about today with her plan to go to 6th and Crotonal with Adam.

Speaking of which…

"Where's Adam and Zia anyway?" she asked, while craning her neck to try and spot them down the hall.

"Adam I don't know about, but Zia had to do some Homecoming committee thing with Rachel Chevner," Josie said as she walked with Mara to Mr. Trenchard's room.

"Oh, yeah, that's right. She told me that last night," Mara remembered. "But where's Adam?"

Josie nudged Mara playfully. "Dating a whole week and you can't live without each other?"

Mara's face turned red. "No. It's just that he usually walks me to class, that's all."

"Uh-huh." Josie eyed her sister knowingly as they arrived at Mara's classroom. "Maybe he's waiting inside for you." She waved as she walked away. "See you after school."

But Adam wasn't in the room. He didn't show up for class at all. After Calculus, Mara texted him to see if he was okay, but he didn't respond. She started to get worried. In the pit of her stomach, Mara knew what his absence meant. Adam's father must have done something to him.

Finishing out the day was utter torture. She desperately wanted to skip school and go to Adam's house to see if he was all right, but seeing as she'd missed the first two days of the week, Mara was too much of a chicken to leave school on her own.

On the bright side, Colt and Kimiko appeared to be as good as Colt's word. They weren't exactly friendly, but they didn't throw her snide looks, either. Honestly, her mind was so focused on Adam, she barely had time to notice if they had their plotting-faces on. Zia promised to keep an eye on Kimiko. She treated the whole thing like an espionage operation, her mission being to try and pump Kimiko for as much information as possible, hoping she could make her slip and reveal what sinister plot she and Colt and were conjuring up. Mara wasn't as sure of the duo's evil intent as Josie and Zia were, but she let her sister and best friend strategize all the same.

Finally, the day was over and Mara could go find Adam. Dropping Josie off at home, she drove directly to Adam's house. Giving him a ride home a couple of days ago, Mara had only been there once, but she'd memorized the route by heart. She hadn't gone inside, though: Adam seemed too ashamed to let her in, so Mara didn't press him.

But she was feeling protective at the moment and she planned on kicking the door down if she thought Adam was in trouble. Parking her car in front of his house, Mara walked to the front door and knocked forcefully. No sense being timid, even though inside she was shaking like a leaf. Her dad always told her barking dogs sensed fear and one needed to fake dominance and confidence so that they'd leave her alone. Adam's dad was basically a big human dog, so she held her head high and tried to hide her terror.

Waiting another five minutes, Mara knocked even harder on the door. She was about to leave to look for Adam elsewhere when the door slowly opened.

Adam stood there.

At first glance he looked fine and Mara was about to feel relief – tempered by a righteous annoyance at his ignoring her all day – but relief that he was okay.

Then she saw the black edge of a giant bruise poking up past his t-shirt's collar.

She reached out instinctively to touch it. He flinched away.

The gaping chasm of how different their lives truly were hit Mara hard. "Are you alright?" her voice was small, all bravado gone.

Before she knew what was happening, Adam pulled her into the house and hugged her tightly. His grasp was so desperate she didn't know what to do except simply return his embrace.

She whispered, "Was it your dad?"

Adam's head nodded into her shoulder.

It broke her heart. He was so vulnerable in that moment.

Nothing she could say would help. Nothing could take back what had happened to him. Nothing could make him feel better. It was such a helpless feeling, it made her want to cry. But she didn't want Adam to comfort her, not when he was the one that needed comforting. It was too horribly selfish to even think about.

"No one has ever cared enough to see if I was okay," his voice cracked.

She never knew her heart could be wrenched so utterly. Mara held on to him tighter and he held her in return. And before she knew what she was saying she said, "I love you." The scary part was: she meant it. She had loved him from afar for three years and now that they were finally together, it was as if something inside her was completed. Of course, as soon she said it, Mara was petrified that it would only scare him off. The thought of losing him was more terrifying than her worst nightmare.

But his words made her whole body sing. "I love you, too."

Adam pulled back enough to kiss her. Feeling him pressed up against her, filled with so much emotion, Mara almost gasped. But she didn't want to breathe, she only wanted to feel his soft lips on hers, as if Adam was her oxygen mask and she'd suffocate without him.

Eventually Adam gently drew back, his eyes full of affection for Mara. Considering how much love she had for Adam in that moment, she could only imagine her expression was the same.

"We should get out of here before my dad wakes up. I don't want him to hurt you." Adam kissed her forehead. "I'm sorry I didn't text you back today."

"Don't be. I get it." Mara reached up and touched his cheek. "I could talk to my parents. Maybe you can stay with us until you turn eighteen."

He shook his head. "No. I'm okay. My dad needs me." Adam said it with such a sincerity that Mara didn't want to argue the matter with him. Besides, she really didn't even know where to begin, so she let it go for the time being.

Adam took Mara's hand and led her out of the house before she could have a good look around. Somewhere in there was Adam's father, asleep after beating his own son. She couldn't wrap her head around it. Violence was abhorred in her family, which was why she'd been so scared her parents were going to ground her for hurting Colt. Growing up in an environment where the only kind of brutality Mara was ever exposed to was in her dreams made Adam's situation surreal. Here he was. Her boyfriend. With bruises all over his body, but only the parts that didn't show. That meant his dad hit with precision and planning, which made it a whole lot worse in Mara's mind. Spur of the moment, mean-drunk-abuse was still horrifying… but a carefully thought-out beating was… evil. There was no other word that described it for Mara.

Adam's father was evil.

Mara took his hand. "Let's get out of here."

Adam didn't argue. She led him to her car and they started driving. Mara decided she didn't want to tell Adam about the "dream location" just yet. This moment needed to be about him and not her, so Mara drove to a park a mile away from Adam's house. They didn't talk on the short ride over. Adam touched her arm as if he needed to be grounded, though his eyes stared out, lost in thought.

The park was secluded, with an outcropping of majestic pines as its backdrop. The perfect place for escape. Only a handful of kids played on a jungle gym in the front of the park, with their parents' looking on. It was peaceful and serene even though clouds were gathering, grey and swollen, ready to rain.

Mara took Adam by the hand and led him deep into the small forest until they were the only two people in sight. She didn't want anyone around. She didn't want anyone to see them. Mara simply wanted to be alone with Adam, the rest of the world be damned.

The fifty-foot pines towered overhead, protecting them from the elements as it began to rain. The soft thumping of water drops were loud against the silence between them as they stared at each other. It wasn't weird. It wasn't awkward. It was intense.

Adam couldn't hold back anymore. He leaned down and kissed Mara as if he hadn't seen her in decades. Mara responded back, feeling the same way. His hands pulled her in tighter, making her want him more. His lips were fevered with desire and desperation. She knew from the strength of his embrace that she was all he had.

Mara never felt more alive than she did in that moment. His touch, his lips…

The heat from his body against hers in contrast to the cold was numbing and the wet air blowing through the trees only intensified the sensation. Mara pulled on Adam's shirt, lowering him to the ground with her. He was gentle in his movements, continuing to kiss her as he lay Mara on her back. She drew him in closer so she could feel him against her.

The rain seeped through the pine needles, falling on Adam's back and onto Mara's face, but it was refreshing and exhilarating.

Mara knew she was ready.

She wanted to be with Adam more than anything in the world.

Even out here, in the cold, with dirt and twigs digging into her back, she wanted Adam to be her first.

Adam sensed where this was headed as well when he admitted in a whisper, "I've never done this before." His eyes were vulnerable, scared at what Mara's reaction may be.

It made her love him even more. "Me, neither."

Adam's kiss deepened at her confession.

Mara lost all thought and reason as the two of them made love under the trees and rain.

Afterward, Mara and Adam lay on the forest floor in each other's arms. Neither one of them spoke for a while, letting the rain drip through the branches, soaking them completely. But Mara wasn't cold, she was never more warm than at that moment.

"I love you," she said.

Adam turned slightly so he could stare at her directly. "I love you, too. More than anything." He leaned down and kissed her.

When their lips separated, Adam smiled. "This was the last thing I expected to happen today."

She laughed and kissed his cheek. "Me, too." Then her fears crept in. "Do you regret it?"

"Never. You're the best thing that's ever happened to me."

"I feel the same way."

Adam kissed her again. "It's been hard for me to trust anyone ever since my mom left, but I trust you with my life."

It was still a difficult concept for Mara to accept that his mother left him to an abusive father. She didn't want to pry, but she was curious. "Why do you think your mom did that?"

Adam didn't pull away or seem offended by the question. He shrugged. "I don't know. She always used to talk about the two of us escaping to Los Angeles where she promised to take me to Disneyland every day…" His voice faltered from the memory.

"I'm sorry. You don't have to…" Mara began guiltily.

But Adam shook his head. "It's okay. I want to talk about it." He sighed and continued, "We were supposed to leave on the weekend, but I guess she left without me."

Mara's heart broke. "But why?"

Adam's expression was one of both sadness and resignation. "She got scared? Who knows? The bottom line was: she left. My dad freaked. Social services came in and took me into foster care until my dad finally got me back."

"And foster care was worse than your dad?" Mara eyed the bruises peaking above the top of his shirt.

Adam self-consciously moved his shirt to cover the bruise. "One hundred percent."

There was so much loaded into his answer, Mara immediately stopped questioning Adam. Something really bad must have happened to him if being black and blue was a better alternative.

Mara snuggled in close.

Then the warmth of being together suddenly gave way to reality.

"I'm freezing," she shivered.

He laughed, all the dark thoughts of his past shoved aside, "Me, too."

Dream Entry #9

I'm sitting in my car waiting for Adam to get some food from the 7-11. We just left the park and I'm still reeling. We had sex! I still can't believe it! It was amazing. I never imagined it would be like that. Personally, I always pictured it would be in a warm bed in a house or apartment or anywhere but on the ground in the middle of a forest. In the rain! But I wouldn't change a thing. It was like something out of a movie. And my mom wouldn't kill me too much if she found out. We did use protection. I had been a complete dork and kept the condom the Sex Ed instructor handed out in last year's Junior/Senior seminar. I'm glad I did though, since it made my first time with Adam possible.

I never thought I could love anyone this much. It's a weird kind of pain, but it feels really good. I know, I sound insane. Maybe I am, but I'm going to enjoy every second of it.

It was our after-talk that I still can't wrap my head around. I just can't fathom why Adam's mom would leave her son! And why his dad would hurt him! I didn't see how bad the damage was because we kept our shirts on when we did it. But I don't need to see his bruises. It would only break my heart more and probably make me do something stupid, like take a baseball bat to his dad's face or something. Adam obviously loves him despite his abuses, so I'm going to let it be for now.

I'm trying to decide if I should tell Adam about my dream. I really want to try and find that house and its basement, but now I'm wondering if it would be too much for Adam. Or for me for that matter. I'm kind of floating right now.

I mean, for Adam, it might take his mind off of what happened with his father. I'll see how I feel when he comes back. Speaking of which, I see him coming now.

***

Mara stuffed the diary in her bag just as Adam hopped into the car.

"Thanks," Mara said as Adam pulled out two heat-lamped corn dogs, handing one to her and taking a bite out of the other.

"I haven't eaten all day." Adam had a paper bag full of newly purchased snacks.

Feeling hungry herself, Mara gratefully downed the entire corn dog.

Adam smiled. "I see you eyeing these Doritos." He ripped open the bag and offered her the chips.

It was so normal that she almost forgot the enormity of what had just happened in the forest. She wasn't a virgin anymore.

Mara always knew her first time would be special, but she had no idea it would be this mind blowing. It made all her other worries seem insignificant. She tried not to stare at him as she ate her chip. But when Adam caught her eye, he smiled. "Are you really okay with everything?"

Mara nodded. "Are you?"

Adam leaned across the car and kissed Mara softly. "I never expected to feel this way so fast, but yes, I've never been more sure about anything."

"Me, too," Mara confessed.

Adam moved back to his side of the car, handing her another chip.

Mara took the proffered chip and bit into it with pleasure. Claire didn't allow junk food in the house, so Mara and Josie rarely ate anything with "chemicals" in it. As she crunched into the heavenly Dorito, Mara understood that chemicals made food taste good.

"Here. Have the whole bag." Adam handed the rest of the chips to her.

Mara gladly obliged.

"Where to?" he asked with a slight pep to his tone.

She finished eating, then plowed forward. "I think I know where the killer lives."

Adam looked highly impressed. "You're just telling me now?"

Mara's face flushed. "Well, we were busy."

Adam lifted her hand and kissed it. "Good excuse." Then he looked thoughtful. "How do you know where he lives?"

Hoping he wouldn't give her a doubtful gaze, Mara admitted, "I dreamt about it. Or at least I think I did. I want to check it out to make sure."

"So after our fiasco of sneaking into an old murdered man's home, you want to break into a place that could potentially house a killer?"

"When you say it like that, it makes me sound crazy."

"You're so cute when your forehead crinkles like that." Adam reached behind Mara's head with his hand and pulled her face to his. "I'll go anywhere with you." He leaned in farther and kissed her until she lost all coherent thought.

Adam's other hand was on her waist, trying to squeeze Mara closer to him, a maneuver the parking brake and stick shift were barriers to. Adam turned at an angle to come closer to Mara, then flinched in pain.

Mara pulled back. "Are you okay? Did I hurt you?"

Adam kissed her lightly, then leaned back to really see her. "I'm fine. You can never hurt me."

Sometimes the way he talked to Mara was so intense that it would make her heart skip a beat.

"Now let's go find this place." Adam sat back in his seat and grabbed a chocolate bar from the bag, eating it with pleasure.

"Are you sure? I don't want to make you do something you're uncomfortable with."

"Any distraction is a good distraction, I liked our forest distraction better, but I'm willing to take a rest and go to a serial killer's house," he finished his thought with a teasing grin. "Besides, I really want to see how you see things. The fact that you dreamed of this place and it could potentially be where the murderer lives? I'm in. I'm definitely in." Adam was energized.

It made Mara enthusiastic too. She typed the street

intersection in her cell and let it guide her to the location.

On the ride over, they talked about school and how Colt had unexpectedly apologized and Kimiko stayed silent. Adam agreed that Zia should do reconnaissance in regards to Kimiko. He didn't trust the couple either, but he was more of the opinion that Colt simply wanted to look good in public. Colt was guilty as charged in the video, so if he came out sorry for his behavior maybe he could work the situation to his advantage. A Changed-Man story could be just as popular as standing-up-to-a-bully story, and if Colt was trying to befriend Mara, maybe he was thinking of a good angle to save face. Adam was under the opinion that everyone wanted their fifteen minutes of fame and nowadays it was easier to achieve with reality television and YouTube. The average for most peoples' YouTube views was 500 maximum, but over 200,000? Mara was practically famous already.

Mara was content to let Adam *conspiracize* as she liked to call it. Not that she didn't agree with what he was saying, but she secretly hoped Colt's apology was real and that he and Kimiko would be nice to her from now on. A girl could dream.

Part of her still wanted to keep talking about what they had done in the forest and another part didn't want to bring it up at all. Mara was an over-analyzer by nature, so she didn't want to scare Adam off by talking his ear off about having sex. But she wanted to know if she was any good. Did he like it? Was he just being nice? Did he really love her like she loved him? It seemed impossible that Adam could feel as intensely as she did…

But she kept her mouth shut and steered the conversation to Colt or Ed Garner. For some reason conversing about a bully and a murder was way easier to talk about than sex.

After a twenty-minute drive they arrived at 6th and Crotonal Avenue. Seeing the sign in person made Mara's skin crawl. It was suddenly real. A dream come to reality. She had seen this very sign from the window of a nightmare. She pulled over and parked.

Adam must have noticed that Mara's whole visage had changed. "You okay?" he asked, then reached across and touched her cheek. "We don't have to do this? We can make an anonymous call to the police."

Mara shook her head and kissed his hand. "I want to make sure it's worth a phone call first. We'll just peek inside the window and then decide. I don't want to call the cops if all this came from my imagination." She didn't like the thought of alerting the authorities because she was always afraid that she'd be wrong. The subconscious was an unpredictable mess and if Mara had a dream about some old house that wasn't associated with the killer at all and then called the police...? She'd feel like an idiot. A loser. A poser.

"I think we know this didn't come from your imagination. We're here aren't we? This is an actual place. Do you see the house?" Adam obviously believed in her ability whole-heartedly.

It should have made Mara happy, but for some reason she felt pressured instead. Like she had to be right or Adam would never believe in her again. Belief in her dreams was such a fine line for most people, which was why she didn't like talking about it much. She figured people would write her off as a flake or a weirdo or a New Age crazy person. Besides, Mara had never followed up on any of her visions before. Reading about the murders in the news was always proof enough for her. But to be at a location that she'd dreamt about and now, awake, could look inside the potential killer's abode? It was unreal.

Mara and Adam exited the car and she surveyed the block.

"Yes, this is definitely the place," she confirmed. Mara could almost see the balloons with the floating body parts coming toward her. The houses, like her second dream, weren't decrepit and overgrown. It looked like a middle-class suburban neighborhood similar to her own.

She stood next to the street sign and squatted down to see the angle at which she saw it through the basement window. "There." Mara pointed.

The house.

The small rectangular window.

She had found it.

Instantly, she had goose bumps.

Adam's hand grasped hers and he squeezed it for support. Staring up into his worried eyes, she nodded. "We'll just check it out real quick."

He nodded back and the two of them walked toward the house.

It wasn't a big home. Craftsman style in its design, there was a large front porch with a bench and small round table off to the side. It was two stories tall, which made for lots of windows on both levels staring down at them like blackened eyes waiting for their prey. It was almost as if the building itself was the predator, waiting to chomp down on the two of them.

Mara went to the side of the house first and looked through the basement window. Shivers went down her spine when she saw the wooden table. Thankfully, unlike her dream, there wasn't a pile of body parts on it. The fact that the table *was* actually there solidified the reality of the situation. Other than that, there was no one in sight.

"Empty," she confirmed to Adam.

"What did you expect to see?" Adam asked.

"A dead body," she answered frankly.

Adam froze for a moment as if hearing her words frightened him. Then he turned away and suggested, "Let's check out the front."

Mara nodded. They headed toward the front of the house.

As they came closer, Mara saw something that made her stop in her tracks.

A For Sale sign on the front lawn.

"Do you think anyone lives in there?" Adam asked aloud what they were both thinking. He let go of her hand and walked up the three steps that led to the front porch. Mara stayed back on the front lawn.

She didn't know how to interpret this information. In her dream she had the impression that the killer lived in the house. Maybe he still lived there and was selling it? Maybe he was squatting?

No.

This house was from the killer's *past*.

That's why the decrepit memories, the balloons, the body...

Mara chastised herself for not putting it together before. Entering into other people's dreamscapes was like that. She'd see places and things that made the biggest impact on the person, not necessarily in the here-and-now, but somewhere in the person's past. And she suddenly knew with certainty that the woman's murder was at least seven or eight years ago, maybe even a decade.

She didn't know how she knew, she just did. That woman in the basement, her body parts: it had meant the most to the killer because it was probably his first kill like she had thought in the dream.

Adam peered inside the window next to the front door. He turned to face Mara, shrugging his shoulders. "Looks deserted. Do you want to go inside?"

The goody-two-shoes part of Mara started to sweat, but the curious-I-dreamt-of-this-place part of her wanted to go inside. The curious side won out. "How? I don't want to bust in like we did at Ed Garner's." She didn't want to break the law. Again. She couldn't process the potential of doing another illegal act. And yet, she was still planning on going in. She just didn't want to smash any windows or do anything destructive. She was having a serious crisis of faith right about now.

"If this house is for sale, it'll have a realtor's key around here somewhere. My mom used to sell houses: each house has a small 'lock box' where they keep the house keys. The box opens with a combination, but I figured out how to pick their locks when I wanted to stay somewhere else for the night." Adam searched the porch until he found a gray box with a combination lock on it.

Having to learn how to break into houses just so he could get away from his abusive father was no way to live… It was heart wrenching.

After a few minutes of fiddling with the lock box, Adam grinned broadly. "Got it." He pulled out a key.

Mara's conflicting emotions couldn't decide if she was happy or freaked-out by that. She was growing braver by the day, though, because she jumped up the three steps and gently took the key from Adam. "Let's do this," she sighed determinedly.

She opened the door and walked in first. The home was empty and felt bigger on the inside due to its hardwood floors and no furnishings. It was as clean as to be expected, considering the house was for sale, but it still had a beat-up look to it that matched its exterior. There was a stairwell upon immediate entry that led upstairs. On the main level each room was sectioned off as its own space. This was strange to Mara, since she had only lived in a house with one large bottom floor. It made her a little claustrophobic.

It also made her paranoid that someone could jump out at them from anywhere.

After a few moments of searching, jumping back, searching, jumping back, Mara wondered, "How do we get downstairs?"

They both looked for a doorway that would lead to the room she saw in her dreams. Adam found it under the staircase. It was kind of creepy, like a cellar door with gray cracked wood. Mara boldly reached for the knob, opening the door wide enough for them to go through. The stairs were rickety, made of the same faded and worn wood as the door.

"Blair Witch anyone?" Adam smiled, pushing ahead of Mara to lead the way. "I'm not letting you walk into the lair of some crazy killer first."

"We probably should have brought a weapon or something," Mara whispered, already feeling like a character in a horror movie. Stupid. Why would anyone walk *toward* potential danger? She'd always wondered about this when she watched movies like that. Now Mara finally understood: no matter how scared she felt, she needed to relieve her mind that the terrors didn't exist. No one ever believed they'd be killed. It was a weird kind of invincibility trait humans possessed. The fear was there, but the belief wasn't.

Mara felt like that now. She was scared, but the compulsion to move forward despite the possibility of danger was overwhelming.

She stepped onto the cement floor and was instantly back in her dream. This was the place. The actual place.

No one was there.

Which made sense if this was a place from the killer's past. The murderer may not have been here for years. But, even though Mara was fairly certain they were safe from harm, her fear didn't subside. It was as if she had jumped inside her nightmare and she'd be locked in this basement, stuck there forever.

At least Adam was there to help her stay grounded.

"Is this it?" he asked surveying the cement room.

"Yeah, except there was a stack of body parts on that table in my dream." She nodded toward the table. "It was a woman," Mara sighed. "It was so specific. I thought she'd still be here, or that there would be blood stains or something, but now I think maybe it was the body of this guy's first kill? Someone important to him."

"What did this woman look like?" Adam glanced around the room curiously.

"Is this freaking you out? I'm so sorry. We should just leave." First he was beaten to shit by his dad and now she brings him to a creepy basement where a murder probably took place? Mara wouldn't be surprised if he never wanted to see her again.

Adam shrugged. "If we know what she looks like, maybe we can look her up as a Missing Persons or something."

"Oh. Good idea." Mara paused, trying to "reassemble" the

dead woman in her mind. "She had dark hair...It was kind of hard to see her face since her head was in a pile with the rest of her, but I bet if I looked through some pictures I could recognize her." Mara was hopeful that maybe this could help them track down the killer. "I'm pretty positive this is, or was, where the killer lived a long time ago. Maybe now that it's vacant he came back to hide. I'll call the police anonymously."

"Maybe you shouldn't. It's too risky." Adam clasped her hand. "Let's get out of here. Whoever was here, it doesn't look like they've been here in a while, so the cops would be just as lost as they are now. I don't want to give them any reason to suspect you. I'm still not sure Detective Nicholson didn't see us running from the Garner's the other night."

"Yeah," Mara agreed. "Maybe you're right. This was a dumb idea." Just like when Mara was in the Garner's house, she'd wondered why she had even *wanted* to go there. To prove to herself that her dream was real? To feel superior somehow? To feel powerful? All of those things. Who did she think she was? She had only thought about the physical dangers she may be putting herself through, never about the being-framed-for-murder dangers.

Adam leaned down and kissed her gently. "It wasn't a dumb idea. You had to see for yourself. Now you've seen. Just don't involve the police. It's too dangerous for you." His eyes were full of concern. "I don't know what I'd do if anything happened to you."

Mara hugged him tightly, then pulled away. "Let's get out of here." She led him by the hand and they locked up the house.

They were in her car and on the road in minutes. "Should I

take you to my house? I'm sure my parents would let you stay in the guest room."

"No. I don't want your parents knowing about what's happening to me. If they knew they'd report my dad, even if they promised you they wouldn't." Adam placed his hand on the back of Mara's neck, massaging her gently as she drove. "Just drop me off at the Motel 5 off the Interstate. It's cheap and I have some cash."

"They won't tell anyone…" Mara started to argue.

Adam cut her off gently, "Please, Mara. You promised you wouldn't tell anyone. I can't do foster care again. In six months I'll be eighteen and I can leave my dad for good. If I can last seventeen years with the guy, I can hold out for six more months."

Mara nodded. "Alright. But if you change your mind…"

"I won't."

And the way he said it, Mara knew he never would.

Dream Entry #10

When I dropped Adam off at the motel, I went up with him to his room. I can't describe how amazing he makes me feel. The way he kisses me... it's as if we were the only two people on earth. His hands held me so tight. The second time was just as incredible as the first time. Although, to be fair, it was a lot warmer: as romantic as having sex under an outcropping of trees in the rain sounds, it was a little cold. Not that I really noticed at the time, but afterward it took a while to de-thaw.

It sounds cheesy even when I think about it, but I really love Adam. People can lecture me all they want that we just started dating, that there's no way I could love him that quickly. But it's true. He's the one shining light with all this darkness in my life.

I had a dream last night that freaked me out a little. It's probably because of yesterday and going to that house. Part of me wishes I hadn't gone, but I had to see it for myself. I needed to know if what

I saw was real.

I'm not sure what my dream meant, but I was walking on a hill of grass and there were blankets covering a large section of it. When I picked up the blankets, the grass was a dark black color. I walked down the hill and I saw Kimiko standing there, yelling at me to get off the grass, that I was walking in blood.

When I looked down I was drenched in blood all the way up to my knees. I quickly ran off the bloodied grass and moved to the green. I looked at Kimiko and she was very distraught. She knew the people that were killed there. Her eyes were so filled with sadness...

Then, just as suddenly, they turned vacant. It was the vacancy that scared me most. I tried screaming at Kimiko, to get some reaction, any reaction, but she didn't move or say anything. Her skin began to turn pale, then gray. Her eyes whitened, then rotted, until all that stood in front of me was a putrefied corpse.

Then the body spoke. "I love a good party."

I woke up after that.

***

Mara placed her diary in the drawer of her nightstand. She wouldn't need it today. Today was Saturday and her plans consisted of going over to Adam's motel to spend as much time with him as possible. She wasn't sure what her dream meant, but she was starting to wonder why she was dreaming about Kimiko so much. First, the dream about adding pieces to a puzzle she'd already solved and, second, Kimiko knowing who died on a hill of blood and then turning into a corpse herself. Mara knew better than to discount her dreams as stress or something else.

They meant something and she needed to know what Kimiko had to do with it.

Mara's cell rang. She answered it promptly when she saw Zia was on the other line. "Hello?"

"So how did it go with Adam yesterday?" Zia prodded playfully.

Mara suddenly realized her best friend had no idea of the events that had transpired after school.

"Um," she couldn't find the words. Serial killer's houses aside, Mara had lost her virginity!

"That's a loaded *Um*. Speak now before I implode," Zia's voice was full of anticipation.

"Don't freak out, but we had sex," Mara blurted before she could think of an eloquent way to say it.

"What?!"

Mara had to pull the phone away from her ear from the scream on the other end. She had to laugh.

Zia continued, "Holy crap! Why didn't you text me right after it happened?"

"I know, I'm a horrible friend, but I was a little wrapped up in Adam at that moment." It was good to finally share it with someone.

"Tell me everything," Zia sighed in contentment. "I have to live vicariously through you."

"I seriously wasn't expecting it to happen. I picked Adam up from his house…" Mara kept her promise and didn't reveal that Adam was from an abusive home. "And we went to a park near him with a forest surrounding it. We wanted to be alone to talk, so we were really far back so no one could see us. It started raining and we were hiding under the trees and it was amazing."

"Your first time was in a forest in the rain?" Zia asked incredulously, then laughed. "That is both extremely romantic and gross."

Mara laughed with her, "I know, right? I was freezing after, but I didn't notice it during... you know."

"Please tell me you used protection?" Zia's tone turned protective.

"Of course, *Mom*," Mara responded.

"That's my girl." Zia sounded reassured. "Not to change the mind-blowing subject, but I thought you'd like to know that Kimiko was unusually quiet the whole day yesterday. Normally, she's pretty peppy, and now that I know what a bitch she is, obnoxious. But she pretty much kept to herself. It was really weird. I tried following her after school, but she just went home. I stuck around like a stalker for an hour, then I left."

"Something is definitely up with her. I keep having weird dreams about her. Last night she was all corpse-y," Mara confessed.

"She didn't... die?" Zia asked carefully.

"No. It wasn't one of those dreams. She rotted in front of my face and told me she loved a good party. Weird, huh?"

"Yeah. Look. There's a fundraiser for the football team today and Kimiko and Colt are both supposed to be there, since they organized the whole event. You want to come?"

Mara did, but she wanted to see Adam more. "I'm supposed to see Adam today."

"Say no more," Zia replied, amused. "I'll drag your sister with me. We'll see if they have anything to hide. As for you..." Mara could picture the grin on Zia's face as she teased, "You and

Adam have fun."

"Oh, we will," Mara teased back. "Bye."

"You're my hero. Bye."

After Mara hung up with Zia, she quickly dressed and left the house. Her parents grilled her on what she had planned for the day, so she was as honest as she could be. She told them that she was going to spend time with Adam, but she didn't tell them that she planned on making out as much as humanly possible… and other things. Mara didn't think her father would appreciate that type of information. Feeling grotesquely inspired from her dream, she said she was going on a picnic.

It didn't take long to arrive at the motel. As she pulled into the parking lot, Adam was already waiting outside. He held a single rose in his hand, which he gave to Mara with a smile when she exited the car.

"I have plans for us," he grinned. "We need to pick up my car first. I'm taking you somewhere special today and I'm going to have to blindfold you."

"Really?" Mara's butterflies did a few back flips.

He nodded. "It' s going to be a good surprise, trust me."

"Okay," she smiled.

Before long, they had left Mara's car at the motel and Adam was driving them to the undisclosed location. She wore a bandana over her eyes and claimed she couldn't see anything, but could make out some at the bottom. She decided not to peek though. Adam seemed so enthusiastic about surprising her, she didn't want to spoil the fun for him.

They talked in the car about simple things, like school and their classes. It was so nice. So normal. No thinking about dreams or murder or killers. Just Calculus and how Ms. Trant's wig kept shifting sideways during her lecture the day before.

Finally, Adam parked and helped her out of the car, pulling off the blindfold.

Gasworks Park.

One of Mara's favorites.

She turned to Adam and hugged him. "I love this place."

He kissed her. "I thought you would."

The park itself was like a steampunk industrial dream with a rusted metal structure at its center. Varying sized cylinders rose up to the sky, all of them surrounded by a lattice work of pipes, catwalks and ladders. Mara and her family used to ride their bikes down the Burke-Gilman trail and stop at Gasworks. Then they'd picnic on Kite Hill…

Mara's eyes went immediately to the hill in the distance.

It was the hill from her dream.

Picking up on Mara's change in mood, Adam was immediately concerned. "What is it? What just happened?"

Mara didn't want to ruin Adam's plan for their date. He had obviously thought this through and was so excited to bring her there. She pushed aside the grotesque images from her dream as if they had been a scary movie she'd watched the night before. Smiling up at Adam, she decided a half-truth would be easier to believe. "I just realized that Kite Hill was in one of the dreams I had a while back. I didn't recognize it." Then she reached up and kissed him. "But I don't want to think about that. Let's have some fun."

Before he could push the matter further, Mara grabbed his hand and pulled him toward the rusted structure.

She was suddenly a kid again, exploring the park and all its beautiful strangeness. Normally, old industrial buildings would be deserted or torn down, but this one had been converted into a park. It was, however, off-limits to climb on the antique construction for safety concerns, so Mara was content to simply look at the old Gasworks as a giant piece of sculpture.

After an hour or so, they were hungry. Mara spotted a couple of food trucks and the two of them ate gourmet hotdogs with sweet potato fries while sitting on Kite Hill with several other couples and families. Mara's lie to her parents about having a picnic was suddenly real.

She tried not to think about the fact that she was sitting on the exact spot where Kimiko had warned her of the blood in her dream. But it was impossible not to. What had it meant? It couldn't be coincidence that the very next day Mara was at the same location. Did someone die here? *Would* someone die here? The nightmare had ended with Kimiko a corpse. Was it a premonition? Mara had never dreamt of the future before, only the here and now. But the way her mind worked, she wouldn't be surprised if her gift was changing, evolving.

"Tell me about your dream." Adam had been staring at her, but she'd been so wrapped up in her thoughts she hadn't noticed.

"It's nothing, really. I'm sorry I keep ruining things." Mara felt guilty and selfish.

They were both sitting cross-legged on the grass hill facing the Seattle skyline, but Adam turned his body to face Mara. He reached out and took both her hands in his. "You're not ruining anything. Today is perfect just for the weather alone. But your dreams are obviously affecting you. I want to know."

140

Mara told him last night's dream from start to finish. "I don't think it means anything, though," she said with an attempt at a casual shrug, trying to dismiss the whole thing.

Adam shook his head. "So far you're batting a thousand with those dreams of yours." His eyes turned contemplative. "Do you think Kimiko is going to be okay? You don't think she's going to…" He left the thought open-ended.

"Die?" Mara finished his sentence. "No, it was more like a warning. But I do think it's connected to the killer. I don't know how, but I can feel it. That sounds stupid, huh?"

Adam took his hand and cradled Mara's cheek. "Nothing you could ever say would sound stupid. I've never known anyone like you, Mara. I wish I would have talked to you earlier. My life could have been very different."

Mara had the impression that he was referring to his dad. She wasn't sure how different his life would have been, but it might have been happier. She knew her life would have been much better if they had become friends earlier, and her life was already pretty good.

Adam pulled her head to his and kissed her more passionately than he ever had before. It was as if a grenade destroyed all her brain cells in one explosive kiss. She couldn't imagine anyone else ever making her feel this kind of intensity. They belonged together. Mara finally understood every book, movie and TV show that spouted about destiny and true love. She had found it and she never wanted to lose it.

It was as if all sight and sound disappeared in that one embrace. Mara was oblivious to the world around her. She didn't care if people stared. She didn't care if it poured down rain.

Nothing mattered except the two of them.

So when she was yanked away from Adam with some force, she let out a small scream from the shock.

Reality flooded back in full color as Mara realized five police officers surrounded the two of them.

It was such a surprise, she didn't know how to react.

"Mara Johnson, I'm taking you in for questioning in the murder of Ed Garner," Detective Jennifer Nicholson said.

Mara had been too stunned to notice her. Nicholson stared down at Mara with contempt and triumph as if she knew all along that Mara had been the killer and she finally was able to...

"Am I being arrested?" Mara asked. Detective Nicholson's words finally sharpened into clarity: *I'm taking you in for questioning.*

The detective shrugged as if this was just a formality. "You haven't been brought up on formal charges *yet,* but I have 72 hours to hold you. And trust me, I *will* prove that you're guilty."

The cop that had pulled her away from Adam proceeded to jerk Mara to her feet and handcuff her.

Guilty.

Mara's mind froze. Her worst fears coming to life. The Detective *did* think she was responsible for killing Ed.

She would have cried if she hadn't been so terrified.

Adam shoved his way past the detective to get to Mara, not caring about the officers in the least. One cop held him back with his arm, but Adam pushed ahead anyway. "You can't take her! She didn't do anything!"

Mara wanted desperately to defend herself, to fight back, anything. But she was petrified by fear. It was finally happening, being accused of a murder she dreamt about.

When Adam knocked over the police officer that was in his way, Detective Nicholson leveled her gun at him. "Stand down, Mr. Layton. I don't want to arrest you for assault."

Mara found her voice at that. "Adam, stop. Go get my parents. Tell them what happened."

Detective Nicholson holstered her weapon when Adam stopped his tirade then said to Mara, "Your parents have already been informed. They are going to meet us at the station." She nodded to one of the cops. "Get her in the car."

The whole situation was so surreal, it was as if she were stuck in one of her own nightmares.

Then she thought of the dream.

Kimiko had warned her to get off the hill. Mara had been soaked in the blood of the killer's victims, and now she was going to jail.

Adam walked behind the entourage escorting her to a police car, the whole time shouting at her that he would fix this.

How? Mara wondered.

She was going to the police station for at least 72 hours. And from the determination in Detective Nicholson's face, Mara would be arrested for murder soon after.

And there was nothing anyone could do about it.

Dream Entry #11

I can't believe I'm actually writing anything down. I'm writing on a pad of paper the detective gave me. I think she expects me to write a confession. I'm in some kind of interrogation room. Since she can basically hold me here for three days, I'm not sure if I'll get any sleep. So I'm stuck here.

My parents are in the other room screaming at Detective Nicholson, but I don't think it's going to do much good. Nicholson was pretty clear about the whole 72-hour-hold-thing. She really thinks I killed Ed Garner. I can tell by the way she looks at me, like I'm the psycho teenager who thinks she's gotten away with murder, literally. How can someone in a position like hers read someone like me so wrong? Can't she see that I'm as innocent as they come? I don't even cut off the labels on pillows! I could never hurt anyone. Not even Josie, who I've wanted to hurt on many occasions. Speaking of which, Josie and Zia are probably at the football fundraiser right about now.

Unless of course my parents dragged Josie away because I was stuck in the clinker.

I really don't want to be arrested, but I feel like it's a forgone conclusion at this point. Detective Nicholson is out for blood. Mine, to be exact.

My stomach is roiling and I think I'm going to puke. I just want to get out of here. Please, God, if you're listening, help me.

***

Detective Nicholson grabbed the pad of paper out of Mara's hand with force.

Mara was sure her face turned three shades paler from the terror racing through her body.

The detective did a quick read, threw the pad on the table in front of Mara, then smiled.

"You're not fooling anyone." Her smile twisted in a way that said she was smarter than Mara. She reached into her coat pocket and pulled out an official looking piece of paper. "I have a warrant right here to take a sample of your DNA. We found hair particulates and fingerprints all over the Garner's house *after* the murder, and I convinced a judge that they could be yours."

They were.

Mara's neck flushed, to Detective Nicholson's enjoyment.

A technician walked in and proceeded to take a long cotton swab and swipe the side of her cheek. He left just as quickly as he entered making Mara feel like she was in the middle of some kind of Surrealist movie.

Detective Nicholson sat down across from Mara, took a deep

breath, and softened her expression. "Look, Mara, I had a unit follow you to that house on 6th Avenue. I think you know what we found there."

"More hair?" Mara didn't know how to respond she was so scared.

The detective shook her head. "We found traces of blood on a table in the basement. Do you know how it got there?"

Mara needed to say something, anything, but she knew whatever she said would sound as if she were guilty.

But she couldn't sit there being silent, so she said, "Did you read my diary?"

Detective Nicholson nodded slowly. "I did."

"So you know I dream things that happen." Mara wanted to close her eyes from the nightmare she was living. Why would a cop ever believe her? It sounded crazy to her and she lived it every day.

"I know you *think* you dream things that happen," was the detective's response. "But, Mara, I've seen this before. *Thinking* you've dreamt something is your way of coping with what you've actually *done*. You murdered Ed Garner, didn't you? And when we get the results back on the blood samples from the house on 6th, we'll find out who else you've killed, won't we?"

Mara shook her head, tears forming in her eyes. "No! I didn't kill anyone! I would never…" She couldn't finish without crying, so she stopped herself mid-sentence.

Detective Nicholson slammed her hand on the desk and Mara jumped. "Stop lying! The only thing that can save you is to tell the truth!" She grabbed a file from a shelf behind her and began to throw pictures of Ed's dead body in front of Mara.

Ed's tongue was swollen and bloated, sticking out of his mouth in a grotesque way.

The poison had choked the life out of him.

Mara had seen it in her dream.

But seeing it in photos was horrific.

She turned away.

"Look at him!" Detective Nicholson screamed, but Mara refused. "Look at him!"

Mara made herself stare at the photos.

The detective waved the most gruesome one in Mara's face. "You murdered him! Just like your great aunt murdered her husband! Did you want to be like her? Did she tell you what to do? What was your relationship with the Lopez Butcher?"

Mara puked.

All over the photos.

It was too much.

To be accused of murder.

To be compared to her great aunt.

Detective Nicholson took a step back at the giant puddle of vomit that was now dripping to the floor.

Mara would have been severely grossed out if she weren't shaking so violently from fear. She thought she was going to pass out.

The detective was about to leave, presumably to obtain some cleaning supplies when Mara spoke softly, "I can't help that I dream these things. I dreamt about my great aunt killing Uncle John the night it happened. I *saw* everything. I know that only makes you think I'm even more guilty, but it doesn't mean I am." When Mara could see Detective Nicholson gaining more

147

confidence in her belief of Mara's guilt, Mara decided on a different tactic. "The blood you found at the house on 6th. Can your lab technicians tell how long it's been there?"

Detective Nicholson wasn't sure what angle Mara was trying to play, but she nodded.

"You'll find that it's the blood of a woman who died there a long time ago. I know that because that's how my dreams work. Whoever that woman was, she was the killer's first victim, and unless you think I started taking down adults as a little kid and dragging them to houses without anyone noticing, you've got the wrong girl." Mara made sure their eyes met, then said with as much confidence as she could muster, "I *am not* a murderer."

The detective didn't respond. She simply left the room.

Mara sat in the room with a table full of photos of Ed covered in her vomit. Her breath was shallow and her hands continued to shake. A flush of heat rose to her head, causing Mara to stand. Logically, she knew this was a panic attack, but it didn't help. No matter how hard she tried to fill her lungs with air, it was never enough.

Mara kept pulling in deep, slow breaths until she managed to gain control of herself once more. Pacing always helped, so she walked around the room taking large, calming breaths as she moved. Closing her eyes helped as well, though the stench of her vomited lunch on the table threatened to reel Mara back into panic-land.

Detective Nicholson thought Mara was a killer and nothing Mara said would convince her otherwise. The thought of this was beyond frustrating. Like watching a movie where you knew the suspect was innocent, but no one would believe him. That was

Mara. Guilty until proven innocent.

She was in real trouble.

Mara had never been so scared in her entire life. Even her horrendous dreams didn't come close to how she felt now. At least with the nightmares she could wake up at some point to recover. But pacing around her own puke, her eyes closed, made Mara want to cry. She wished someone could be there with her. Her parents must be frantic, trying to find some loophole that would let them come see her. Nicholson knew what she was doing by bringing Mara in for questioning and not arresting her. The detective was all too eager to brag that by law the police department could question Mara without an adult present. Because if Mara *had* been arrested it would be her right to have a lawyer or guardian with her. Sick. Nicholson was so convinced she was right, she didn't even want to consider Mara may be innocent.

Her thoughts strayed to her best friend. Zia must be out of her mind if Josie had told her. And Adam...

Adam had been so crazed to save her. Mara wished she could have comforted him somehow, but she had been paralyzed in terror. After they placed her in the police car, she hadn't said a word, she simply let them drive her away. Away from Adam. Away from his desperate pleas to let Mara go.

What must he be thinking? she wondered. Mara hoped her parents kept him in the loop. She knew Josie would try, but Mara wasn't sure how much Claire and Ben would tell their younger daughter.

Mara felt a shiver run through her body. She wasn't sure if it was because of the temperature or because she was so nervous. Either way, she was cold. Her teeth began to chatter uncontrollably. The panic was surging again.

Mara began to cry. Once she started she couldn't stop.

She was in a police station. For murder.

Mara cried as if the pain would never stop. As if the core of her being was sick and dying. She couldn't imagine ever feeling normal again. The anguish of what was happening to her hurt too much.

Was this a new kind of torture? Leaving her in this tiny box until she fell apart?

Mara had seen enough movies to know that the mirror on the front wall was a giant spying eye glaring at her despair. Detective Nicholson probably thought her anxiety and crying were admissions of guilt. Mara could almost hear the detective laughing at her.

After what seemed like an hour a janitor came in to clean up the now half-dried vomit. Mara offered to help seeing as it was hers, but he politely refused and had the table and floor clean in no time. He left behind a pad and pencil for Mara on Detective Nicholson's instruction. That lady really wanted Mara to confess. But she already had. Mara had told her about her dreams, but the detective didn't believe her. Why would she?

Once the janitor was gone, Mara was alone again for hours. At one point she thought she heard her father yelling somewhere out in the hall, but nothing ever came of it. She knew Detective Nicholson was purposely keeping her away from her parents. The detective was trying to sweat Mara out. Make her break.

Mara paced the whole time while she was alone, afraid to sit down for fear of a panic surge.

With no windows in the small room, Mara had no idea what time it was. Based on when she arrived and how long it seemed like she'd been in there, she assumed it was night. Mara could be wrong, but she was sure five or six hours had passed, making it 8 P.M. at least.

Running on empty now, exhaustion threatened to overtake Mara completely. Pacing in a circle for hours and hours, adrenaline and unease pumping through her veins, crying non-stop, Mara's body began to suffer the aftermath of what she had gone through today.

It hit her hard and fast. She almost stumbled to the floor.

Finally, she sat back down and lay her head on the table to rest for a bit.

If Detective Nicholson wanted to watch her, then she'd have to watch her unconscious, because Mara had trouble keeping her eyes open. She couldn't remember when, but fatigue finally took over and she drifted off to sleep.

***

Well, this sucks. Mara thought in her head.

She was in the killer's head again. The FREE killer. The killer who she was taking the rap for! Mara wished she could wake up and tell them where he was! But now that she was looking around, she wouldn't have known what to tell the cops anyway: there was nothing recognizably familiar.

The killer walked through the hallway of what appeared to be a rundown apartment complex. Mara tried to see out of the corner of his eye some kind of clue as to this location, but all she could see were the wrought iron numbers nailed to each apartment door. She noticed that the killer had on the same leather gloves that he wore when he murdered Ed Garner, and the same dark clothing. She assumed the syringe he'd used to kill Ed was in the same place as well, tucked inside his jacket.

Mara knew that, if the killer took someone's life tonight, the cops would be forced to set her free, but she'd rather stay at the police station than see another person die. So it was a strange mix of emotions as she watched him head toward his yet-unknown destination.

A strange sense of wishful thinking filled her as she saw through his eyes. What if he was going home? What if the universe was giving her a glimpse into his head so she could tell the police where the real murderer lived? Then no one would die tonight and she could stop him before he slaughtered anyone else.

But when he pulled out a lock-picking tool and began his work on apartment number six, Mara knew she was about to witness something sinister.

He opened the lock in quick work and entered the home. It was dark. Whoever lived there was asleep or gone. She prayed they were gone so he wouldn't succeed in his mission. Mara desperately tried to jump out of his head so she could see his face, but when the killer passed by a hallway mirror she saw that he wore a ski mask again.

A bright light from outside lit the living room of the one-bedroom abode. It was flashing and neon. Mara focused as hard as she could to try and make out what the sign said. When the killer moved toward the bedroom door, she managed to garner a good look. The neon spelled the word: A – r – r. Arr? That didn't make much sense. Maybe it was only a part of the sign. Mara knew she wasn't wrong though and she committed the strange word to memory.

The apartment was messy: clothes strewn all over the floor, a ratty couch situated in front of an old tube television, a mound of dishes stacked a foot high in the sink of the disgusting kitchen. Take-out containers and crusted food adorned every free space of counter. Whoever lived there, cleaning wasn't a priority.

The killer slowly turned the knob of the bedroom and soundlessly opened the door.

The bedroom was just as messy as the rest of the house with more clothes on the floor and a foul looking bathroom off to the right. A man slept in a queen-sized bed, tangled in a melee of sheets and a comforter.

Mara could hear the snores of the man as if he was in the room with her.

The killer pulled off his ski mask, just as he'd done at Mr. Garner's place. He wanted his victim to see him. To see who was taking his life. It was the opposite of an executioner, who wore a hood to stay anonymous. It was as if at the last moment before death, the murderer wanted his victims to know who had killed them. As if he were punishing them…

That was it.

The killer believed these victims deserved to die and he was the one chosen to carry out those orders. She didn't know how, but Mara knew she had tapped into a part of the killer's mind and caught a glimpse of why he killed.

Then she saw it.

He pulled out a syringe like the one he'd used on Mr. Garner.

With efficiency, he quickly injected the sleeping man's neck with his poisonous cocktail.

The man jolted up to sitting position, grabbing at his neck.

When he saw the killer, his eyes went round from the initial scare, then turned annoyed and angry. "What the fuck…"

He was going to say the killer's name, Mara knew it, but he never finished his sentence.

The poison worked faster than it had with Mr. Garner. In less than five seconds, the man fell back onto his mattress. Dead.

Pulling the ski mask back over his head, the killer left the room, leaving the dead body behind.

***

Mara jolted awake. She was instantly on her feet and pounding on the one-way mirror, screaming for Detective Nicholson. Not knowing what time it was, she had no idea if anyone was even around to answer her.

Within seconds, a cop entered the room. "Calm down. What's the problem?" he asked.

"I saw him. I saw the killer! I have to talk to Detective Nicholson!" Mara was shocked that she woke up right after the kill. "Maybe there's still a chance to catch him if you guys can figure out where a neon sign with the letters 'A,' 'r,' 'r' is. It could be a part of a bigger word. I don't know, but the man that was just murdered lives by it!" Mara knew that her words were rambling, but she needed to get it all out, fast, in time for the police to catch the killer.

"Miss, calm down," the cop tried to reason with her. "Detective Nicholson has left for the night. It's three in the morning. You can tell her whatever it is you need to tell her in four hours when she gets here."

"But it'll be too late! You guys could catch the actual killer instead of locking up innocent teenage girls!" Even Mara heard the attitude in her voice, but she didn't care. She wanted this guy caught. Not just for her own freedom, but to save anyone else he decided to kill.

The cop wasn't buying it. "You had a bad dream. Go back to sleep and I'll send the detective in here first thing. She'll be here in four hours. Deal?"

"Go back to sleep? On a freaking metal table! No thanks!" Mara was frustrated. Time was slipping away and she knew it was too late. Even if the cop had believed her, finding the letters of a neon sign? That could take hours unless someone happened to know where it was, which was highly unlikely. The fervent worry the nightmare had left her with had faded slightly in the reality of waking up.

Slowly, she nodded.

The policeman appeared relieved. She could tell he didn't like interacting with seventeen-year-old girls. Still, he tried to be soothing once again, "Now, try and sleep, okay?"

"Seriously? I have a chair and a table. Keeping me here should be illegal, I'm a minor."

The cop actually looked like he felt sorry for her. "Legally, we can keep you here for 72 hours…" he began the mantra.

Mara interrupted him, "Yeah, yeah. This is torture. You know that, right? And no one is even interrogating me." She grew more and more angry. "You're just leaving me here for what? So that I go bat-shit insane and confess to a crime I didn't actually commit?"

"Look, sleep or don't sleep, but you've got to stay inside." The cop left before she could respond, locking the door behind him.

Mara yelled at the mirror, "Fine! But when you find the poor guy that just died, you'll wish you had listened to me! 'Arr!' Look it up. Someone look it up!" Mara shuddered in embarrassment at pronouncing 'Arr' out loud. She sounded like a pirate.

After a whole lot of nothing in response, Mara figured no one was listening to her.

They didn't care that they had a chance to catch him — because they thought they had already caught the real murderer.

Her.

Mara sat back down in her chair.

The victim knew the killer.

It was going to be a long four hours.

Dream Entry #12

I *swear it's been four hours already. I've been wide awake ever since I had my nightmare. The killer is long gone by now. But I can tell the detective so many details she'll have to believe that, at the very least, I'm not guilty. I mean, I was in this stupid room all night! She'll probably think I'm working with someone. I just hope she has enough common sense to see that I'm harmless. I can't even hurt spiders! I mean, really can't hurt them: I always set them free when I find them in the house and I'm terrified of their creepy, crawly legs! I'm so angry at Detective Nicholson's idiocy that I can hardly breathe. And, yes, I know she's going to read this. Hi! I'm innocent, Detective. And last night proves it! So get your butt over to wherever 'A-r-r' is and LET ME GO!*

***

When the door opened to the interrogation room, Mara stood up to plead her case to the detective.

Detective Jennifer Nicholson walked in with a sour expression on her face. Coming in next to her was an attractive Native American woman who, from the aura of authority she emanated, looked like Nicholson's boss or something. They both wore suits, though, and the only reason Mara suspected the second woman was the detective's superior was because she carried herself in a way that said she shouldn't be messed with.

"You're free to go, Ms. Johnson," Detective Nicholson snarled.

So much hostility, it brought out Mara's people-pleaser gene. "I know you think I'm guilty, but I swear to God I didn't do it. I don't know if the cop from last night told you, but I had another dream last night and the killer murdered someone new. It was in a gross apartment and there was a neon sign outside his window with the letters: 'A,' 'r,' 'r.' You have to believe me. I can describe the victim. I saw his face, but I didn't see the killer's." Mara couldn't stop herself from babbling. "He knew the killer. I think he was about to say the killer's name, but the poison killed him before he could."

Detective Nicholson only appeared angrier at Mara's information, but she sighed. "We know about the second victim. That's why Agent Piper is here. It's a federal case now."

The Native American woman's eyes had an edge to them. She viewed Mara with fascination. "I'm FBI Agent Raven Piper. I'm assigned to this case."

Then she leaned in closer to Mara. "I'm very interested in what you have to say." She said it like a scientist talking to an experiment volunteer, clinical and reassuring at the same time.

"Do you want me to tell you everything I dreamed last

night?" Mara asked.

"No, I've already heard the key points. After the second body was discovered and the FBI was alerted I went to the crime scene. The 'A – R – R' is from a liquor store downtown called Larry's Liquor.

"And," she eyed Detective Nicholson with some disdain, "as far as your involvement with visiting the Garner house... You have to come clean. Why were you there?" Agent Piper asked.

Mara didn't want to drag Adam into this, so she acted as if she had gone in alone. "I thought if I could see where it happened, I'd be able to find something the police missed. It was stupid."

Agent Piper was thoughtful. "It wasn't stupid. I've read your diary and your dream about Ed Garner gave the precise details of the incident. Did you find anything when you were there?"

Agent Piper genuinely wanted to know. She believed Mara. Wishing she could give the agent a better answer, Mara shook her head. "I didn't find anything."

Detective Nicholson's skeptical expression at this only made Mara certain that she still thought Mara was guilty of the crime in some way. With no proof, though, there was nothing the detective could do about it, thank goodness.

Mara nodded. "I'm sorry. I thought I could help."

Agent Piper nodded encouragingly. "I think you will be able to help, Mara. But for now, I don't want to keep you here any longer."

Mara stood up cautiously. "What about the Crotonal house? Detective Nicholson said they found blood. Did you guys figure out who it was yet?" She needed to know. Mara was absolutely certain that, as soon as she left, she'd be out of the loop as far as the official investigation went.

The detective stared at Mara with curiosity and loathing, but she nodded. "The blood we found there was eight years old. How did you know?"

"I tried to tell you: I dreamt of the killer and just knew it was his first murder," Mara explained. "I didn't know exactly how old it was, but I guess he's been doing this a long time."

"The detective took you in before checking to see if there was any sign of a foul play that took place in the residence *recently*." Agent Piper looked at Detective Nicholson in a disapproving manner. She really didn't like her. And from what Mara could tell, the feeling was mutual. "Which there wasn't. So." She took a deep breath and continued, "On behalf of the police department and the FBI we apologize for the mistake…"

Detective Nicholson interrupted, desperate. "We can still charge you on breaking and entering based on your own admission and the testimony of the officer I had following you."

Agent Piper gave the detective a look that shut her up. "You will not be charged for breaking and entering and you have our apologies. Isn't that correct, Detective Nicholson?"

The detective shrugged angrily. "Yes."

Mara still needed to explain. "I know it's weird, but I swear, I just dream things. I always have. Like last night. I can tell you everything." She focused on Detective Nicholson. "And I know you think you can explain it away as me working with someone else, but you should know as a detective that you can plan something all you want, but the way it goes down never works out that way. But I can tell you *exactly* what happened. If I had conspired with someone, I'd only be telling what was *supposed* to happen, not what *actually* happened. Right?" Mara had thought a lot about how she could convince the detective of her innocence and now, with her dream murder taking place while she was being held in police custody, she knew that her logic made sense. When she saw the wheels turning in Detective Nicholson's head, Mara pushed forward. "I will tell you every single detail that I saw, from the dishes in his sink to the shirts on the victim's floor. I'm telling you I SAW it."

Agent Piper smiled. "The Bureau has worked with psychics before. I know your value even if the detective does not. And from your diary, I can tell you're one of the best. Speaking of which…" She handed Mara back her diary. "From now on, I'll speak with you directly. I'm sorry for this invasion of your privacy."

Mara cringed at the thought of the two of them reading her innermost thoughts, especially in regards to Adam. "Thanks," she muttered, embarrassed. Then Mara had to know, so she asked the detective. "Why did you think I did it?"

Detective Nicholson softened slightly at the way Mara asked the question. "I've done this job long enough to know when someone is hiding something."

Agent Piper stopped the detective with her hand. "It doesn't matter." She placed her hand out for Mara to shake. "What matters is how we move forward, Mara, what do you say you help us find this guy?"

Mara took her hand and shook it. It *did* matter to Mara, though, because she didn't want Detective Nicholson believing she was a murderer, but Agent Piper genuinely seemed to believe in her dreams.

But more importantly, Mara wanted to catch this guy and

maybe with the FBI's help, she actually could.

***

The rest of the morning was paperwork and describing every last detail of her dream. It was weird talking to the FBI and police about her nightmares, especially since she knew half of them thought she was full of crap, but Agent Piper listened in rapt attention. From the way she asked questions Mara knew the Agent had dealt with people like her before. It was as if Piper understood how the whole dream-thing worked, from not seeing the killer's face, to jumping out of the dream right when he killed. Agent Piper appeared extremely fascinated when Mara told her how she had been stuck after Ed Garner died and couldn't wake herself up. It had been strange for Mara as well, but she never thought it would interest anyone else. Or that it meant anything other than her subconscious simply didn't want to wake up.

But Agent Piper didn't volunteer any theories on the matter, which made Mara frustrated. It would have been nice sharing with someone who had experience with other people who had her gift.

After agreeing to meet with Agent Piper the next time Mara had another vision, she was finally allowed to go home. Claire and Ben grabbed her in a tight bear hug as she exited the interrogation room. Ben made all sorts of threats as they were told Mara was free from questioning. But Mara knew his threats were empty. He was just angry and scared. Ben always said he'd protect his girls no matter what, and even though Mara knew her situation was out of his control, he obviously let it get to him.

The press was a whole other nightmare. Unfortunately, word got out that Mara had been taken in for questioning for Ed's murder and due to the high number of YouTube views from her excursion with Colt, it had made the story even bigger. Feeling somewhat responsible for the chaos, Detective Nicholson led Mara and her parents out the back way to avoid the growing crowd of reporters outside the station.

Once they were in the car, Claire turned to Mara who sat in the back seat. "Are you sure you're okay?" Her mother continued without waiting for an answer, "I can't believe they kept you there all night. It has to be illegal. They wouldn't even let us stay in the lobby. They made us leave! But I stayed in the parking lot all night, just in case they let you out early…"

"Mom, you're rambling," Mara interrupted her mother with a smile.

Claire and Ben chuckled and Ben said, "I think she'll be fine."

"I *am* fine. The FBI is on the case now, not just the local police, and Agent Piper believes that my dreams are real, so I don't think they'll be bringing me in again." Mara hoped this was a true statement.

Claire kept her attention on her daughter. "It's not Agent Piper that worries me it's that woman detective."

The fact that her mother didn't bother saying Detective Nicholson's name indicated the deep hatred Claire felt towards the lady.

But Mara had to agree. "She really thinks I'm guilty. She doesn't believe for a second my dreams are real. She's probably looking for evidence right now to arrest me for real next time."

"They just better find the guy before that happens," Ben

added, keeping his eyes on the road.

Claire switched topics, not wanting to consider the possibility of her daughter being brought in again. "Well, with that whole YouTube thing, you're front page news and your Principal doesn't think it's a good idea to go to school for a while. He's going to have Josie bring your homework, but Adam will tutor you since he's the only one you know in your advanced classes."

Adam. Being alone with him sounded really good to Mara right then.

"Have you heard from him?" Mara asked. "I didn't get a chance to say anything when they took me in. I was kind of in shock."

Claire's whole face lit up. "Oh, Mara, he is such a thoughtful young man. He's been in constant contact with me the entire time you were inside. He even stayed with me a few hours in the car last night, hoping they'd turn you loose. He really cares about you."

Even Ben chimed in, "He's a good kid."

Wow. That was the highest praise Mara ever heard from her father. He had always made it quite clear that no one would be good enough for his daughters, so to admit that Adam was *a good kid* was a raving review.

After the whole 'suspected of murder' ordeal, this new turn of parental attitude made Mara surge with happiness. Of course, she wasn't about to tell them that she and Adam had had sex. Her father wouldn't be singing Adam any praises if he knew *that* particular piece of knowledge. No sense in ruining the mood.

"Zia and Adam are waiting at the house," Claire explained. "Zia spent the night in Josie's room. We've all been train wrecks

164

since they took you in and wouldn't let us see you. I still think it's illegal…" Then she went off on another tirade that lasted the rest of the way home. Mara didn't mind. It was nice to hear her mom exploding with passion over how her daughter was wronged. If Claire knew that Mara had been stuck in the interrogation room with her own vomit for an hour, she'd be a lot more pissed off. So Mara kept her mouth shut on this matter, too, not wanting to poke the mama bear too much. The last thing Mara wanted was more attention.

Spoke too soon.

When they drove down her street, Mara had to slink down in her seat: there were news trucks and reporters everywhere. Even more than when Ed Garner was murdered. They were all salivating for Mara to arrive back home.

Seeing the crowd camped in front of his house, Ben had a few choice words that he muttered under his breath. Claire outright yelled at them through her open window.

Mara's heart surged when she saw Adam walk out her front door with Zia and Josie. They acted like directors of traffic, shoving the press aside, carving a path for Mara's parents to park by setting up cones in the driveway. It was an important precaution, because even then Ben almost hit a few overzealous journalists as he parked by the side of the house.

Adam opened Mara's door and put out his hand for her to take, which she gladly did. She wanted to hug and kiss him forever. But seeing as the world was watching and, more importantly, her parents, she settled for holding his hand.

Once inside, Claire picked up the phone and called the police. She began the screaming match that would hopefully lead to most of the press leaving their home. At least Mara hoped so. But she did feel safe inside. This was her home. And, once the door sealed them inside, it shut out most of the noise and gave her relief.

Zia hugged her first, though Adam never let go of Mara's hand, but Zia didn't care. "I can't believe they took you into the station. What did they want? Did they think you killed Mr. Garner?"

Mara nodded. "Detective Schmucko did. She still does, I think, but the FBI is taking over and they seem to *want* my help."

Zia and Josie perked up at this, very impressed. Adam, though, became more concerned.

"Your dreams are what got you in trouble in the first place, Mara. Now suddenly they believe you?" He was angry at what had happened, and not surprisingly, defensive.

"Well, this Agent Piper said she's had some experience with people like me. I'm telling you it was just that detective lady who thinks I'm guilty." Mara wished Detective Nicholson would drop her vendetta against her, at least in the short term, so Mara could find the killer, but there was no way to be sure if the detective would obey the Feds.

Claire, meanwhile, continued to scream at the police on her phone in the background.

Ben nodded to the teenagers. "You guys should let Mara rest."

"I just got home. I don't want to rest." Mara *was* exhausted since she'd only had a few hours of sleep in a metal chair, but the thought of Adam and Zia leaving was excruciating.

Ben nodded, seeming to understand what his daughter needed. "At least go upstairs and try to relax. Your friends can stay with you."

Mara, Adam, Zia and Josie all trudged upstairs to Mara's room. Her sanctuary.

Josie sat at the desk while Zia sat on the window sill blocking the view of any stray correspondents who might be trying to take a peek inside.

Mara and Adam sat on the bed.

She decided to tell them about her newest dream while stuck in the interrogation room – and everything Agent Piper had said to her.

When Mara finished, Zia questioned worriedly, "I can't believe you two went to that house. What if the killer had been there?"

"I know, we were stupid. But at least we know now the killer probably hasn't been there in years. They said the traces of blood they found on that table were eight years old."

Adam's expression turned thoughtful. "Do they know who it was?

"If they do, they didn't tell me," Mara sighed in disappointment.

More to himself than the others, Adam spoke aloud. "So, this guy has been doing his murder thing for at least eight years, maybe longer."

Zia tried to puzzle it out. "You were probably in the killer's dream space or something, seeing his past. I mean, I'm pretty sure the balloons with body parts didn't really happen, either. That would have definitely been on the front page news."

"Yeah," Josie joined in, "maybe he's like you and he dreams stuff too. In your other dreams you're more like an observer watching the killer and the victim, but with this guy you can't get out of his head. Maybe that's on purpose."

That idea creeped out Mara beyond thought. She knew she was connected to the guy, but imagining he was like her made her skin crawl. If he was, the killer could be way more powerful than her, which maybe was why he was able to keep her stuck inside him, watching through his eyes, an audience to his murders. What if he could make her do things in her dreams? Or worse, what if he could control her body in her sleep? These weren't rational thoughts, but Mara's imagination was running wild.

Adam seemed to be working things through as he responded to Josie, "But Mara wasn't in the killer's head when she dreamt of that house. She was just in someone else's dream." He glanced over at Mara for approval. "Right? I mean, if this killer guy *is* powerful enough to keep you inside his head while he's killing, then he'd be powerful enough to stop you from seeing the house where he killed his first victim. Maybe there are two different people involved in this somehow."

Mara pondered that for a moment. "So, you're saying this house where the old blood is may not be connected to the killer of Mr. Garner and that Larry's Liquor guy's killer? That it was some other killer's dream I jumped into?"

Adam shrugged as all eyes turned to him. "Yeah, maybe. I just think that, if this guy *can* keep you from seeing him, that he'd never let you into his dream space. Especially, to a place that could potentially convict him of murder."

They were all silent for a moment, mulling over Adam's theory.

Zia stood up as if she had just solved a difficult math problem.

"Wait a minute. This is going to sound crazy, but what if we used your Ouija board? I mean you said last night's victim knew the killer? Maybe he could tell us."

Adam looked at her skeptically. "Are you kidding right now?"

Zia placed a hand on his shoulder supportively. "I know you're new to all this, but your girl has been connected to whatever it is you want to call it: psychic world, dream land, whatever. We've had some pretty crazy experiences on ye olde Ouija board."

Josie chimed in, "We should totally do it."

Adam shrugged. "I'm up for it if Mara is."

Everyone focused on Mara.

She wasn't sure how she felt. Though it sounded like a cool idea, something about it scared her. She had just seen these two men die and now to talk to them through a *game board*? It didn't seem anywhere near the realm of reality. But what could she really lose? Not much. If anything, she could always tell Agent Piper that she'd dreamed who it was, if the killer's latest victim named their murderer.

"Yeah, I'm in," she nodded. "But let's eat dinner first and wait until its dark."

***

Most of dinner was spent with Claire and Ben frantically planning the next week. Their lives were in more of an upheaval than Mara's. She found she was distancing herself from the craziness of what was happening and focusing on finding the murderer so her life could go back to normal. There hadn't been this much excitement and worry at their house since her great aunt killed

Uncle John. The press had been relentless then, too, but it was focused on her aunt's trial more than their family. No one but her parents and Josie knew about Mara's dream back then and they weren't about to let a seven-year-old take the stand talking about her nightmares.

This cut far closer to home for Claire and Ben, but it had the same type of intensity. And when it came to the safety of their daughters, they didn't like it one bit.

After dinner, Zia and Adam went upstairs with Mara and Josie. Ben set the time for everyone to go home at ten o'clock. It was only eight now, so that gave them a couple of hours to try their Ouija experiment.

Josie pulled the game off the shelf, laid it out on the floor and the four of them sat in a circle around the board.

"This is so crazy," Mara said of the game. "Do you think it'll work?"

Zia smiled. "Put your hands on the disk and we'll find out."

Josie looked spooked. Adam seemed freaked by the whole notion, but he was the first to put his two fingers on the plastic pointer. Mara was next, followed by Zia, then Josie.

Zia took the reins. "We want to talk to the young man who was recently murdered," she called out to the air.

Nothing.

Not even a slight shove.

Zia tried again. "We know you recognized your killer. We want to catch him so he can't hurt anyone anymore."

Nothing. It was as if pointer was made of lead. Not that it wouldn't move, but it seemed as if it was being held in place. Mara noticed the whites of Josie's fingers from the force of too much pressure. "Josie, you're supposed to hold on to it as lightly as possible."

"Sorry." Josie blushed. "This is nerve wracking."

She lightened her grip.

Swoosh!

The pointer flew over the letters, stopping briefly at each.

"Adam, write it down!" Zia ordered.

Adam didn't look too happy to be the stenographer, but he did as he was told, letting go of the plastic device.

Josie's face was pale from fear, while Zia lit up with excitement. She spouted out each letter as the pointer went to it.

"What are they saying?" Zia asked of Adam.

"Your dreams will.... That's all it says so far, keep going." Adam eyed Mara worriedly.

Mara didn't like the sound of where this was headed.

Then suddenly the pointer stopped.

As in no movement at all.

Zia was flustered and her excitement turned into fear as she saw the expression on Adam's face. "What is it Adam? What did they tell us?"

Adam's eyes met Mara's and he looked scared as he said, "Your dreams will make you pay."

Dream Entry #13

*L*ast night was crazy. After the doozy revelation the Ouija board gave us, it went completely dead. We tried again for at least an hour before we decided to give up and Adam and Zia went home. Even though I was beyond exhausted, it took a while before I finally drifted off to sleep. I was too scared I'd have another dream, especially after the message from the board: Your dreams will make you pay. What did that mean? It sounded like a threat, like I'd be punished for having my dreams. I feel like I've already been punished for them. Going to the Garner's, then breaking into that house where the lady was chopped up is the reason I was arrested in the first place. Maybe these Ouija ghosts are a bit behind on the news front. I know that isn't it, but thinking too hard about it is making me sick.

When I finally did get some Z's, I had another dream. It was powerful, but it wasn't a vision. I wonder if whoever talked to us on the Ouija board sent it to me. I know it's important. I just don't understand it.

I was standing inside an old mansion decorated with nothing but antiques. Next to me was an intricately carved grandfather clock, but the clock face was digital instead of using hands like I would have expected. It was 12am. I knew that couldn't be right, though, because I could see sunlight filtering in from outside through the mansion's gauze curtains. The draperies were floor to ceiling, covering a set of French doors. As the wind blew them gently aside I saw a wooden balcony. It had no railings.

Curious, I walked onto the hanging structure. Once there, standing on what was really nothing more than an open ledge, I realized the house was perched on the very edge of an enormous canyon. The canyon's walls went on forever, its deep chasm so wide and empty that no one would be able to travel to the other side without a plane or a helicopter.

Though the grandfather clock had said it was nighttime, the sun was at its apex in the sky and completely viewable to the human eye.

But that wasn't what caught my attention. Making a perfect circle in the sky, all the planets of the solar system surrounded the sun in breathtaking imagery, each one the size of a beach ball. I could even see Jupiter's moons and Saturn's rings as if I was close enough to reach out and touch them.

Excited by what I was witnessing, I ran back inside the mansion to tell someone.

Great Uncle John and Kimiko both stood there staring at me. For some reason I didn't think this was strange. I began pleading with them to come out and see the spectacle. Finally, after some effort, I convinced them to walk out onto the balcony. But, to my horror, when they looked into the sky...

They couldn't see anything.

I was so shocked because it was as clear as day to me. They both went back inside without another word.

I gazed at the planets and suddenly had an urge to go to the bottom of the gorge. Not knowing how long the sunlight would last, I left the giant, looming house and began to climb down the cliff face.

It was as if I was floating down the rocky terrain. The journey was so much easier than I had anticipated.

But the moment my foot touched the canyon floor, the sun went down all at once.

In utter darkness, I heard the sound of a car engine coming closer and closer. Before I could think to shield myself my own VW Bug whizzed by, almost hitting me. As the car zoomed away I saw that the person driving the vehicle was me. The car and my doppelganger were gone before I could process what I had seen.

Looking up at the sky, the blackness swirled and churned until it transformed into angry dark clouds. Rain fell at full force, soaking me to the bone instantly. All I could do was run toward the canyon wall to try and climb back up to the mansion. As I struggled to make my way up, strong gusts of wind blew me off course.

I held onto whatever I could: rocks, dirt and plants. After what seemed like hours, I finally crawled to the rim of the cliff face and ran inside the mansion.

Great Uncle John was still there. He pointed to a window. I followed his gaze and the biggest, nastiest tornado imaginable came straight for us.

"Here it comes," he said softly to me.

But, just before the tornado hit the mansion, it was swept inside an oil tower that suddenly formed outside the house and remained trapped. The roaring tornado spun and spit, trying desperately to escape its new prison. It wanted to destroy. It wanted to consume. But the oil tower kept it in place.

Great Uncle John disappeared, replaced by Kimiko. She placed her hand on my shoulder, staring at the captured tornado, and said, "I don't remember Dorothy getting to Oz this way."

I woke up after that.

I have no idea what this dream means, but know it means something. It's the third time I've dreamt about Kimiko. I need to talk to her, as horrible as that sounds. My dreams are telling me she's important somehow. My arch nemesis and personal bully for the last few years. Somehow, she's connected to all this.

Zia told me there's a party tonight at Kimiko's house and that Kimiko went out of her way to invite me. Zia doesn't want me going after everything Kimiko has done. In fact, Zia wants to boycott the shindig herself, but after about ten minutes of me convincing her we could find out more information, she finally gave in.

I don't want to go either, but I know I need to.

***

Mara tucked her diary in the drawer and shut it closed. She was relieved Agent Piper had returned it to her, but was still a little humiliated that God-knew-how-many-people had read it.

She didn't think last night's dream was particularly relevant to the case, so she decided against sharing it with the Feds. It was probably just her subconscious on overdrive after the whole Ouija board experience. Maybe her dreams were *making her pay* by being so ridiculously hard to translate. She knew in time everything would be revealed. It always seemed to work out that way. Like at Gasworks Park and Kite Hill. Once she was taken into custody she knew that was why she'd dreamt of the hill being covered in blood. Running down the hill, trying to escape being blamed for Ed Garner's murder. The only thing that hadn't clicked for her in that nightmare was why Kimiko had turned into a corpse.

Mara hoped it wasn't some kind of premonition. She didn't like the girl, but she didn't want her dead, either. If Mara was gaining some kind of special glimpse into Kimiko's future, she needed to be warned. Or at least Mara needed to try and figure out how Kimiko was related to all this.

Zia called later that morning to make sure Mara was still going with her to the party. She tried again to convince Mara that they should boycott the whole thing, but Mara assured her best friend that she needed to go. And if Colt and Kimiko had a revenge plan brewing, maybe Mara, Zia and Adam could figure out what it was at the party.

Mara's parents weren't too thrilled about the idea, especially with all the news trucks still camped out in the front of their house. So Mara laid on them a long guilt trip about trying to fit in and forgetting about what was happening to her. They gave in.

The rest of the day Mara watched as the minutes drew closer to her doom. Social events were like that for her. Doom. She couldn't help but suspect that she was walking into some sort of setup. Like Carrie in Stephen King's book. Maybe that was what the blood really meant in the Gasworks dream. Kimiko planned on pouring it over Mara's head.

She took a deep breath and tried to ignore her paranoid

176

thoughts. Claire had stayed home all day to somehow protect Mara from over-bold reporters, but her mother had to work most of the day on her laptop, which left Mara on her own pretending to study. Finally, Josie came home from school and she had someone to talk to.

Josie plopped down Mara's bag and collapsed on the desk chair. "I have a bunch of homework for you." She pulled out a stack of papers and couple of text books from her bag. "Adam should be here soon to show you how to do all this stuff." Josie handed Mara a Calculus workbook. "Your classes suck."

"Thanks," Mara smiled as she took the workbook from Josie's hand. "I'm going to get so far behind," she groaned.

"With Adam as your tutor, I completely agree," Josie teased.

"Shut up," Mara joked back. She hadn't told her sister that she was no longer a virgin and she didn't intend to. Gossip like that was ammunition in the sister-world. It was a get-out-of-jail-free-card for Josie. If her sister was about to be punished for something all she'd have to say is: *Mara had sex!* Josie would be free of all charges because Ben would implode on impact. No. Though Mara would love to share the news with her sister, it was too risky.

"Have you thought about the whole Ouija board thing last night?" Josie asked. Mara noticed that her sister seemed wary, as if she had been thinking about it all day.

"Not much to think about. I can't control my dreams." Mara shrugged. "And if they're going to *make me pay*, there's nothing I can do about that."

"I guess," Josie agreed thoughtfully. "But it was creepy, right?"

Mara nodded. "I wonder who we were talking to."

"Yeah… Maybe Mr. Garner. He always seemed a bit gloom and doom," Josie suggested.

"He did not. He was always nice."

Josie shook her head. "Now that he's dead, kids are talking at school. I guess he didn't always used to be such a good guy."

Mara's attention immediately focused on Josie's words. "What do you mean?" She'd been trying to find out any dirt on the Garners since the whole thing happened, but had come up with nothing. She knew that what she was about to hear was most likely hearsay, but sometimes there was an inkling of truth in rumors.

Josie leaned forward, excited to share the news. "Craig Flont said that Mr. Garner used to beat his own kid. He called it 'discipline,' but I guess back in the day he'd come to school all bruised and bloody."

"Robert, right? Don't you remember him? He used to do yoga on the front lawn." Mara suddenly remembered the image of a sixteen-year-old boy doing stretching poses in the early morning hours.

Josie shook her head. "How long ago was that?"

"I don't know, eleven years maybe? I was about six, I think. He must be almost thirty now. Adam said that he and his mom used to clean the Garner's house and that they were all really nice."

"Well, Craig said that his older brother went to school with Robert and that no one did anything about the abuse because Mr. Garner had some weird sway over the community." Josie sat back, waiting for Mara's response.

Mara was doubtful. "There's no way someone didn't report

him if that was true. Our parents for one. Don't you think we would have noticed if the kid across the street was all bruised up? Mom and Dad would never let us near that place if they suspected anything, and Dad was more excited about Mr. Garner's Halloween candy than we were."

"Look," Josie put her hands up in supplication, "I'm just telling you what Craig told me. His brother said that Mr. Garner had it coming and he wouldn't be surprised if their son was the one who killed him."

"Where *is* Robert Garner, anyway?" Mara mused aloud. She could have missed Robert if he had stopped by his father's place, but Mara hadn't seen him at all since long before the murder happened. She thought for sure Robert would at least stop by the house to pack things up or something.

Mara suddenly wanted to talk to him. Maybe there was more to Mr. Garner's son that even Adam knew. What if Robert was the killer? If she could just look at him. Even if Robert didn't admit to anything, she was sure she'd be able to sense if he was the killer or not.

"I heard Robert came in for the funeral and he's staying at a hotel." Josie nodded toward the Garner's home. "You should ask Adam. If Adam knew Robert all those years ago, maybe he could tell you if Robert was abused."

There was a knock on the front door downstairs. Josie perked up. "Speak of the devil." She gave Mara an excited smile and rushed to her sister's door. "I'll go get him."

Her sister took off and Mara pondered Josie's last suggestion. Adam had said he barely knew the Garners, but maybe he'd blocked some of it out. It was over eleven years ago. Maybe with

179

a little prodding he could remember something that would be helpful.

When Adam walked into her room, his smile melted her utterly. He had his book bag with him and tossed it on the bed next to her. Then he scooted in as close as he could and kissed her neck.

Mara almost gave into the temptation, but her mind was too focused on the Garners. "Josie said Robert Garner was abused."

Adam pulled away with a slightly crestfallen expression. "That's not important."

Mara was shocked. "Not important? Wait a minute, you knew?"

Adam sighed and flopped back on her pillows. "I didn't want to tell you because you'd think Robert did it. He didn't. Yes, I knew him more than I let on before. But listen, Robert is a good guy. He always looked out for me. We did have a lot in common and he was the one who taught me to be better than my asshole dad. Robert would never hurt anyone."

"How do you know that? Maybe he snapped, which would be pretty freaking understandable. His dad beat him. A child. You of all people should know what that's like. Adam, if you told me you just killed your dad, I'd understand and I'd be happy. I think anyone who can beat up a kid doesn't deserve to breathe." Mara was furious. She didn't realize how much Adam's constant abuse had affected her psyche. The thought of someone causing bodily harm to her boyfriend made her livid, especially imagining him as a child. In the past she always saw all sides. Now, knowing Adam and knowing he was being methodically abused, it made her want to tear his dad's heart out like some kind of creature on

180

a supernatural TV show.

Adam pulled her onto his chest. "Well, I appreciate your permission to off my dad, but I think I'll pass."

She looked up at him and he smiled gently.

"My father does what he does because that was the way he was raised. He doesn't know any different. Robert taught me that. He was the one who told me to hide the bruises by provoking fights with bullies. He was the one that told me that once I was eighteen life would be different. I won't have to put up with guys like my dad ever again. I owe him, Mara. And when we first met and decided we were going to solve this... I didn't know how you'd react to me knowing him. Robert is very important to me. I didn't want you to go after him."

"Can I just meet him?" Mara asked carefully "I believe you, but I need to see it myself. I'll know as soon as I talk to him." She didn't want to anger Adam.

Adam leaned down and kissed her until her head began to spin, then he pulled away. "Alright, if you really want to meet Robert, I'll go over to the Garner's house now and invite him to Kimiko's party."

"He's over there now?" Mara instantly peered out the window, but the Garner's house appeared as empty as ever.

"Yeah, I had to go in through the back. Not even the press knows he's in there."

Mara turned back to Adam. "You'll really bring him to the party?" Upon seeing Adam's nod of affirmation, Mara perked up. She had a surge of... relief? She wasn't sure, but she knew meeting Robert would either put her mind at ease – or she'd have to sit Adam down and tell him his friend was a killer.

181

"I'd do anything for you." Adam kissed her again. His lips were soft and she became lost in the moment.

Separating was difficult for both of them, but they finally parted.

"We should do our homework now," Mara said grudgingly.

"Right. Homework." Adam shook his head to focus.

The two of them spent the next two hours going over all of Mara's subjects.

When it was time to go, Adam kissed her good-bye.

"I'll see you at Kimiko's," he smiled.

Mara nodded, then Adam left the house.

Now, at least, she had two missions at this dreaded party: talk to Kimiko and talk to Robert.

***

It wasn't long after Adam departed that it was time to leave. Zia picked Mara up and, driving away, they almost ran over three reporters trying to grab a statement from anyone coming out of the house. Mara wondered how long the news would care about her or what she had to say. Surely, they had better things to report on than a girl who was taken in for questioning on a murder case. Until they figured out who the real killer was, though, Mara guessed that she was stuck with them for a while.

The more she thought about Robert, the angrier she was that there were people who had known about his abuse but did nothing to stop it. How did her parents not see? How did *she* not see? And if people knew about Mr. Garner's dickhood, why *wouldn't* Robert be a suspect? Where were the cops? Where was

Detective Nicholson? Or Agent Piper? Mara didn't know the first thing about solving crimes, but she would have thought that Robert Garner, abused son of victim Ed Garner, should be the number one suspect. It didn't make sense.

Unless…

Unless he had an iron-clad alibi. She nodded to herself inwardly. That was probably it, but still…

Mara wanted to talk to the guy.

She hoped he'd agree to Kimiko's. Robert was in his late twenties, so showing up at a high school party would most definitely be a little awkward, to say the least. Still, Adam seemed to think he would, so she decided to have faith.

Arriving at Kimiko's house, Mara was immediately struck at its similarity to the mansion from her dream last night. She knew for a fact that Kimiko didn't live on the lip of a giant canyon, she could see that for herself, but the house had the same dark wood and architecture as the place in her vision.

People were spilling out of the doors as if everyone from school had made it to the event. For lack of room, Zia had parked her car a block away and the two of them walked toward Kimiko's.

"Hey, wait up," Adam's voice came from behind.

Mara and Zia turned to see Adam and…

Robert Garner.

At least she assumed it was him. Robert was older than she remembered, of course, clean-cut, brown hair, brown eyes and in really great shape. He looked more like his mother Millie than Ed, which was definitely a good thing. His demeanor was guarded but light as he approached Mara and Zia.

"I'm Robert," he introduced himself.

He held out his hand and Mara shook it.

Nothing.

She didn't feel a thing.

Mara had thought she might get some kind of impression from being close to the guy. But Robert's eyes were kind and thoughtful.

"I hear you have some questions for me," he prodded nicely.

Mara wasn't sure how personal this conversation was about to get. And, since Adam probably didn't want Zia knowing about his abuse, she turned to her best friend and said, "You go on ahead. I'll meet you in there."

"I'm not going anywhere." Zia wasn't budging.

Mara admired her friend's loyalty, but put her convincing-face on. "I'll be fine. I promise. You know Adam has my back."

Zia eyed Robert warily, then gave Adam the stare of intimidation. "I'm counting on you."

Adam wrapped his hand around Mara's protectively. "You know I'd never let anything happen to her."

"It's because of that, that I'm leaving," Zia hugged Mara, then nodded toward Kimiko's house, "but if you're not up there in ten minutes I'm hunting you down."

"Duly noted," Mara smiled.

And with that, Zia left with a few backward glances over her shoulder.

When Mara was sure no one could hear them, she figured she might as well be bold. "The cops brought me in for murdering your dad, but I didn't do it," she blathered nervously.

That was when she saw a flicker in his eye. It was gone before she could analyze it, but it had been there. Something. What was it? Fear? Anger? She couldn't tell, it happened too quickly.

"I know you didn't do it." He seemed genuinely concerned. "They didn't hurt you, did they?"

It was as if Mara was some kind of psychoanalyst, constantly trying to study every move, gesture or expression from Robert. His size. Did he match the guy from her dream? Maybe? She couldn't really tell from an outside perspective. But aside from the one brief second of… something… he appeared perfectly normal and terribly worried that she had been wrongfully accused.

"They didn't hurt me physically, but mentally it wasn't much fun," Mara answered. "I just want them to find the guy already."

Robert nodded slowly. "Me, too." Then he paused, looking at Mara thoughtfully. "I'm glad you and Adam found each other. He's a whole new person."

Adam blushed from Robert's words, and that was when Mara knew…

He saw Robert as family. The older brother he never had. Someone that looked out for him and treated him with kindness and respect. Who did Adam have other than her and Robert? A mom who abandoned him and a dad who beat him?

Mara suddenly felt a growing warmth for Adam's friend. "Well, I'm glad you two had each other, too. I think I would have gone insane going through what you did."

Robert nodded. From the expression on his face, he obviously knew Adam had told her about their relationship and their shared abuses. "We do have that in common, but it doesn't define who we are. We're better than our fathers. And better than our mothers who sat back and let it happen."

There was an edge to his voice as he said his last words. It was almost as if he was reciting some kind of mantra. Mara assumed he probably was to a certain degree. How else does one survive what they went through? What Adam was currently going through.

She immediately was apologetic for ever suspecting Robert and found herself saying, "I'm sorry I was so suspicious, it's just that, after what Mr. Garner did to you… I figured… I mean, I wouldn't have blamed you if you killed the guy."

Robert raised an eyebrow at her statement. "You wouldn't have?"

"Well, you know what I mean. To spank a kid is bad enough, but to beat them bloody? There's a special place in Hell for people like that." Mara was overcompensating for her guilt, but she wasn't lying. Even seeing a peek of Adam's bruises made her want to hurt Adam's dad.

Robert laughed and nudged Adam affectionately. "She's a firecracker."

"You have no idea." Adam kissed Mara lightly on the forehead.

Robert watched them with genuine regard. "Well, it would have been impossible for me to rid the world of Ed Garner because I was at a conference in Portland the night my father died. I was notified the next morning and believe me: *I* was their number one suspect at first. That detective lady who took you in interviewed every single one of my co-workers who drank with me at Gordo's bar the time he was murdered. I guess I was lucky I decided to go out. I almost turned in early that night."

Solid alibi. Exactly what Mara suspected.

Too solid.

Mara told herself to shut up. If he was with his co-workers at a bar when his dad was killed, then there was no way he could have done it. None. Zilch. Nada.

Then why did her mind always go back to not trusting Robert? Mara forced herself to stop thinking bad thoughts. She was simply being overprotective of Adam. That had to be it. And maybe a little jealous. Robert and Adam were obviously close, they had a bond that anyone could see. It made Mara wonder just how strong *her* bond was with Adam. Would it ever be as solid as theirs? She knew it was irrational, but she couldn't seem to shake the feeling.

Breaking Mara out of her reverie, Robert clasped Adam on the shoulder. "Look, I should go, but if you want to talk to me some more, I'll be staying at my parent's house."

"It was nice meeting you." Mara tried not to sound too pathetic. Her own insecurities aside, she had dragged this poor man to an under-aged party and he had been nothing but polite.

"You too," he said.

There it was again. Mara couldn't pinpoint it, it was just instinct, but he was hiding something.

Stop it. Stop it. Stop it.

Mara knew she was turning nothing into something. Her own petty jealousies were making her see things that just weren't there.

Robert left, leaving Adam and Mara alone on the sidewalk.

"Better?" Adam asked insecurely.

Mara nodded. "Much." She reached up and kissed him. "He's a really cool guy."

For a brief second, Adam's expression turned distant. Then,

as he stared into Mara's eyes, he came back to his normal self. "Yeah, he is. After my mom ran off, I don't know what I would have done without Robert."

Mara inwardly flinched.

There it was again: knee-jerk reaction to Adam's praise of Robert. It bothered her. She chastised herself for being such an annoyingly possessive girlfriend. Internally, Mara may have been green with envy, but outwardly she put on a positive face and said, "Well, I'm glad you two found each other."

Adam's face lit up and he kissed her passionately. When he tugged her in closer, Mara's stomach did flip-flops. He gently pulled away. "I love you so much."

"I know the feeling." She practically yanked his lips to hers, needing him to be closer.

Before they both lost themselves on the sidewalk in front of Kimiko Thompson's house, Mara forced herself to break away. "Maybe we should go inside?"

Adam smiled, kissing her softly. "Do we have to?"

Mara sighed. "Unless you want Zia to come out here and kick both our asses."

"I definitely don't want that," Adam laughed.

Taking Mara by the hand, Adam led the two of them up the stone walkway and into Kimiko's house.

It was beautiful inside, though it was almost impossible to tell, what with the giant crowd covering every inch of free space. The décor was modern, with an open concept downstairs like Mara's house. It was furnished quite sparsely, but Mara assumed that was because Kimiko had moved some of the furniture to make room for guests.

It was a surreal moment, though, standing in Kimiko's residence. Mara never thought this day would ever come, nor had she wanted it to. But having such intense dreams about the girl made Mara change her mind: she was worried her enemy's life was in danger.

Zia fought her way through the crowd to Mara and Adam, then whispered in Mara's ear, "She's over there with Colt."

Adam held Mara back with his hand. "I don't want to see Colt right now."

She didn't blame him. Aside from his father, Colt had beat up Adam almost as much.

But they didn't have a chance to run.

Colt and Kimiko saw the three of them and walked over as if Mara and Adam were the only two people in the room, the crowd seeming to part in front of them. Even Zia appeared to mean nothing to Kimiko and that shocked Mara the most. Her whole life Kimiko was always trying shove Mara out of the way so that she could steal Zia away from her. So seeing Kimiko ignore her best friend only made Mara realize that something was definitely off.

Then Mara saw it in Kimiko's eyes: fear.

Something had her spooked.

Colt stepped in at this point. "We want to start over." He turned to Adam. "With both of you."

Adam instinctively took a step back. "What's in it for you?"

Colt didn't seem fazed or offended by Adam's slight retreat. "I'm turning over a new leaf. I don't want to be the guy that everyone is scared of."

It all sounded wrong.

False.

Something wasn't right.

Colt was over confident.

Kimiko shifted uncomfortably. She was worried. But about what?

Mara forced eye contact with her. "Are you okay?"

Kimiko's fake smile drowned out any real emotion she might be having. "Of course." Then she motioned to the rest of the room, acting as a perfect host. "You guys enjoy yourself. There's food and drinks, anything you want." Before Mara could respond, Kimiko reached up and kissed Colt's cheek. "I'm going to make the rounds."

And she was gone. Disappearing into the crowd without a trace.

Colt wasn't phased at all. His eyes grabbed Mara's. "Can I speak to you alone?"

"No way," Adam said boldly.

But Colt acted as if he didn't hear him. "Please. Just for a second. Adam and Zia will have eyes on you the whole time."

Adam tugged on Mara's hand to lead her away. "You don't have to listen to this guy."

But Mara wanted to. This was her chance to find out if Colt and Kimiko were up to anything. She turned to Adam and Zia, who were both staring at her like a protective wolf pack. "It's okay, guys. I want to talk to him."

Neither one of them seemed pleased by that statement, but they knew better than to argue with Mara.

Zia gave Colt the stare of death. "We'll be watching you."

Colt nodded humbly. "Like I said, I would expect nothing

less."

After an overly tense moment, Colt led Mara to a corner of the living room. It was somewhat empty considering the amount of people crowding the house. To Mara and Colt it was practically abandoned.

Mara waited for Colt to talk.

With one more glance over at Zia and Adam, Colt focused all his attention on Mara. "I know you think I'm evil, but you really don't understand everything that's going on right now."

The fact that *Colt* said that made Mara feel that he was right, but she didn't want to show it. "Then tell me what I'm missing."

Colt kept looking around, paranoid, as if the students near him were listening or recording this conversation. "I can't tell you here. Too many eyes and ears. But I can tell you that you need to watch with both sets of your eyes."

It sent a chill down Mara's spine.

The exact words Great Uncle John had said to her in her dream: *Watch with both sets of your eyes.* It was followed up with: *You'll need them to save what you love most.*

Mara was so shocked, she couldn't say anything. She still didn't understand what it meant, not from her Uncle and certainly not coming from Colt. She finally found her voice. "What do you mean: 'Both sets of eyes?'"

"You know what I mean." Colt seemed sure of himself.

"No. I really don't." Mara felt like a fool.

Colt didn't look like he believed her. "I know about your dreams. And I know they're *real*. They're your second set of eyes. You have to trust what you see in them *and* what you see when you're awake."

Mara wasn't sure what shocked her more: Colt's apt observation – or the fact that he knew about her dreams.

"How did you know about my dreams?" She decided to ask first.

Colt did another visual sweep of the room. "It's not important. What *is* important…"

Mara cut him off, "It *is* important. How did you find out? Did someone tell you?" *Are you the one I've been connecting to in my dreams? Are you the killer?*

Colt grunted with annoyance. "Kimiko told me. Zia told her years ago."

A stab in the gut.

Zia? Her best friend? The one she trusted most in the world. Her mind was dizzy with betrayal.

"Don't be mad at her. I'm telling you it's really not important that I know. I just want you to know that I do." Colt forced eye contact with Mara. "Mara, be careful. I know it sounds weird coming from me. I've been nothing but a jerk to you and Adam, but I…" He was at a loss for words. For some reason it scared her. Then Colt continued, "I don't know, you deserve better, I guess."

Mara couldn't comprehend what Colt was telling her. All Mara wanted to do was confront Zia and ask how she could betray her to her worst enemy.

Her mind was brought back to reality when Colt's hand brushed her cheek. On instinct, she swatted it away forcefully. "What are you doing?"

Colt's face dropped. All the emotions Mara never expected to see in the football quarterback: insecurity, hurt… embarrassment.

She instantly regretted it, but before she could utter a

response, Kimiko arrived at their side. "What's going on here?"

Mara wasn't sure how to respond. Just knowing that Kimiko knew about her dreams made her physically ill.

"Nothing," Mara finally responded. "I thought Colt was going to hurt me so I smacked his hand away, but he was just trying to lean in so I could hear him." Mara wasn't sure why she was covering for him, probably because... awkward.

Colt's expression showed relief. Then he lazily wrapped his arm around Kimiko. "Remember what I said. We're just trying to look out for you."

"Yeah, thanks." Mara looked around the crowded house. "You know, I think I'm gonna go. Parties really aren't my thing."

Kimiko shrugged as if Mara's words were offensive. "I love a good party."

I love a good party.

Just like in Mara's dream.

Except, when Kimiko had said it in her nightmare, she had been a corpse.

Dream Entry #14

I *just got home from the party. Not much happened after talking to Kimiko and Colt. It really freaked me out when Kimiko repeated what she had said in my dream. I never thought I'd care whether or not Kimiko Thompson lived or died, but I do. She seemed so upset about something. And what was up with Colt touching my face all affectionate-like? It was creepy. The whole confrontation was just plain weird. So much so I didn't even deal with Zia afterwards. I chose to suck it up and pretend everything was fine. I could tell Zia and Adam knew something was wrong, but they obviously chalked it up to my conversation with Colt.*

I know eventually I'll have to confront Zia about what she did, but my psyche couldn't handle it all in the same night. I can't explain how I feel anyway. It's somehow embarrassing that Zia told Kimiko about my dreams. All that time Kimiko knew something so personal about me. I feel so exposed and vulnerable and all because I trusted my best friend. Why would Zia do that? It hurt so badly I can't talk about it. I almost want to forget about it completely, but I know eventually it'll eat me up until I have to talk to Zia about it.

The bottom line is that Colt and Kimiko know about my dreams. The biggest surprise of all was that they believe the dreams are real. Most people shrug off the possibility that a "Sixth Sense" or whatever exists.

Despite how odd the conversation with Colt had turned, though, him telling me to keep both sets of eyes open, just like my great uncle had told me, somehow seems the most important takeaway from the night. Now I know what Uncle John meant: I need to pay more attention to my dreams, even the ones that don't make much sense. If my subconscious is trying to warn me about something, I have to figure it out before anyone is hurt.

Zia and Adam had me home by 10, just like I promised my parents, and I can tell they are liking Adam more everyday Adam and I talked more about Robert Garner as well.

We both agreed that there's a fairly strong possibility that the police and the Feds have no idea of Mr. Garner's past. I wonder if I should tell them. Because if Ed Garner secretly beat his kid, then he was capable of so much more evil. Which means he probably had enemies, people who wanted to kill him…

…Who wanted to inject him with poison and watch him die.

The key would be finding out what Ed Garner and the second victim had in common. Maybe they knew each other? Maybe they pissed off the same person?

I have a lot to process. I'll stay quiet about Mr. Garner's child abuse for now. I just hope they find the murderer sooner rather than later because I don't know how much more I can take of being stuck in his head for every kill. I hate that we have some kind of connection. I want to sever it, but I don't know how.

And honestly, if having dreams about this guy helps catch him, then it will be worth it.

***

Mara woke up after having a dreamless night. It was such an odd sensation that she almost high-fived the air and jumped up and down for joy.

Taking out the homework Josie and Adam had brought her from school, Mara attempted to distract herself from everything that was going on in her life. She couldn't fight the gnawing ache that churned inside of her at the soon-to-be confrontation with Zia, but schoolwork was a good start at masking it. Besides, she didn't want to get too far behind. Mara had already been accepted to her top three schools, but she wanted to fill her head with as much knowledge as possible so college wouldn't overwhelm her. After everything she was currently going through, the two out-of-state colleges were looking better and better.

Claire stayed home again, so Mara, not wanting to be alone, joined her mother at the kitchen island and they worked in peaceful quiet. It was nice. The first time in a long time when Mara felt normal. She could tell her mother appreciated the day as well because, out of the corner of her eye, Mara saw her mother smiling at her every half hour or so.

Most of the homework Mara could puzzle out. It was just Calculus that gave her trouble. She'd have to wait for Adam to arrive and explain some of the more complicated equations.

Josie came home first, followed quickly by Adam.

Mara and Adam went upstairs to her room to go over her Calculus questions. She pulled in a chair upstairs from the den so that they could both sit at the desk. It was hard to concentrate on what Adam was explaining to her, though. Mara kept focusing on his perfect lips attached to his perfect face. When he asked her how she would solve the next problem, she imagined the blank stare on her face made it pretty obvious she hadn't been paying attention.

Adam shook his head, smiling. "Did you listen to a word I said? Because I probably want to be doing Calculus as much as you do – which is about zilch right now."

"I can't think straight when you're around," Mara admitted.

"Is that a fact?" His hand traced the line of her cheekbone, making her physically shudder.

"You're dangerous," she whispered, leaning over and kissing him.

Adam's lips pressed against hers and his hands squeezed the back of her shirt, making Mara dizzy with emotion.

"I love you," she said between kisses.

"I love you more," he responded breathlessly.

Everything melted away in that second. Time. Space. All the things that threatened to break up this perfect moment. It became just the two of them.

Mara wanted to be with Adam so badly in that instant she almost lost her breath.

Adam lifted her from her chair and laid her gently on the bed. His body pressed against Mara and she desperately wanted his shirt off so she could feel his skin against hers.

197

She began to pull his shirt up when she saw the black bruising on his stomach.

From the expression on her face, Adam self-consciously looked down. He sat up and gently moved his shirt back over his wounds. "Sorry," he said, embarrassed.

Mara's guilt meter went into haywire. She lifted his shirt and kissed his stomach. The blackness of the bruises broke her heart, especially since it went all the way up to his throat. The constant pain he must be in all the time had to be unbearable.

Adam lifted Mara's head with his finger. "You don't have to do that."

"Am I hurting you?" She suddenly worried that even kissing his wounds would cause more pain.

"No. I've learned to tune it out." He lay back on her pillows and pulled her down to rest against his chest.

"You shouldn't have to stay with him. I know my parents would let you stay here."

Adam absently stroked her hair, lost in thought. "I know you want to help, but I'm really okay."

Mara softly traced her finger on his neck. "You're the strongest person I've ever met."

He peered down at her and smiled. "I doubt that." Then he kissed the top of her head. "Besides, I'm not strong. I'm a coward."

Mara sat up at that. "No, you're not. I don't care what your father tells you or anyone else. The fact that you haven't turned around and beat the crap out of your dad takes more courage than his yellow-bellied-weakling-asshole self ever could."

"That made zero sense," Adam laughed.

The fact that he could laugh at the horrors in his life made Mara love him more. She laughed with him. "You know what I meant."

Adam placed his hand behind her head and pulled her to him, kissing her gently. When he pulled away, his eyes were sparkling. "Yes, I do, and I love you for it."

Mara knew it that moment: she'd do anything for Adam. She trusted him explicitly and she never wanted to be without him. She knew it was obsessive, but it also felt right.

She was just about to tell him when there was a knock on her door.

As if they had been building a bomb, Adam and Mara leapt off the bed and back into their chairs.

"Come in," Mara announced, trying to sound as calm and casual as possible.

Zia walked in. From the look on her face, Mara could tell that Kimiko had let the cat out of the bag.

"Can we talk?" Zia asked quietly.

Adam's puzzled eyes went back and forth from Mara to Zia. "Am I missing something here?"

This is happening. Mara put up her walls and stated loudly, "Zia told Kimiko about my dreams." Looking at Zia, she continued, "How long ago? Months? Years? Tell me, *best friend*, how long has the person that tortured me known about my most personal secrets?"

"I'm sorry. And you know I had no idea she was that mean to you. You kind of hid that from me, if you recall," Zia responded defensively.

True, but still. "It doesn't matter. Even if she was the nicest girl on the planet, that was my secret! You had no right to say anything to *anyone*."

"Should I go?" Adam squirmed with awkwardness.

Mara and Zia ignored him, too involved in their conversation.

Zia shook her head. "It freaked me out. I didn't know if I believed you or not."

Ouch.

Seeing the expression of pain on Mara's face, Zia continued quickly, "I didn't mean it like that. Of course, I believed that *you* believed. I just didn't know how or what to think."

"You know that's worse, right?" Mara's insides surged with anger.

Zia sighed. "I'm saying everything wrong. As soon as I tell you what I'm about to tell you, I never doubted you again."

"So you needed proof. Great." Mara wasn't letting Zia slide. Every word stung. Every ounce of doubt Zia had of her was painful. "So, what? You had a laugh with Kimiko about me? *Let me tell you about the crazy girl?*"

Zia's shouted angrily, "I would never do that! How could you think that?!"

Adam stood up. "I'm really going to go."

Mara whirled on him. "Why aren't you defending me?" She knew it was unfair, but with Zia confessing to being a horrible friend and Adam wanting to leave because he was uncomfortable, it all made Mara feel abandoned.

"Don't bring Adam into this," Zia intervened.

Mara knew Zia was right, but her emotions were too high to control. "Just say what you're going to say and let Adam and I be alone."

It was the equivalent to a slap in the face, but Zia handled it smoothly. "Do you remember the first dream you told me about?"

Mara remembered all her dreams. "The old lady who was walking her dog and some psycho pulled her into an alley and slashed her throat. Not hard to forget."

"Yeah, but do you remember what you told me about her. About what she did?" Zia prodded.

Mara would always remember that dream. The lady had had no fear. Even as she was being dragged away, all she cared about was getting her little Yorkie to safety. She had let go of the leash and screamed for him to run. Instead, the little dog tried to fight the attacker, but the woman commanded him to 'Go protect her Chichi!' and the dog finally ran away. Mara could remember the peace the old woman felt when she knew her dog would be safe and that he would find her beloved 'Chichi,' whoever or whatever 'Chichi' was. Even as the murderer cut her throat, the old woman had been ready to die. She said a prayer as he attacked and then Mara had woken up. "The dog and the dying in peace thing?" Mara asked, not knowing where this was headed.

Zia nodded. "I found Kimiko in the locker room after gym that day, crying. Her grandmother was the woman you dreamt about, Mara, and…"

"And…?" Mara was afraid she already knew the next part.

"Kimiko is 'Chichi.' I had to tell her, Mara. I had to tell her that her grandmother found peace and that her last thoughts were of her."

Mara paused. Her anger transformed into guilt, washing over her like a blanket of slime. She didn't know what to say or how to react. It had been such a powerful vision – and to find out that the sweet old lady had been Kimiko's grandmother? It left her numb.

Finally Mara found her voice, "Why didn't you tell me? I would have understood."

"I don't know. I just couldn't. I knew how much you hated Kimiko and how much it would hurt you if you found out I'd told her. I never thought you'd find out." Zia took a step closer. "And, Mara, as mean as she was to you, she *never* used that knowledge against you. That has to mean *something*. She could have thrown that back in your face anytime she wanted to, but she didn't."

Mara was suddenly awkward and unsure.

Zia seemed to pick up on this. "Do you forgive me?"

Mara took a moment to let things sink in. Then after a long pause, she nodded and walked over to her friend, hugging her fiercely. "I'm sorry for doubting you."

When the two pulled away from each other, Mara saw tears in Zia's eyes, which instantly made her eyes water, too. Mara pointed at her. "Don't cry! You're going to make me cry!"

Zia wiped away a few tears. "I can't help it. I was so scared you wouldn't let me explain."

Mara brushed aside her own tears. "I should have known better."

"Okay, now I'm really going to go," Adam announced. "You guys need to be alone."

Mara and Zia suddenly noticed Adam's existence and the two of them broke into laughter. As if reading each other's minds, they both hugged Adam.

"Group hug." Mara settled in to the embrace and Adam

physically relaxed.

When they all pulled away, Mara thought of something. "You're right about Kimiko. Why *didn't* she call me out? She ridiculed me for pretty much anything and everything. *Being psychic* would be perfect fodder for her."

Zia shrugged. "I don't know. I thought for sure she'd say something to you. That was two years ago."

Adam offered his opinion, "You've been dreaming about Kimiko lately. Maybe she's like you?"

"Maybe," Mara mused. "I saw her in my dream as a corpse. I just want to make sure she's safe." She turned to Zia. "You should go to her. See if you can get anything more out of her. Tell her about my dreams, anything, see what she says. I know she knows more than she's letting on. I'm telling you, she was scared last night. We need to know what of."

Zia nodded. "Okay. I'll see what I can find out."

Zia hugged them both and headed to the door just as Claire walked in, followed immediately by Agent Piper.

It was so surprising that Mara couldn't speak, so she simply stared. It wasn't that she hadn't thought she'd ever see Agent Piper again, she simply hadn't expected her to come to her home. Her room. Her sanctuary. It made Mara a little nauseous.

Claire spoke first, "Mara, Agent Piper wanted to talk to you about something. We've already discussed it and if you'd like to do it, your father and I will support you."

"Do what?" Mara didn't like the sound of that.

Claire's eyes shifted uncomfortably to Agent Piper, then back on her daughter. "I've given her permission to talk to you alone. I think you'll feel more at ease if she can explain it to you herself."

Agent Piper stepped in, "I promise I only have your best interests in mind. I have an idea that I'd like to share with you." She focused her attention on Adam and Zia with a kind expression. "But I do need to discuss it with Mara alone. Would you mind, Mr. Layton, Ms. Quinn?"

Zia took her cue. "I was just leaving anyway." She turned to Mara. "I'll call you later."

Adam turned to Mara to see what she wanted. He would have stayed if she had insisted, but Mara didn't want to involve him any more than she had to. "It's okay," she assured him. "I'll see you tomorrow?"

Adam kissed her hand, not wanting to be too intimate in front of Claire. "Text me later."

Mara nodded and the three of them left the room.

"Do you want to sit down?" Mara asked politely.

Agent Piper took the other desk chair and pulled it away from Mara a few feet, sitting down.

Mara appreciated that the FBI agent was trying to give her space, so as not to be intimidating. Not really working, but Mara appreciated the effort. More than that, though Agent Piper was strong and beautiful. Her dark almond eyes and straight pitch-black hair only accentuated her heritable Native American high-cheek bone structure. She carried herself in a way that made Mara want to be completely honest just to impress her. Like a good teacher or parent, Mara found she didn't want to disappoint Agent Piper in any way.

"I want you to know I've worked with a lot psychics," Agent Piper began – then stopped when she saw how Mara flinched at the word 'psychic.' "You don't like that word, huh?"

"It sounds flakey or something," Mara admitted. "Like I'm a crazy person."

Agent Piper smiled. "Let me re-phrase then. I've worked with a lot of people who have your gifts. Better?"

Mara nodded, wondering where this was going.

Agent Piper continued, "The amount of detail you've written in your journals blew my mind. As I've said before, I've never met anyone as talented as you."

"Thanks?" Mara left it as a question because she never thought of her nightmares as a *talent*.

Agent Piper laughed, then turned serious. "It think there's a lot more detail up in that head of yours that you haven't even tapped into."

Mara had immediate thoughts of brain machines and lab rats. "And?"

She must have looked terrified because Agent Piper tried to appear as comforting as possible as she rushed to say, "I would never hurt you. And come on, do you really think your mother would agree to let me in here if she thought you'd be in any danger?"

Good point. "What do you want me to do?"

Agent Piper sat back and took a deep breath. "I want to hypnotize you."

Dream Entry #15

*T*oday is the day I get hypnotized. Agent Piper is coming over this morning with an expert that will supposedly "put me under," as she calls it. I'm a little nervous. I can't imagine being hypnotized. I feel like I'm only going to irritate them because I won't be able to stop laughing or something.

My dreams last night were a non-stop jumbly ride of nothing that made any sense. Kimiko was in them again, which isn't that much of a surprise after the whole Zia-trauma-thing. At least Kimiko wasn't a corpse this time, but she was crying a lot. Every time I tried to go up to talk to her, she'd somehow be just out of reach. It was very frustrating.

On the non-dream side, Zia went over to Kimiko's house last night, but her mom said she was out with Colt.

So, the current plan is: Zia will talk to Kimiko today at school. I really don't know what we'll find out. It's not like I think Kimiko is *the killer or anything. I just have a gut feeling she knows more than she's letting on.*

After dreaming all night, I don't feel much rested. Maybe that will help make me fall asleep easier for the hypnosis session.

We'll see.

***

Mara lay back on her bed and eyed the three women staring at her: Claire, Agent Piper and the hypnotist, Joanne Barker. She had a kind face and her long hair was loose and wavy over her shoulders. She was dressed casually in a t-shirt and jeans, a stark contrast to the ever-rotating array of power suits that Agent Piper sported. Everything about the hypnotist was relaxed and laidback, which put Mara at ease.

Her mother had insisted on being present at the hypnosis session. Mara was grateful for that. She knew her mom would have Mara's best interests in mind and wouldn't let Agent Piper delve too deeply into Mara's head. Mara barely knew what was going on in her own mind, so to have someone poking around in there made her feel vulnerable.

What if she started spouting about the fact that she wasn't a virgin anymore?! The idea of *that* actually coming out terrified her. Well, at least it would be her mother that would hear it first and not her father. Mara just hoped that bit of information would stay hidden from the watching crowd!

Joanne, the hypnotist, leaned a little closer to Mara and smiled warmly. "How are you feeling? Relaxed? Nervous?"

"Nervous," Mara answered truthfully.

"That's completely normal. I guarantee by the end of this session you'll be calm and focused," Joanne offered thoughtfully. "Why don't we get started," Joanne breathed deep. "I want you to close your eyes and focus only on my voice."

At first, Mara was too stressed to even laugh like she thought she would have, then she realized that being so nervous made her too hyper focused. Yes, she was concentrating on Joanne's voice, but she was analyzing ever second of it and wondering if she was ever going to be hypnotized. *This isn't working,* she thought with frustration, and was about to call the whole thing off...

...when she saw the silhouette of the killer.

The sensation was so surreal Mara didn't know what was happening at first. Gradually, though, her surroundings formed around her as if she was in some kind of virtual reality. Mara understood that she was officially, "under."

When the scenery stopped shifting, she recognized where she was immediately: Ed Garner's bedroom, the night he was murdered. Ed Garner was awake, looking up at his killer, but nothing was moving. Both killer and victim were motionless. It was as if Mara had stepped into a 3D picture, except, instead of being inside the killer's head, this time she was standing next to him. His mask was off. It was the moment where Ed Garner gasped his last breaths.

Mara moved to stand in front of the killer, trying to see his face, but he was blurred.

It was as if she required glasses to see him. No matter how hard she tried, he was simply a silhouette.

Then she heard Joanne's voice, "Take off the killer's gloves."

Mara did what Joanne suggested, sliding the killer's gloves

208

from his hands. When she did, Mara was happy that she could see them clearly. They were young, strong hands, no wrinkles or sunspots. Definitely male. She didn't recognize them, but who really pays attention to people's hands?

And yet…

They did have some familiarity to them.

Compelled to move on, Mara pulled the syringe out of the killer's jacket. She examined it closely. It looked like an ordinary syringe one would find in a hospital, nothing unique to set it apart.

Mara placed the weapon back into his jacket.

Then her environment fell into a million pieces. It slowly started to rebuild…

Mara was now standing in the second victim's bedroom.

It was frozen in time again, just like the first vision displayed.

The killer stood before her, unmasked, watching the man die.

But, try as she might, Mara could not identify the murderer. It was as if someone had smudged a photo, but only on his face.

Chills raced down her spine.

The killer was controlling this.

Mara knew it to the core of her being. He didn't let her see his face because he knew she was looking.

He *was* like her, tapped into the unexplainable. The two of them were connected and it terrified her. That was why Mara saw through his eyes. She wasn't just a witness, she was an active observer, trapped inside a murderer's mind, forced to see him inject his victims with poison.

Just when Mara thought she was going to have a heart attack she slowly started to calm down.

The room collapsed around her, then rebuilt itself into…

Hogwarts?

A thrill of excitement raced through Mara as she stood in the dining hall from the Harry Potter books.

Then her eyes opened and she was back in her bedroom.

She was completely relaxed, but still held a bit of the happiness at being inside one of her favorite stories.

Joanne smiled at her. "How do you feel?"

Mara was suddenly unsure if she hadn't just fallen asleep and had a very strange dream. "Good. Did it work?"

Agent Piper replied, "It worked fantastically. You gave us some interesting information."

"I did?" Mara was pleased. Then she eyed the clock. An hour had passed. "Whoa."

Claire stood up and took her daughter's hand. "You did great, sweetie."

"At first I was sure it was working, but when I woke up it felt like I had just been dreaming."

Joanne explained, "It feels like that when you're deeply under. Everything you saw in your dream, you described to us aloud. I left you at Hogwarts because your mother said it would bring you out of your terror. You started screaming."

That was why Claire seemed overly protective. But Mara conceded, "Good call, Mom. That was awesome."

Her mother laughed at that, though she still appeared shaken.

"I didn't see his face, though. I don't see how any of what I saw could help you," Mara complained, defeated.

Agent Piper tried to dispel Mara's feelings of failure. "You told us he was young, athletic, connected to you. Connections this strong usually indicate it's someone you know in waking life, so maybe he's a student. The point is we now have a better place to start." Agent Piper stood up and nodded gratefully. "I don't want to keep you any longer. You should rest. Thank you, Mara. I know this is hard, but if we can catch this guy, it will largely be in part to you."

Her words made Mara feel better, relieved.

After a few pleasantries, Claire showed both women out of the house, leaving Mara alone in her room.

Someone she knew?

Mara tried to picture the silhouette for height, weight, anything that might be recognizable.

A name appeared in her head.

Colt.

But did he seem like the kind of guy who had dreams like hers? Maybe. It could be the reason why he'd been so violent with Adam. Maybe he couldn't handle the dreams and decided to act them out? Maybe that was why he'd apologized to her, because he recognized that she had been in his head the night of the murder and was afraid she'd I.D. him. Maybe his "warning" at the party was really a threat?

Although…

Colt did say to *keep both sets of eyes open* and if he was the killer, then it would only be a matter of time before she found out it was him.

So many Maybe's and not enough facts.

Part of her knew she might be reaching, but there was enough belief in her theory that she needed to check it out. If she could follow Colt around she might be able to at least see his hands. It wasn't definitive proof, but it would be something.

Mara waited impatiently for Adam to arrive and told him her theory. He seemed more interested in the hypnosis process than her revelation, but when Mara had finished the re-telling he was on board with following Colt.

"It makes a weird kind of sense." Adam mused. "It never took much for me to provoke the guy. With a fuse that short, he could be capable of anything. The question is: how do we get out of here to follow him? You kind of have the entire Seattle news team on your front porch."

"We'll have to sneak out." Mara had been planning all day. "I told my mom that we had to get some things for Ms. Potts's writing project, so she's going to help us make an escape."

"Based on a lie – to your mom – your mom is going to create a diversion for us to leave the house? Shouldn't we tell her the truth if she's going to go through all that trouble?" Adam asked with a guilty expression.

Well, when he worded it that way… Ouch.

But Mara knew her mother would worry needlessly if she was honest. Besides, Mara had no intention of being anywhere near Colt Lennox. She was going to watch from a distance. If she saw anything that confirmed her suspicion, then she'd call Agent Piper. Simple. "Telling my mom puts her in danger and I don't want to do that," she explained. "What she doesn't know keeps her safe."

Adam shrugged. "Okay, your call." Mara could tell he didn't quite agree, but he was going to follow her lead.

When the time was right, Claire stepped out of the house and motioned for all the reporters to come over to her. After four days of radio silence, the press salivated at the prospect of a statement. Within seconds they surrounded Mara's mother eagerly awaiting what she had to say. While the correspondents were busy with Claire, Mara and Adam snuck out the back on foot, cutting across the neighbor's back yard, then over to the next street behind them, to finally reach Adam's car parked a few blocks away.

Once inside and driving away, Mara's adrenaline pulsed through her. "I have no idea where Colt lives. Maybe we should follow him from football practice?" she suggested.

"I know where his house is," Adam admitted. "When you let a guy beat you down, you tend to find out where they live." He tried to comfort her, "Not that I was going to do anything to him… you're looking at me funny."

Mara hadn't realized that she was looking at Adam in any way that would suggest she doubted him, but she sensed he was sensitive about the topic. "I'm not saying a word. I'm just glad you know where we're going." Then she asked, "What else do you know about Colt?"

"Not much. I never stalked him or anything. I just wanted to know where his house was in case… you know… in case… I don't know. I always thought I'd have the courage to beat him back or something. Stupid." Adam didn't like sharing anything he saw as a weakness.

Mara tried to cheer him up. "It's not stupid at all. I've had many fantasies of punching the lights out of Kimiko. The important part is that neither one of us acted on it. We're better as observers, not fighters."

His body relaxed visibly, so she figured she'd done her job as a supportive girlfriend.

They parked a few houses down from Colt's. It was one of the bigger houses on the block, yellow paint, white trim craftsman style. It was exactly what Mara imagined his house to look like.

It didn't take long for Colt to pull into the driveway and exit his Mustang. He was dressed in sweats as he grabbed his duffel and went inside his house.

"What now?" Adam asked.

Mara hadn't thought of that. In the movies, some huge event would happen when detectives or spies staked out a suspect. But in real life? The guy had simply walked into his house.

"I guess we have to go up there and look through the windows or something?" Mara suggested, her voice betraying no desire to do any such thing.

Adam chuckled softly. "What did you think was going to happen? A syringe would fall out of his gym bag and we'd catch him red-handed?"

Mara shrugged, smiling at her own naivety. "I'm crazy. We should head back."

Adam turned his car back on, then shut it off abruptly.

"What is it?" Mara asked, seeing Adam's curiosity.

He nodded toward a car driving up. "That's Colt's dad." But Colt hadn't pulled his car all the way forward, so his dad had to park on the street.

Not a big deal, Mara had to do this numerous times when her mom or dad had done the same thing.

But Colt might as well have robbed a bank, his dad looked so furious. The tall, heavyset man was positively fuming as he stormed up the front walkway and flung the door open, slamming it behind him.

"Let's go see what happens." Mara already had her door open.

"Maybe we shouldn't…" Adam seemed leery of the idea, whereas moments before he had been gung-ho.

Mara realized it might be exceedingly close to Adam's own life. Colt's dad was extremely angry. If he was abusive, it could be too much for Adam to witness.

"I'll go. You stay here." Mara exited the car.

But Adam was immediately close behind. "I'm not letting you go alone," he said taking her hand as they rushed forward to hunch behind a large section of bushes next to the house. It was perfect cover from nosy neighbors, but if anyone was looking out from inside Colt's house, they'd be spotted instantly.

It didn't matter though.

The screaming was so loud Mara knew no one would be paying any attention to the side of the house.

With every boom of Colt's father's voice, Mara flinched. Adam was silent as he watched. This behavior was "normal" to him, but Mara knew she could never get used to it. When the sound of crashing furniture and the thuds of fists punching body parts went on for more that a few minutes, Mara had had enough.

She ran.

Ran all the way back to Adam's car.

She couldn't listen.

It was one thing to dream of abuses and murder, but it was entirely different being awake and present while it was actually happening.

A terrible thought suddenly struck her.

Mara had left Adam there.

Alone.

To witness what had happened to him his whole life.

She felt horrible.

What kind of person was she?

But Adam was quickly by her side hugging her. He didn't seem to care that she had abandoned him, his embrace was protective and loving.

Mara knew she should be the one comforting him, but she was too distraught to stop him.

"Let's get out of here." Adam opened the passenger door for her and she sat inside.

So, Colt was abused by his dad.

She should have known, but it was easier to hate him as a bully than to think it had been learned behavior.

Adam started his car. He was about to pull away when three black vehicles surrounded Colt's house.

Mara's first instinct was that it was the cops arresting Colt's dad for child abuse, but then she saw Agent Piper exit one of the cars.

Mara and Adam exchanged wide-eyed glances as, only a few minutes later, Agent Piper and a handful of Feds came out of the house with Colt Lennox in handcuffs.

But in that moment, watching Colt's terrified expression, and truly focusing on the shape and silhouette of his body…

Mara knew.

Colt was innocent.

Dream Entry #16

*I*t's 3am. I can't sleep. I just had another vision. I'm still shaking from my dream. I hate that it affects my body so much. I'm sweating too. It feels as if I break a fever whenever I wake up from a vision like this!

The killer has struck again.

I'm sensing a pattern here. He seems to kill whenever someone else is accused of his crimes. Is he trying to show off? Is he so sick that he needs the authorities to know that they caught the wrong guy? Of course, the Feds currently think they have the right guy, but I knew when I saw Colt being dragged to their car that it wasn't him. But it's not like Agent Piper could simply take my word for it. She obviously thought she had evidence that tied Colt to the crimes. If it was anything like the evidence they had on me, hopefully he'll be out by morning.

The killer was in an old abandoned house. I can't say where, but it wasn't in the greatest shape, so it was either in a poor part of town or it was one of those houses that people ignore on their block.

A homeless man was living in the basement. He had a rubber strap wrapped around his upper arm and there was a burnt spoon and a syringe carelessly lying beside him. A junkie, I guess. The man had a pleasant look on his face, so he was definitely high.

The basement was cluttered with newspapers and dirty blankets, which made me think that other people were squatting there as well. But there was no one else in sight when the killer arrived. He wore his leather gloves and black outfit. Since the only light source was the moonlight filtering in through the basement window, he blended in with the dark shadows of the room so well that the homeless man didn't even see him.

Once the killer stood in front of the junkie, he pulled off his ski mask and held the syringe in his hand, ready to strike.

The homeless man finally noticed the killer. He looked up and, like the others, recognized him immediately. He asked the killer what he was doing there, and the killer told the junkie that he already knew the answer to that question.

Instead of fear, the junkie simply nodded, then he said: "Do it. I deserve what's coming."

The killer obviously agreed because he injected the syringe directly into the homeless man's neck. But this time death was instantaneous. No choking. No gasping. The man simply closed his eyes and was gone.

Pulling the needle out of the man's skin woke me up.

The homeless man thought he deserved to die. More importantly, he seemed to look at the killer as a righteous executioner. Like he deserved the death penalty for his crimes. It makes me wonder why *the killer chose these three victims. They all knew him. Maybe they did him wrong and he wanted revenge?*

It seems like a logical explanation, but I just don't know...

***

Mara put the journal back in her drawer. Sleep wasn't her friend lately. If she wasn't dreaming crazy "message" dreams, she was inside a murderer's head watching him kill. She just wanted a good night's sleep. Was that too much to ask for? In her case, probably.

Mara closed her eyes and took a few deep, calming breaths, relaxing her body and mind.

If she could just fall asleep...

***

"Mara?" Colt's voice came from the darkness.

And just like that she was officially asleep. As she turned to see the high school jock, colors and shapes exploded all around her, until they all fell into place. Mara and Colt stood in a jail cell. Her heart went out to him. He was a jerk, but she knew what it was like to be accused of crime you didn't commit. The *same* crime.

She didn't know if she was actually with Colt in a vision, or if she was simply dreaming about him. She wouldn't be surprised by either.

The cell itself was small. There were two beds cemented to the wall, but Colt was alone, which was good. Sharing a closed space like that could be dangerous.

"Hi, Colt," Mara answered. Even if it was a dream maybe her subconscious needed to tell her something important.

Colt seemed sad. He sat down on one of the beds and stared down at his feet. "You know I didn't kill those people, right?"

Mara sat next to him so their legs were practically touching. "Yeah, I know."

He turned to her. "Do you know who the real killer is?"

Mara shook her head. "I can't see his face. I think he dreams like me and blurs it to protect himself."

Colt nodded. "I know who it is." Then he stared back down at his feet.

Subconscious or not, Mara wanted to know who Colt thought was the murderer. "Who is it?" she asked.

He sighed deeply. "I can't tell you."

"Why not?" Mara didn't want to hear that.

Colt's eyes met hers again and they were full of terror and grief. "I'm scared of what he'd do if I tell."

"More scared than being arrested for what he did?" Mara questioned.

Colt nodded, his face frozen in horror. "Yes. But I fixed it. He can't hurt me anymore."

The way he said it made Mara pause. "How did you fix it?"

He ignored the comment and stood up, then he looked at her once more. "Good-bye, Mara. Tell Kimiko that I really did love her."

"You can tell her yourself. Trust me, Colt. The killer struck again tonight. They'll have to let you go, like they did with me."

His smile was sad but content. "I found my own way out."

Mara was about to ask him what he meant, when her body was thrown back against the bars.

The inside of the cell transformed and Mara saw what was truly there:

Colt.

Dead.

A sheet wrapped around his neck and tied to the bars.

He had hung himself.

***

Mara woke up screaming.

Claire ran into her room, instantly by her side. "Mara, what is it? Did you have another dream?"

Mara fell into her mother's chest and started to cry.

Claire's hand stroked Mara's hair. "Do you want to talk about it?" Claire asked gently.

"They arrested Colt Lennox yesterday and he just hung himself. He wasn't even the killer," Mara choked out.

"Oh my God, Mara. I'm so sorry." Claire held her tight as if she could hug all the pain away from what her daughter had to witness.

Mara didn't say anything after that because the truth was: she thought it was all her fault. Logically, she knew it wasn't true, but she couldn't help it. Even considering Colt as the killer made her feel guilty. Going over to his house, invading his privacy, watching him be beaten then arrested, knowing full well that he was innocent at that point. Why hadn't she called Agent Piper? She would have listened. She might have even let him go. His father was still an a-hole abuser, but at least Colt would be alive. He was eighteen. He could have left.

But Mara had stayed silent.

And now he was dead.

Slowly, she gathered her wits and wiped the tears from her eyes.

Glancing at her clock by her bed, she noticed it was 6AM.

Claire followed her gaze and gave Mara one last squeeze of support. "Why don't I make us some breakfast?" Mara could tell her mother didn't know what else to do, so falling into a "normal" pattern was as much for her to cope as it was for Mara.

Mara nodded and her mother left to the kitchen.

It was early and she was exhausted, but the thought of dreaming again made her nauseous. She went into her bathroom and splashed some water on her face, making her feel a little better.

Colt had been speaking to her. It wasn't her subconscious. His spirit reached out to her and she was able to hear his last words. He knew who the killer was, but didn't want to say. And he loved Kimiko. Both thoughts haunted Mara. She knew she should care more about the fact that he could identify the murderer, but Colt's love for her nemesis stuck with her the most. Mara knew she'd have to tell Kimiko what Colt had said. At least she knew Kimiko would believe her.

Mara was afraid that Colt's suicide would solidify that he was guilty to the Feds. She took a deep breath, picked up her cell phone and called Agent Piper.

"Hello?" The agent's voice sounded as if she'd been awake for a while.

"Agent Piper? It's Mara. I had another dream last night. Two actually. One just happened though. Colt Lennox is dead. He just hung himself a few minutes ago. He was innocent. He wasn't the killer from my vision." Mara had to stop from the catch in her voice and from the anger she felt rise inside her at Colt's false arrest that led to him taking his life.

There was silence on the other end. For a moment, Mara wasn't sure if their call had been disconnected. Finally, Agent Piper spoke, her voice distraught by Colt's actions, "We were going to let him loose today. I arrested him to try and get him to talk." She sounded choked up as well. "We must have pushed too hard. I made him think we had evidence against him to try and scare him…" Her voice became steady again. "I pushed too far."

The admission only made Mara feel worse. She didn't want to talk about Colt anymore at the moment. It was too fresh, but she needed Agent Piper to know what he said. "Colt said he knew who the killer was, but he wouldn't tell me."

After another long silence, Agent Piper admitted, "We knew there was a connection between him and killer. And now your dream confirms it."

Physically and emotionally, Mara couldn't talk or think about Colt anymore, so she switched gears. "I need to tell you about the other dream," she said it almost shyly. She didn't really want to re-live yet another horrifying vision, but she knew she had to.

Mara told Agent Piper everything she could remember about the dream of the homeless man's murder.

After Mara was done, Agent Piper was distant, almost cold. "Is there anything else you can tell me?"

It threw Mara off, hearing the agent switch moods so fast,

but she answered, "No. That's it." Then bravery took over and she asked, "Do you even have any *real* suspects?" Even she cringed at her abrasive tone, but Agent Piper's mood swings set her off for some reason.

"I've already discussed too much with you. You are still technically a civilian." Her voice went back to being kind when she added, "I think we're close though." She laughed quietly, "You'll probably know who he is before we do."

Mara did not want that to be the case. If the killer knew how to find her, and knew that she was talking to the authorities, he'd probably come after her. The thought was paralyzing.

"Well, I hope you find him soon," Mara replied lamely. It sounded stupid, but she meant it.

After the phone call, she went down and ate with her mom. Josie and Ben were still asleep though she knew they'd be up soon. Out the window, she could see that there weren't as many reporters parked out front as usual, maybe only one or two. Word must have leaked about either Colt's arrest or his suicide. Either way, Mara Johnson wasn't as news worthy any more.

Mara called Zia after breakfast and asked her to bring Kimiko over to her house after school. It would be a long wait for Mara, but she had to talk to the Homecoming Princess. She told Zia everything and her best friend promised to deliver Kimiko.

The rest of the day went as slowly as possible. Trying to distract herself with homework only reminded Mara of school. Colt and Kimiko had always been such a sore spot for her teenage existence. Now one of them was gone, dead, and in his spirit's last minutes he had decided to come to Mara. Of course, out of all the people Colt knew, he understood that Mara was probably the only one who could communicate with him, but it was intimate in a way Mara couldn't shake.

Thoughts of their dream conversation inevitably led back to Colt admitting that he knew the killer. Unfortunately, the guy was popular, so that could mean half the school if the killer was a student. Mara wracked her memory, trying to recall who Colt hung out with, who he seemed to like, who he seemed to hate… Was he scared of anybody? It didn't seem so, but apparently Colt was a good actor. She never would have known that his dad beat him. Although, she didn't know Adam's dad beat him either. Apparently, Mara wasn't very good at certain observations. She guessed the reason was because her dreams were so violent that seeing it in real life didn't register when she was awake. But others didn't know, either. Adam and Colt hid their secrets well. Even from someone like her.

As if Adam were reading Mara's mind, he texted her: *whatcha doing?*

She texted back: *Aren't you in class? They're going to take your phone away.*

Adam: *Don't care. It's worth it to talk to you.*

Mara: *ur cute.*

Adam: *no ur.*

Mara smiled. She knew where this was going. A long battle of determining who was the cutest between the two of them. It meant he was bored. And adorable.

Mara: *we'll have to meet tomorrow though. Kimiko is coming over today. You know, after everything that happened.*

Mara had told Adam about her dream earlier that morning by text, so he understood immediately.

Adam: *no worries. I'm surprised she even came in today. Maybe you can help her.*

Mara: *I hope so.*

Mara and Adam's texting match went on for another hour or so until Mara heard a knocking on the front door.

Signing off with Adam, Mara walked to the door and took a deep breath. When she opened it, Zia and Kimiko were waiting outside. Zia gave Mara a look of encouragement, while Kimiko's whole demeanor was of devastation. Colt's death had wrecked her.

"Come on in." Mara held her hand out for the two to enter.

They settled on the couches in the living room and Claire brought out some snacks.

Mara sat across from the two girls.

Kimiko's eyes were red from crying. It was as if she was a broken toy that no matter how many times you try to wind it up, it just won't move.

So Mara decided to start. "I know you know about my dreams."

"Yeah, so," Kimiko replied. Even in her grief she could still give attitude.

Mara chose to ignore it under the circumstances.

"Colt wanted me to tell you that he loved you." Mara hated it when she saw psychics on TV telling audience members that their dead relatives had some kind of message for them. It always seemed fake, rehearsed, as if they were taking advantage of people's grief to garner attention for themselves.

Kimiko wiped a fresh set of tears away and turned to Mara. "My grandmother had your gift," she said suddenly. "I think

226

that's why you saw her. Sometimes I see things, too." Her voice was raw from crying.

Sudden clarity flushed through Mara. "You knew about me before Zia told you, didn't you? That's why you hate me."

Kimiko nodded. "I don't really hate you anymore. I did for a long time, but I'm just too tired now." She continued before Mara had time to digest that. "I saw you once in my dreams. You were watching someone getting killed, and I was watching you. It was the worst nightmare of my life. I've never had any kind of dream like that again, thank God. When I woke up my grandmother told me that you were like her and that I should be kind to you because what you see is such a burden."

"Didn't really listen to her on that one." Mara was appalled that Kimiko had not only ignored her grandmother's advice, but did exactly the opposite.

Kimiko shrugged. "I don't know why I treat you the way I do. I just see you and all I can see is that nightmare... and that man... being slashed to pieces." She shuddered. "I just want to kick you or something. Like it would erase the images from my head." Kimiko appeared to be growing angrier by the second. "And when when Zia told me you saw Grandma die? I hated you even more."

Before Kimiko turned into a raging bitch, Mara decided to bring the conversation back to Colt. "Well, Colt visited me after *he* died and just wanted me to tell you how he felt."

Kimiko's anger subsided. Fresh tears formed in her eyes. "Was that all he said?"

Mara watched for Kimiko's reaction when she said, "Colt said he knew who killed all those people."

227

Kimiko's eyes widened. She glanced around the room as if the killer would jump out of the woodwork. "He told you?" She was incredulous.

Mara's heart almost stopped. The way she said it implied that Kimiko might know who the murderer was so she nodded, seeing if Kimiko might slip.

But Kimiko shook her head in frustration. "He wouldn't even tell me." Her expression was fearful. "Who is it?"

And fail.

Mara decided to come clean since she wouldn't be able to keep up the ruse much longer anyway. "He didn't tell me. I thought you might know."

Kimiko was instantly angry again. "You're playing games with me? After my boyfriend killed himself?!" She stood up. "I have to go."

Mara stood up with her. "Please, Kimiko, don't go. I know you're connected to this somehow. I'm sorry I tried to trick you. I just… I have to find this guy. I can't take this much longer."

Kimiko softened a little, but still had an air of defensiveness. "You think I wouldn't go to the police if I knew? The only thing I'm sure of is that Colt knew the guy." Kimiko sat down, leaning back on the couch. "Colt started spending more and more time away from me. At first I thought he was seeing another girl, but when I followed him one night I could tell he was with a guy. I never saw him though. I was so relieved he wasn't cheating, I ran. I asked him about it later and he got so angry with me." She unconsciously touched her cheek. "He hit me. Remember when I didn't come to school for two weeks last spring?"

Best two weeks of Mara's life. "Yes."

"I had to wait until the bruising went down enough so that I could cover it up with make-up. Colt was devastated. I don't know if you know, but his father hurts him. He hides it with football, telling his teammates that he bruises easily. He's…" her throat caught from emotion.

"Colt was terrified of becoming his dad. I forgave him, of course, but he became super-paranoid. He didn't want me knowing what he was up to or who he was seeing. Then one day he just became normal again. He still left for hours at a time seeing whoever it was he was seeing, but I didn't question it because he was acting like his old self. He never hit me again and I thought everything was back to normal.

"It wasn't until you hurt him at the café that Colt changed again. He got so violent. I thought for sure he was going to hit me again. He told me what I needed to say and how I should act. He said it was because the video put a spotlight on him. It scared him more than anything, especially when the press followed him around. That was why he didn't come to school and he wouldn't let me, either. He was afraid I'd say something. I don't even know what he thought I'd say." Kimiko seemed happy to be unleashing her load on Mara and Zia. "That was when he told me he knew the killer. That the guy was some sort of psychic and that you dreamed all of his murders. I knew your visions were true because of my grandma, so it scared me even more. I thought I was going to die."

Images of Kimiko's rotting corpse from Mara's dream played in her mind. She tried to focus.

"Do you think Colt was protecting the killer?" Mara wondered. Colt said he knew the killer in Mara's dream, but he refused to name him. Was that because they were friends? He could have been scared because he was afraid his friend would get caught. But he seemed scared for his life. But why would he be scared for his life if he killed himself? Death wasn't his ultimate fear, obviously. Was he scared for someone else's life? Kimiko's? None of it made sense.

Kimiko shrugged at a loss. "I really don't know if Colt was protecting him or not. But Colt said that you and the killer were really connected. That the killer could feel you inside his head. This is all too weird for me." Tears welled up again. She blew her nose in a tissue.

Terror seized Mara.

The killer knew. *Really* knew that Mara could see through his eyes. And he knew there was a connection, too.

Mara couldn't shake the feeling…

That she was next.

Dream Entry #17

If I keep waking up in the middle of the night I think I'll go insane. My nightmares are getting more and more chaotic. Kimiko took off after her confessional and it left me feeling even more unsettled than ever. This guy that was running around murdering people knew I was in his head. It was confirmed by Kimiko. I had suspected, but now I knew and that made it all the more terrifying.

The dream I had tonight though, it was telling me something. I just have to figure out what.

I was tracking down a serial killer. In the dream, I was some kind of hunter that knew how to find them. I was afraid, but I was ready for a fight as well.

My surroundings were strange and surreal, as if I was in some kind of apocalyptic forest with overgrown trees and plants, mixed with jagged cement blocks and the ruins of a city.

I was suddenly in front of the biggest tree I had ever seen. Its trunk was the circumference of a small house and I couldn't even see its top the bole was so tall.

But I knew the killer was inside, waiting, drawing me in. Whoever it was, he knew I was coming and he knew that I was there already.

I looked down and saw a syringe in my hand. The syringe. I had the killer's weapon and I planned on using it if I had to. I gripped it tightly and found the entrance to the inside of the tree.

The interior was dimly lit, but I could see every detail. Though the ground was soft soil, the walls and ceiling were draped with red velvet. It almost seemed like blood, the red was so vibrant despite the small amount of light.

I saw the killer then.

Lying on a bed of velvet.

I approached cautiously, surveying the room for traps or hidden attackers.

When I was near enough to see him, I stopped in shock.

It was me.

I was the killer, laying there, staring at me.

I wasn't sure what to do.

Then my doppelganger spoke. She told me that I was born to kill. That the purpose of my dreams was to show me the right path.

I knew she was wrong, but I couldn't speak. It was as if she had some kind of power that prevented me from talking.

In my dream I somehow knew that she had caught some kind of virus. A virus that turned you into a serial killer. If I didn't kill the virus I knew that I would become her. I would become my darkest nightmare and finally succumb to everything that I'd seen. As if it hadn't been real. As if my own mind had made it all up and now I'd have to act on it. As if I'd been seeing all these horrendous things over my lifetime because it was my destiny to kill.

Her face began to transform and stretch as if the virus turned her into some kind of creature or demon. She tried to snatch my arm, but I pulled back. Her skin rotted before my eyes and she screamed that I had to do what I was born to do, or I would melt like her. I froze in place from the grotesque sight. I wanted to help her, but I didn't want to go near her.

The syringe in my hand began to burn.

I lifted it, thinking I should end her agony.

Instinct, though, told me it was trap. She wanted me to kill her. Once I did we would somehow fuse. She was the darkness inside me. She was the virus itself.

If I killed her, I'd become her.

Then I heard another voice behind me.

I turned and saw Great Uncle John. He was scared and worried as he held out his hand. I found the ability to move and reached for him. Grabbing me, he yanked me out of that dream space inside the tree and brought me to the sunflower garden in his backyard.

I instantly felt safe.

He touched my cheek affectionately, then said, "I love you, Mara."

It was so real my eyes filled with tears. I missed him so much. "I love you too, Uncle John."

Then he turned his head toward the sky. The sun slammed down, just as it had before in my other dream. It was immediately almost black it was so dark. Only the silhouettes of my uncle and his sunflowers remained visible.

I heard his voice coming from the shadows, "You can find the answer in the files."

I asked him what files he was referring to, but he didn't elaborate. He simply pointed to the profile of one of his flowers and said, "You're in danger, Mara. Watch out for the sunflower."

Then I woke up.

I had been so close to melding with "evil-me." I'm trying to figure out what it means, but it seemed more like a movie, too disjointed to gain any real meaning. I had a millions guesses, but nothing solid.

If my great uncle hadn't pulled me out I think I'd still be stuck in that tree. But what he said to me was still ringing in my ears: You're in danger, Mara. Watch out for the sunflower.

Not creepy at all, but since my uncle said it, you can bet your ass I'll be looking for sunflowers.

The one thing he did say that made a little more sense was: You can find the answer in the files.

I'm assuming he meant the police files? Or the FBI files? Good places to start, anyway.

I guess I'm calling Agent Piper in the morning.

***

Falling asleep was a lot harder than Mara anticipated, but eventually she dozed off and even managed to grab a few real hours of sleep. As soon as she woke up she called Agent Piper and asked if she could meet her at her FBI office, but Agent Piper informed her that she was at the police station that day. Mara really didn't want to go down to the police station again, she'd much prefer an "FBI safe-zone," but she figured Agent Piper would probably have the files with her. So wherever Piper was, that was where Mara needed to be.

Agent Piper offered several times to come to her, but Mara insisted that her mother didn't want the FBI around for a while. It was a complete lie, but eventually Agent Piper relented.

Mara explained to her mother that Agent Piper needed to see Mara at the station because the FBI had some pictures to show her. Lame excuse, but at least Mara wasn't lying about where she was going. Hopping in her VW Bug, she drove to the station in less than ten minutes. She wished Adam was with her. It would help to have someone distract her from the anxiety roiling around in her belly. Mara didn't want to think about how she was going to pull this caper off. It would come to her when she got there. She hoped.

As Mara entered the daunting building, she began to lose her gumption. But keeping one foot in front of the other, Mara found herself at Agent Piper's temporary office in no time. She had passed Detective Nicholson along the way, but the detective barely acknowledged Mara's existence. She figured Nicholson was still a little bitter about how everything had gone down.

Once this killer was caught, everyone would be happy, including the detective. So, Mara had to see those files. Her great uncle seemed to think that as soon as Mara read them, she'd have everything figured out.

"Come on in." Agent Piper waved for Mara to enter.

Mara did as she was told and sat down on the chair across from the FBI agent. The room was cramped, with a metal desk in the center and a row of filing cabinets on the left side.

Mara's heart raced when she saw a small stack of files on Agent Piper's desk lying before her. Since Agent Piper had just been thumbing through them before she walked in, Mara knew they were about the case.

"Now, what was it that you had to tell me that you couldn't tell me at your house?" Agent Piper eyed her curiously.

Mara played it cool. "I probably could have told you there, I just had to get out for a bit, you know?"

Agent Piper seemed to buy it, nodding, then asked, "Did you have another dream?"

Yes. But Mara didn't want to discuss it with her. It was too personal. Too weird. And she wasn't quite sure what it all meant yet, so she decided to keep it to herself. "No, but I think I know what my other dream with Kimiko means and I wanted to see what you thought." Not true, but Mara needed Agent Piper interested.

Which she was. "Please." She waved for Mara to continue.

"Do you think I could have a glass of water?" Mara asked as pathetically as possible. She was relying on the fact that Agent Piper was well-mannered and would leave her desk to go retrieve water for Mara.

"Of course. There's a water cooler, just outside my office." She nodded toward the door.

No such luck.

"Uh, thanks." Mara now had to leave. Awesome.

Quickly standing, she trudged out to the dispenser. As the large bottle glugged water into Mara's paper cup, she was at a loss. Now what?

She took a sip from her cup, wishing she'd called Zia or Adam for help.

From where she stood, Mara knew that Agent Piper could see her. Desperate times called for desperate measures. She called out as quietly as possible. "I'm just going to go to the bathroom real quick."

Agent Piper nodded and stuck her head back into the files.

Mara walked toward the bathroom and her hands began to sweat.

She had an idea.

The office level of the station was a maze of cubicles, which was perfect for what she had planned.

When she was out of view from Agent Piper's office, Mara pulled out her phone and brought up Agent Piper's number. Ducking into an empty cubicle and praying that whoever's desk it was wasn't coming back, Mara picked up the phone and dialed.

She was always good at making her voice sound different. Her imitation of Taylor Swift was legendary. At least to her family anyway.

The other line picked up. "This is Agent Piper."

Mara went for it, speaking in an unrecognizable higher pitch. "Hi, this is Gretchen from records. Colt Lennox's father is insisting to see you in person. I don't know what to say to him."

"Why would he be in records?"

At least she didn't outright recognize Mara as being on the other end.

"My thoughts exactly. Detective Nicholson told me to call you. She said it was your problem." Mara cringed, hoping she wasn't taking it too far.

She wasn't. Agent Piper sighed heavily. "I'll be right there."

A rush of adrenaline coursed through Mara mixed with a little bit of guilt. Bringing up Colt's dad felt like a dirty trick, but Mara had to see those files.

She peeked her head around the cubicle and watched as Agent Piper left her office.

Mara casually walked back and went straight for the pile of folders on her desk, constantly looking over her shoulder for Agent Piper's inevitable return.

She wasn't sure what she was looking for so she started at the top. Mostly it was information on the arrests, hers included. There were even some notes about Mara's dreams. Agent Piper really did take her seriously. It made her like the Fed even more. Another file was dedicated to the entire hypnosis session. If Mara had more time, she would have been curious to read more, but she knew that wasn't what her great uncle wanted her to find.

Finally, Mara found a document labeled: Profile.

That sounded promising.

She read Agent Piper's notes:

Young, probably in his late teens, early twenties.

Definitely comes from an abusive home. Some kind of vengeance killings? The victims aren't connected, but they all have a history of violence and child abuse.

Trying to find a common denominator.

Foster care? The second two victims used to be foster parents until they were both charged with neglect. Victim number two had been accused of multiple rapes of the minors he had in his care, but was never charged.

The killer may have been in the foster system.

Maybe he's killing for someone else? Some kind of mentor? A gang? More than one person taking out their abusers?

Robert Garner has a sold alibi. He was in Portland that night, four witnesses can attest to that. But something about him rubs me the wrong way. Maybe he's the mentor?

Then who is his student?

Mara Johnson broke into the Garner's house, but why? This is something that killers often do to re-visit the scenes of their crimes. But Mara isn't the killer. I'm positive about that. Did someone tell her to? I found it hard to believe she just wanted to view the crime scene to see if the police missed anything. She's never done that before or since. So why then?

Mara's my only link to the killer because they have some kind of connection whether the killer knows it or not. Maybe he's like her. Maybe he has the visions as well...

Mara stopped reading. Her insides froze.

Adam.

Everything in that profile screamed his name.

Abused. Foster homes. Re-visiting the scene of their crime.

But it couldn't be.

It was just a coincidence.

Adam could never... He would have told her... about the killings... about his dreams... lies... so many lies...

Mara thumbed through the papers, looking for anything that would dissuade her from the line of thinking that ultimately ended in her boyfriend being a serial killer.

That was when she saw it, and the truth was nauseatingly clear.

A picture of the locket from her dream. The locket with the engraved rose that belonged to the dismembered body of the woman from the Crotonal house. It was draped around the neck of a beautiful woman with green eyes and long brown hair.

Mara's heart almost stopped when she read Agent Piper's

scribbled notes on the picture. *DNA match to Joy Layton, Adam Layton's mother. Could he be the student? Did he befriend Mara to insinuate himself in the investigation? Bring him in for questioning.*

Adam was the killer, and Agent Piper was right about Robert Garner. He *was* the mentor. It all clicked into place. Robert talked Adam into this. Mara knew it in her soul. Robert killed Adam's mom to make him think she had abandoned him and convinced him to murder Ed Garner. It took Robert eight years to talk him into it, but Adam finally gave in.

The grotesque body parts hanging from balloons. Those images had come from Robert's twisted mind, not Adam's.

Mara had to get out of there. She needed air.

Not waiting for Agent Piper to return from her ruse, Mara left the station the back way, so no one would see her. As much as she had been trapped at home the last couple of weeks, now it sounded like heaven. She had to think things through. How on earth would she confront Adam? Would he inject her with poison to shut her up? If he was connected to her, maybe now he knew that she was on to him. *Insinuate himself in the investigation.* Was that why he stayed with her? Because she was involved with the case? Would he come after her? Would Robert?

Too many questions raced through her head.

Hurrying across the parking lot, Mara unlocked her door and slid inside.

She was about to turn the key in the ignition when she saw a sunflower growing in the median in front of her car. Mara couldn't believe that she hadn't noticed it before.

Terror seized her.

Watch out for the sunflower.

240

Danger.

On instinct, Mara grabbed the door handle and tried to fly out of her car. Before she could, a cold metal blade pressed up against her throat.

"Normally, I'd inject you with a tranquilizer, but I can't have you falling asleep. I don't know how powerful your mind is and you might warn my boy. You're the only one he'd turn against me for."

Robert.

Mara had met him only once, but she recognized his voice.

Mara had the faint stirring of hope at Robert's words. *You're the only one he'd turn against me for.* Adam. Maybe he wasn't completely gone. Maybe he could be saved.

Maybe I won't die.

It wasn't looking good at the moment, though.

Mara almost puked.

#18

*W*here are we going?

I'm so scared right now, I don't know what to do.

Robert is sitting behind me, telling me where to drive. From the brief encounter I had with that knife, (it's huge!) he could probably stab me right through the seat.

I'm terrified for my life, but I'm more terrified that Adam killed all those people.

Adam!

He is so gentle and kind and loving. How could he have done those things? Agent Piper's notes said the killer only killed people who were abusers themselves. So is Adam some sort of vigilante? When I saw the bruises his father made I'd wanted to kill his dad myself. But I would never actually do it!

I never wanted it to happen, either. Jail, yes. Punished, yes. But death? Death?

I'm seriously going to barf.

Of course I am connected to the killer! He's my boyfriend! How could I have been so blind?

Because I didn't want to see it.

I felt so safe with Adam.

I still love him.

Robert hacked Adam's mother to pieces and then brainswashed him. He must have. Even Agent Piper thinks that there was some kind of teacher/student thing going on.

I want to cry.

I can't justify Adam's actions no matter how hard I try.

And I want to.

I want to with all my being.

I love him, and he loves me.

Robert said so himself. He's afraid that Adam will be loyal to me, not to him.

Robert doesn't want me to fall asleep because he thinks I'm powerful enough to contact Adam. Is he serious? Could *I do that? If I can, I've got zero clue as to how.*

If Adam is like me maybe I could talk to him while I'm unconscious. He could tell Agent Piper what happened and they could rescue me. If he wants to rescue me. Maybe he doesn't. Maybe he wants me dead so he won't get caught or, worse, so he can kill some more. He must be way more experienced than me with the whole dream thing. I can't control shit, but he was able to control his dreams to prevent me from seeing him! He has way more abilities than I do.

Maybe that can save me.

I don't want to die.

"Turn here," Robert instructed Mara.

They were somewhere in an industrial area on The Sound. The stench of polluted water filled Mara's nostrils with disgust. But she'd give anything to jump into the decrepit, freezing water just to swim away from Robert and to safety.

Mara didn't want to die, but she knew she was going to.

She was going to die and she was still taking directions from the man that planned on doing it.

Why?

Why was she still driving? She should crash her car and run. She should swerve into a pole. Anything! But no matter how much she wanted to. Mara couldn't. It was as if Robert controlled her. As if she was a puppet and was trapped inside her own body with no power over her actions.

Why?

The fear of the knife was too powerful. The immediate danger outweighed the abstract danger. She still thought she could run away once they parked. Mara was too afraid she'd die trying to escape before then, and it froze her to inaction.

"Up here, park there." Robert pointed with the knife.

Like the marionette she was, Mara did exactly as he ordered.

"Out." Robert held the knife to her throat as Mara opened the door and the two of them exited the vehicle.

They were parked between two large warehouses, abandoned years ago. Mara wondered when the last time anyone had ever set foot in this area besides the Charles Manson wannabe over here.

Adam had.

If he was Robert's protégé then this must be their hang out.

Or protégés.

Colt.

It made sense now. Colt was also one of Robert's underlings. He was protecting Adam that night he killed himself. That must have been the "secret friendship" Kimiko stumbled upon. And the fear in Colt's eyes was of Robert not Adam. Colt must have thought that Mara would have turned Adam in if Colt confessed to who the killer was. Or worse: Robert could have hacked up Adam like he had chopped up Adam's mother.

Mara wished Colt had had more faith in her, but she understood his reasoning.

She probably *would* have turned Adam in. Not because she wanted Adam punished, but because she wanted him to stop. If Mara could reverse Robert's brainwashing, then maybe Adam could be normal again. Screwed up, but not murder-y.

Feeling the tip of the blade pressed sharply against her back, Mara let Robert lead her inside the warehouse to the right.

Inside, Mara changed her opinion of this being their hangout. From the inch of dust on the floor, she could tell no one had been inside for a long time. Then it occurred to her that Robert would never take her to a place Adam knew about. If Robert was worried about Adam flipping sides, then he'd take her somewhere Adam would never find them. Where no one would ever find them. Like Robert had done with Adam's mother when he murdered her.

Fantastic.

Prodding Mara with the knife, Robert guided her to a small office in the corner of the giant empty space. A stack of chairs rested against the wall. Grabbing one with his free hand, he motioned for Mara to sit. Since no one had paid the electricity bill in a while, the only light came from a skylight on the roof.

This was the moment.

Kick his groin and run.

But the knife… his strength… his bulk… his speed…

If Robert wanted Mara dead, she'd be dead already.

Right?

The instant of hope passed as hard plastic zip ties locked Mara's hands and feet to the chair. The chair was against a wall and Mara rested her head against it in an attempt to calm her nerves.

Once she was secure, Robert rummaged through his jacket and pulled out a syringe.

It was more horrifying than the knife. All Mara could see was the memory of her dreams and the poison injected inside of the victims. "You're going to kill me."

"No, but I need to give this to you." Robert took a step closer.

On closer observation, Mara realized that the liquid inside the syringe was a different color than the concoction used on Mr. Garner and the others. "You're not going to give me drugs, are you?" Mara sounded just as horrified. "Anyone who knows me knows I would *never* do drugs, so if you have some stupid plan to make it look like I overdosed or something, it won't work. No one will believe you. And Agent Piper already suspects you. She's already figured out that the killer has a leader or something. So she's on to you, asshole." Mara wasn't sure why she was revealing so much to him, but the thought of being injected with something like heroin or any other drug was almost as terrifying as being injected with poison.

Robert squeezed out the excess liquid from the vial and walked over to her side. "Relax. It's just adrenaline. I told you, I don't want you falling asleep."

He stuck the needle into her neck and Mara felt a sharp pain as he injected the substance.

Mara felt an instant rush. It was like drinking eighteen cups of coffee all at once.

She couldn't breathe.

Mara gasped and her whole body shook. She was going to die. Die. Something went wrong. Whatever Robert had just done was going to kill her. Kill her! The world spun, her vision grew dark. She was about to pass out.

SLAP!

Mara jolted out of the sensations that threatened to take over her body. Robert was shaking her shoulders.

"You're having a panic attack and I can't have you passing out," he said sharply. "Breathe in for five counts, hold it, then out for five counts and hold it."

Mara was so desperate to not feel like dying, she did as she was told. Within seconds, she was charged with an adrenaline high, but relaxed enough that she wasn't panicking.

"Why are you doing this?" Mara couldn't fathom why Robert was going through all this trouble if his plan was to kill her.

"Because, despite what you think, I don't want to kill you, Mara. You're one of the good guys. *I'm* one of the good guys. I know you don't see it yet, but I brought you here to convince you," Robert pleaded.

Mara was incredulous. She stared at him for a few seconds in disbelief.

Then finally she found her voice. "Are you kidding me right now? You kidnap me by knife point, bring me to some crazy-ass abandoned warehouse, tie me to a chair, inject me with a liquid panic attack, and *you're* one of the good guys? I'd hate to meet a bad guy." Mara didn't mention Adam's mom for fear of Robert killing her on the spot. If Adam ever found out, he'd probably try to kill Robert. No. She had to keep that particular piece of knowledge to herself.

"You've met many bad guys. Hundreds of them. In your dreams. You're just like Adam. Special. I first met him eleven years ago when Adam's mom used to clean our house. I saw his bruises and knew his dad was the same kind of monster as mine. A few years later I volunteered at abuse shelters and his mother had brought him there, trying to get away from his dad. His mother only lasted two days in the shelter before she realized how hard it would be to live on her own while supporting a ten-year-old." Robert spoke of Adam's mother with disdain. Considering how he'd chopped her up, Mara wasn't surprised at his tone.

"My mother was worse, of course. Complete denial. My father's favorite pastime was beating me. To 'teach me respect and make me a man.' All bull shit. He loved feeling the power and he loved getting away with it. Everyone in the neighborhood thought he was the greatest guy on earth. I bet you even liked him, didn't you?" Robert prompted Mara.

If he was talking, she had a chance of escaping, so Mara nodded. "No one knew he was violent, if that's what you're asking."

Robert sat on the edge of a metal desk, contemplative. "His violence went beyond a standard abuse." He laughed, though there was no humor in it. "Ed Garner would have been better off if he had just hired a sadomasochist and been done with it. I still have scars." Robert pulled his shirt up to expose long worm-like marks stretching up his chest.

"Can you skip to the part where you talked my boyfriend into killing your dad?" Mara's patience had run dry. She would almost feel sorry for the guy if he weren't… crazy! Sure he had been through a lot. Sure he had been tortured by his own father but…

What was the 'but'?

Mara was conflicted.

Robert was the product of a cruel and horrible man's sickness.

She was angry because he seemed to have inherited the *sickness* part by talking a ten-year-old boy into becoming a murderer.

Robert sighed. "I know you think I'm a monster for shaping Adam into who he is today. But he's *free*, Mara. He's free from ever feeling helpless again! I showed Colt the way as well, but he was older and already set in his fear. It was too much for him and he took the easy way out."

He walked over to Mara and kneeled before her. "Adam and I have a mission and you're getting in the way." He smiled. "But you can join us. You can help us find the people who don't deserve to live on this planet. The people who hurt innocent people. That's what Adam is trying to do with his gift. He's our eyes. But you could be our eyes too." His face was full of hope.

"So you're saying those two other men he killed after your dad were from his dreams? That he somehow tracked them down and killed them?" It would be impossible to find a connection between the victims if Adam was picking them based on his

249

visions. But they both recognized Adam. He *knew* them and they knew him.

Robert answered, "Using dreams, that's our plan for the future. But those two men were different: they did unspeakable things to Adam when he was in foster care. Not just to Adam, to other kids as well. Adam saved a lot of lives by taking them out. And you could too."

"Or what? You'll kill me? *I'm* an innocent. According to your little code, you can't kill me." Mara tried to catch Robert in his holier-than-though logic spiel. Although she already knew he was willing to break that code when he murdered Adam's innocent mom.

"There's always collateral damage," Robert confirmed Mara's point. "If I have to, yes, I will kill you." His optimist energy returned. "But I don't want to, Mara. We can work together. You can be a part of our mission."

Her heartbeat on overdrive due to the adrenaline pumping through her system, Mara thought her eyes were going to pop out of their sockets. "I can't kill people, even if they're murderers." Mara didn't want to justify herself to someone like Robert, but it was the truth. As horrendous as the visions of crimes she had experienced in her life, Mara could never exact revenge on them. Not even on her great aunt, who killed the only grandfather figure she'd ever known. It wasn't in her. Sure, in theory, what Robert suggested was very Punisher-esque: kill the people who kill. But in reality it was so much more.

"You wouldn't have to hurt anyone. You and Adam would just tell me where to find the killers and Adam and I would handle the rest." Robert tried to assuage her fears.

But that was when she knew.

Robert had the virus.

The disease from her dream. The insatiable desire to kill.

Robert had enough of a conscience left to want to target and kill the "bad men," but he still had an impulse he couldn't shake. Probably ever since he had his first taste after murdering Adam's mother.

Mara knew Adam had killed three people, but she couldn't believe he was like Robert. Maybe he could still be saved. Adam had no father figure that was worth a damn and the one guy who understood him, taught him how to hide his bruises, who treated him the way a father should... told him to kill.

Adam had been ten.

It was no wonder he had finally given in. The fact that it had taken Adam eight years to agree to take a life, after being constantly beaten down physically, then beaten down mentally...

Adam may have killed, but he was just as much a victim as the men he murdered.

And Mara needed to talk to him.

How?

Sure, Robert seemed to think that it was possible to somehow dream-talk, but Mara wasn't so certain. She knew it could be done by the dead – Colt had talked to her, Uncle John – but the whole point was *not* to die. Adam was apparently good at the task, but it was the middle of the day. He was at school. It wasn't like he took naps or anything. Even if he did Adam wouldn't know to look for Mara. Nope. She was royally screwed. She had to get the heck out of there.

But Robert was never going to let that happen without Mara

agreeing to work with them. She was tempted to just lie and say she was on board, but she knew on some level that it didn't matter what she said.

Robert planned on executing Mara whether she agreed to his terms or not.

She had dreamt of enough psychopaths to recognize one.

In Robert's eyes, Adam's mom had planned to take Adam away from him and now so was Mara.

The only way Mara was escaping was to get help.

And the only way she could get help was to escape.

"Why are you so worried about me falling asleep? Mara asked. "Adam is awake. It's not like I can connect to him."

Robert was very adamant about keeping her from sleeping. He had to know that Adam was in school. So why was he so scared?

Robert stared at her for a few beats, thinking who-knows-what, then he answered, "Adam doesn't tell me much about his gift."

Mara guffawed, trying to appear as is she were relating to Robert. "Join the club. I didn't even know he had dreams like me. But that's all they are: dreams. If I could talk to him in his head, I'd be able to do that awake a lot better than asleep. And as you can see, no one is coming."

She could tell Robert was feeling out whether he could trust her or not. "Better safe than sorry, right?"

Mara didn't answer. His answer basically added up to a never-ending streamline fuel of adrenaline until she either died of a heart attack, or had perma-insomnia. Both options were pretty horrible.

Even though she had been trying to gain a tiny bit of Robert's trust, part of what Mara said really did bother her. Adam had never told her about his dreams. She'd been so honest with him and he had flat-out freaked out when she first told him. Was that reaction faked for her benefit? Maybe hearing how detailed her dreams were made him think she'd find out that he was the murderer? Adam must have already known about her gift. Why else would he have randomly decided to text her the morning of Ed Garner's murder?

At this point she could speculate all she wanted, but Mara had to free herself first. If she could convince Robert that she was willing to play ball, maybe she could find a way out. Mara tried to be as persuasive as she could saying, "Okay. I'll do it. I'll join your little club. I just want to talk to Adam first."

Robert watched her carefully. After a few agonizing seconds that felt like an eternity, he finally nodded. "You'll have to understand that I don't trust you yet. I'll give you some time to think things through, then, maybe… I'll bring Adam here."

"I don't have to think things through. I'm in," Mara pushed it.

Robert shook his head. She was losing him. "You need some time alone. But since I can't have you falling asleep…" He pulled out a small medical bottle full of the same liquid as before and filled the syringe again.

Mara panicked. "No, please. I'm so amped up. I swear, there's no way I could fall asleep!"

"Well, this will guarantee it." Robert had an expression of sympathy, but his eyes told another story. He enjoyed torturing her.

Mara had to brace herself as he injected her with another dose of adrenaline.

Her heart raced uncontrollably, but she tried to hide her discomfort from Robert. She didn't freak this time. Her body was growing used to the flush through her system. It made her a little nauseous, but Mara managed to keep the contents of her stomach in check.

It went on for hours like that. Talk for a bit. Robert drilling her on her intentions, trying to catch her in a lie, seeing if she was really on Team Killer. She'd had enough dreams in her life to know what to say, but Mara knew it would take more than a day to convince him, if ever. His kill-face had let up a little, though, and she marked that up to baby steps.

Robert left a few times throughout the day to buy food, or do something nefarious. Mara had no clue. She tried to break free, but the zip ties were solid.

He fed her a fast food hamburger with his hands. In those moments Robert was so nurturing, so caring, making sure she chewed every bite before placing the burger back in her mouth. She could see how an abused child like Adam would feel instantly connected to Robert. Being fifteen years older, he must have been the older brother Adam always wanted and secretly prayed for.

The nicer Robert was, the more she hated him. Hated him for doing what he had done to Adam.

It was easier to hate him when he pumped her full of adrenaline. He kept the dosages regular, one every couple of hours or so. Mara had never been so awake in her life. She knew it couldn't be good for her. She hoped she lived long enough to escape.

They were in the middle of a philosophical discussion about why she and Adam were given the gift of visions when Robert's phone rang.

Instantly, Mara's heart raced and not from the adrenaline shots. Was it Adam? She readied herself to scream for help, but Robert must have had the same idea because before answering the phone he grabbed a roll of duct tape and stuck a piece of it across her mouth.

Stepping outside the office, Robert answered his phone. His voice was muffled, but Mara could hear his end of the call.

Robert's voice sounded calm and sympathetic. She knew at once it wasn't Adam. Whoever was on the other line was someone Robert wanted to impress.

"Yes. Hello." Beat. Beat. "It's a little late, but, no, I'm not busy at all. I'd love to meet you, just tell me where." Beat. "Perfect. I'll see you in an hour."

Robert walked back into the office and ripped the tape off Mara's mouth. His eyes were sad, distant. "I'll be back in a bit." Then he shrugged. "It's your fault, really. You're the one who told me Agent Piper was on to me. Thank you for that. But now it looks like she's going to have to have an accident."

Agent Piper.

She was with the FBI and she already suspected Robert. There was no way he could gain the upper hand on her.

But he was so confident. A true predator.

"Wish me luck," Robert said as if he were talking about going out on a date.

Mara stayed silent, not wanting to provoke him into killing her on the spot.

Mara groaned inwardly as Robert gave her another shot of adrenaline. "Can't have you sleeping while I'm away."

His mind shifted to his destination and he left the office.

The most important part of his phone call: when he'd said "It's a little late…"

Darkness had fallen hours ago, only Robert's flashlight gave any illumination to the room, but…

Mara prayed it was late enough for Adam to be sleeping. She knew what she had to do.

When she heard the clanking of the warehouse door shut closed, Mara was alone. With the adrenaline surging through her, Mara knew she only had one choice to make it to dreamland.

Here goes nothing.

Mara smashed the back of her head against the wall as hard as she could.

She had a faint smile of satisfaction as she lost consciousness.

#19

I'm back in my old dream with the trapped tornado and the mansion, but Great Uncle John and Kimiko are no longer with me. I'm standing in front of the oil tower that holds the tornado in place. I'm not sure what to do. Should I call Adam? Why am I here? Is my body okay back in that warehouse? I've left myself so vulnerable to get here and now that I'm here, I don't know what to do.

I'm dreaming, I know that: I'm conscious of the fact that I'm dreaming. That has to be a good sign, right?

This is all too weird. How on earth can I find Adam while I'm unconscious? I was counting on the fact that he is so much better at this than me. But, even if Adam finds me here, will he even want to talk to me? What if he already knows Robert has me and he doesn't care? How much of our relationship has been real?

Looking at the tornado is insane. It's huge, especially up close, and more violent than I remembered.

My mind took me here for a reason. The more I think about it, the more torrential the wind blows, to the point where I need to back up a few paces just to keep my footing.

I'm screaming out Adam's name as loud as I can… but nothing.

I figure I'm in my own dream space, so I have no idea if he'll hear me.

After a few moments of waiting, I peer over the edge of the cliff. It is a long way down, but I went to the canyon's floor the first time around in this dream locale, so I feel like I should do the same now.

The sun is up and the planets are surrounding it in a circle, large as life, same as before.

If I climb to the bottom of the canyon, it should become night, like last time.

I feel blocked from indecision.

But I'm on a time clock because Agent Piper's life is in danger now too.

"Adam!" I can hear my scream echo down the canyon. "I know you killed those people! We need to talk!" Maybe he was scared that I didn't know he was the killer yet.

The tornado is growing in front of my eyes, the metal of the oil tower screeching in protest. I don't know how much longer it can hold in the storm.

I keep thinking of Kimiko and how she told me in the last dream I had in this place that she didn't think this was the way that Dorothy found Oz.

Then it hits me.

All my dreams about Kimiko were really about me. She had just been the messenger.

My subconscious was trying to tell me the killer was Adam from

258

the beginning.

Like she had said in my first dream of her when she 'needed more pieces to a puzzle that was already solved.' That was me having Adam in my life, the puzzle was completed, but I kept shoving in new pieces to create a different picture, a different future.

And this tornado.

It contains all of the rage, the violence, the visions — all wrapped up in a whirlwind of black debris and destruction. Trapped inside me, fighting to let loose.

And, like Dorothy, the lesson was that the answer has all been in front of me the whole time.

Adam killed those people.

My subconscious knew it.

My awakened self ignored it.

The tornado instantly disappeared in a single puff of smoke, now all that's left is an empty oil tower.

"Mara?"

I turn around and see Adam standing in front of the mansion. His expression seemed confused and terrified, all rolled into one.

I want to run into his arms and tell him we'd fix this. We'll find some way to repair everything he had done, but I can't. I can't change what he did. I can't bring those people back to life.

So I stay where I am. "Adam, I know everything," I confess.

His eyes start watering and he quickly wipes the sudden tears away. "I never wanted you to know."

I take a step closer to him. "Why?" I can hear my voice turn cold as I sputter, "You seemed to enjoy it."

Adam looks horrified. He shakes his head. "No. I never enjoyed it. I did what had to be done. You have to believe me, Mara. My dreams have been leading me to this path my whole life. Robert showed me the way, how I was destined to see these monsters so I could hunt them down and do good in this world."

"It's not good to kill people," my voice chokes out.

"It is when they're evil. You have no idea what Ed Garner did to Robert his whole life! And Derek? He raped all the girls in my foster home and no one did anything about it! And Frank was a crack addict who beat one of my foster brothers until he died. I did the world a favor, trust me." As he confesses, his body language grows more confident.

"You could have gone to the police." I'm hearing what he's saying and my heart wants to accept that what he did is right, but my mind holds me back.

Adam laughs. "The police? That's a joke. I did go to the police, many, many times and you know what they did?"

I shake my head.

"They'd transfer me to a different foster home. That's it. I know you have all this faith in the system, but you don't know what it's really like out there, Mara." He takes a step closer to me, we are only a few feet apart now. "You are so lucky, you have no idea. You have a family and friends who love you and believe in you. I never had any of that until I met Robert."

Seeing Adam in front of me, so vulnerable…

Robert had taken the essence of a sweet little boy and turned him into an executioner.

Before I can speak, he continues, "I wanted to stop after I killed Ed Garner. I puked all night afterward. But when I saw you on the news the next morning, I knew. I knew you had been with me the whole time in your dream. I recognized you immediately. Even though I had seen you every day for three years, pining over a girl who was way out of my league... I had never seen it before. And when you walked into class, it was like I saw you looking back at me in my dream."

I wished I had had the same revelation that day, but I hadn't. I had been too wrapped up in my feelings for him. "But you lied to me so many times, Adam! You faked your reaction when I told you about my dreams and my aunt," I can't seem to control my anger as I vent at him, "And you went along with everything! Going to the crime scene, me meeting Robert, following Colt... Didn't you think that I'd find out?!"

"Mara, I wanted *you to find out. It was killing me not telling you and hiding this secret. When you shared your secret with me, I wanted to tell you then, but I was afraid... I didn't want to lose you." Adam's eyes look haunted with fear.*

More and more deceptive moments play back in my head. "If you were actually friends with Colt, then was that whole situation at the Café fake?"

Adam seems desperate to explain, "When I knew you had dreams like mine, I had to see what kind of person you were so, yes, I staged that fight with Colt at the café. When you attacked him... It was the best thing that ever happened to me." Adam takes another step toward me and reaches his hand out, touching my face. I let him. Part of me wants to punch him and the other part wants to hold him close and tell him everything is going to be okay.

Adam takes his hand away and his eyes turn distant. "Robert was furious at Colt and me when the video went viral. He was afraid it would draw too much attention."

"Then why would you kill again so soon afterward? Or at all if it

really upset you that much." I take a step back from my rising anger.

Adam acts frantic. "I had to! They'd arrested you. When the cops went to the Garner's and found your DNA, I thought for sure you'd be blamed for what I had done! I couldn't let that happen! If killing that asshole rapist could save you, I had to do it. Your life is more important than his and you'll never be able to convince me otherwise. I didn't regret it the second time. Maybe because I had seen what he had done. I knew he deserved it. I'm sorry, Mara, but he did."

He murdered someone to prove I was innocent. It's either romantic or disgusting. I can't decide which.

And like my other dream, more pieces of the puzzle fit into place. "And you killed the third guy to protect Colt."

Adam nods. "He should have known I'd save him. He knew what I did for you." He looks devastated at losing Colt.

"Colt didn't want to do what you were doing. I see that now. The way he talked to me. He thought he was saving himself from hurting anyone."

My chest aches. Who was braver? Colt: for committing suicide so he wouldn't have to be a murderer? Or Adam: for finding it in him to execute men who lived to hurt innocent people?

Tears flow down Adam's face. "I don't want to do it anymore. I can't. I told Robert last night. I told him I wasn't going to hurt anyone again. I don't care how evil they are. He was so mad, Mara. I don't know what he's going to do." Adam reaches forward again and gently holds my hand. Even in the dream, I can feel the warmth of it. "I went to your house today to tell you everything, but Robert stopped me. He told me you'd hate me forever. I chickened out." His eyes grow round with hope. "But you figured it out anyway. And you're here." Adam tentatively lifts my hand and kisses it softly. "I'm *turning myself in. As soon as I wake up, I'm going to the police and telling them everything. You'll never have to see me again. I promise."*

But that isn't what I want.

Robert should go to jail, not Adam. Or, if Adam does go to jail, it should be for temporary insanity. He wasn't in his right mind. I can see it in his eyes, he doesn't have the psychotic virus. He doesn't relish the kill. He is nothing like the monsters I have nightmares about.

He's a kid that was horribly used and beaten into becoming what he hates most.

To have to live with the kind of dreams I've had to live with and be beaten and coddled by a psychopath? It isn't fair. Adam had been dealt a bad hand and he did the best he could with it. He really thought he was killing monsters, like in a video game, or a movie about justice in vengeance.

I hug him. I just need to hug him. To feel my arms wrap around his fragile soul and try to heal him in some way. Nothing ever can though. He will always be broken. But maybe confessing his crimes will start the mending process. "I'll go with you, so you don't have to be alone." I whisper in his ear.

"I love you so much, Mara."

"I love you, too."

And I do. I truly do.

We are going to get through this together.

I had become so lost in the moment, I had forgotten my current situation. I yank away from him suddenly. Adam looks shocked, but then his chest falls in disappointment. He thinks I've changed my mind and that I want nothing to do with him.

I grab his hand to reassure him. "I came here for a reason, Adam."

He squeezes my hand back, his expression changing to concern.

263

"What's going on?"

"Robert. He kidnapped me this morning. He's keeping me in some kind of abandoned warehouse by the docks, near downtown. He knows I know everything and I was an idiot and told him Agent Piper suspected him. He's on his way to meet her now and I think he's going to kill her. And Adam," I can't hide the fear from my voice. "He's going to kill me too. He thinks I took you from him. He's been shooting me up with adrenaline all day so I wouldn't find you in my sleep, but I smashed my head against the wall pretty hard so I could find you. But, outside of this dream, in the real world, that means I'm still tied to chair and completely vulnerable."

"This is all my fault! I should have turned myself in before I told him anything! I should have known he'd do something like this!" Adam is pacing now, terrified and worried. Then he turns to me and holds my arms with his hands. "I have to wake up now, but I'm coming to get you. Okay?"

I nod. "Just hurry."

He hugs me one last time, then disappears.

***

"Mara, Mara, wake up," Adam's voice called to her.

Mara squinted as she slowly came to. Her heart was still racing from the adrenaline and her head pounded with pain.

It seemed as if she had just left Adam in her dreams, so to see him in front of her was discombobulating.

Her hands and feet snapped free as he cut the zip ties with a Swiss army knife.

She had never been so glad to see someone in her life.

In person, his eyes were tentative and unsure. "We have to get out of here," he instructed cautiously.

Adam obviously wasn't sure how the "awake" Mara was going to act toward him.

But Mara understood Adam better than anyone. She knew what it was like to dream of killers all of her life. If her parents had abused her and she had been influenced by Crazy-Town, she might have gone down the same path. It was impossible to say and, for her, impossible to judge.

All she knew was that she loved him and he loved her. Adam was there to save her, that was all that mattered. She hugged him as fiercely as she had in the dream. His arms were wary at first, then held her tightly in relief.

He examined the back of her head. "It's bleeding. We have to get you to a hospital."

She nodded and let Adam support her as they left the office. "How did you find me?"

"I drove down every single one of these warehouse rows until I found your Bug. Mara, he didn't even hide it." His eyes met hers and he looked frightened.

"He was going to kill me no matter what," she confirmed.

"I called Agent Piper, but she didn't pick up, so I called Detective Nicholson. She said they've been searching for you all day. Your parents are a wreck." Adam handed her his phone. "You should call them."

"Your phone gets one bar of signal. Let's get outside," she said woozily, her world spinning from the combination of the adrenaline and the injury to the head.

The warehouse door swung open.

Through it walked Robert, dragging in a zip-tied Agent Piper.

His eyes went round with fury and shock when he saw Adam and Mara on their way out. Then he smiled angrily. "I knew it. I knew you'd pick this whore over me."

Mara made eye contact with Agent Piper. The agent shifted her eyes toward Robert as if trying to tell her something. Mara tried to see what the woman was signaling to, but she couldn't figure it out.

Adam took Mara's arm off his shoulders and placed her behind him for protection. "I'm going to the police, Robert. It's over."

"It's not over until I say it's over!" Robert screamed, yanking Agent Piper for emphasis. "I'm going to place these lovely ladies into your whore's car and drive them off the dock."

"Not going to happen." Adam guarded Mara fiercely.

Robert's face turned red with frustrated anger. "After everything I've done for you, this is how you treat me?"

Adam nodded toward Mara and then Agent Piper. "They're innocents, Robert. We can't kill them. That's not what you taught me."

"Yeah, well, your mom was innocent too, but she had to die," Robert growled with irritation.

Adam's face turned white. "What?" His voice was small.

"She was going to take you away from me too, run away to Los Angeles or something ridiculous. She was my first kill and it was worth it. You became *mine* that day." Then he looked at Mara with venom. "Then your new little bitch led you straight to the house I killed her in. Right to the table where I hacked her into pieces!"

Mara knew all this, but it broke her heart to see Adam finally learning the truth.

Robert unbuttoned the top button of his shirt to reveal the necklace from her dream: a locket with a rose engraved on its surface. It had belonged to Adam's mother. And Robert wore it as a trophy around his neck. He ripped it from his body and threw it at Adam. "Take it, you ungrateful worm!"

Adam's hands were shaking as he slowly knelt down to pick up the necklace.

Mara could only imagine what was going on in his head. His mother. She hadn't left him. She hadn't deserted him to his abusive father.

Robert had killed her.

Adam stood up, staring at Robert with fury and betrayal. "I won't let you hurt them! You'll have to go through me!"

Robert shook his head.

Mara saw in that instant that Robert was officially "over" Adam.

Before she could react, Robert's words echoed through the warehouse, "You know what? Not a problem."

BAM!

Adam clutched his stomach as the bullet from Robert's smoking gun tore through him.

No.

Mara went to her knees with Adam, his eyes filled with terror. "Adam," she cried out.

When Adam's eyes met hers, he coughed. "Karma, huh?"

"No." Tears streamed down Mara's face.

"Isn't this sweet?" Robert rolled his eyes. "Don't worry, you'll be joining him soon enough. But first…" he turned his gun on Agent Piper.

And Mara saw red.

Adam didn't deserve to die.

Robert did.

Despite her dizziness, Mara used all the adrenaline the monster had injected her with and charged across the three feet that separated them, knocking him to ground.

It took Robert by surprise and caused him to drop his gun.

He was much stronger than Mara, though. He lifted her from his chest and tossed her off. She hit the ground with a thud.

Adam slid his Swiss army knife toward Agent Piper.

She grabbed it, cut her restraints and picked up the fallen gun. Aiming at Robert, she kept her cool as she ordered, "Get up."

Robert carefully stood up with his hands behind his head.

"Mara, grab my cuffs. They're in my back pocket," Agent Piper instructed. Mara did as she was told and the agent continued, "You're going to have to restrain him so I can keep the gun on him, okay?" She spoke calmly to keep Mara steady.

The last thing Mara wanted to do was go near Robert Garner, but she started to walk over there despite her fear.

It was like a horror movie, waiting for the bad guy to attack despite the gun leveled at his body. Mara flinched three times before she was even in arm's distance.

Robert leapt at her.

Mara screamed.

BAM! BAM!

Robert fell to the floor screaming in agony. Agent Piper had shot both his kneecaps.

"I was hoping he'd try something like that." Then she shrugged with a relieved smile. "He should be easy to cuff now."

Agent Piper was on her phone as soon as the writhing beast was secured in his manacles. She called an ambulance for Adam, then Detective Nicholson for police back up.

Everything happened so fast after that.

Mara was put in the ambulance with Adam and before she knew it they were both admitted to the hospital sharing a room.

She had a slight concussion. Robert's bullet had gone clean through Adam. It was going to take a while, but he'd recover. He confessed everything to Agent Piper when she arrived in their room, but she told him they'd talk later. She wasn't surprised by his confession after hearing their conversation in the warehouse. Plus, Mara knew the agent had suspected Robert had a protégé all along.

Detective Nicholson was in hog-heaven arresting Robert, but it was obvious at how she treated Adam, that Agent Piper hadn't told her yet of Adam's involvement. Mara was surprised at how apologetic the detective acted toward her. Mara knew Detective Nicholson had been doing her job and thought she'd caught the killer when she brought Mara in for questioning. The detective's instincts had been right: Mara *had* known more than she let on. But Mara had also been innocent and, by the way Detective Nicholson was treating her now, it was clear that the detective was trying to make up for it.

Mara's family and Zia came to see them, not knowing about Adam's confession either. It was better that way: Mara would tell them later. Adam needed some love and attention right now, not judgment and accusations.

When everyone left and it was just the two of them, Mara slipped out of her bed and crawled into Adam's. He placed his arm around her, gratefulness beaming out of every pore.

"I can't believe you're still talking to me," he whispered.

"If you hadn't found me, I'd be at the bottom of The Sound in my car." Mara knew how close she had come to death.

Adam wasn't letting her give him any credit. "If it wasn't for me, you would have never been put in that position."

"I'll never regret being with you." Mara didn't care if she was being reckless. She had been thinking a lot about what had happened, wondering how she hadn't guessed the killer was Adam. And she realized... she hadn't guessed because Adam was a good person. Messed up, yes. Manipulated, yes. Guilty, yes. But he had done all those horrible things because he thought it was justice for everything that had been done to him and others like him.

"I'll be going to jail for a long time," his voice quavered. "But I'm okay with it."

"I'm not," Mara confessed. "Look, I know what you did. I saw what you did. But you helped save my life and Agent Piper's life. That has to count for something." She was already playing out the trial in her head.

"We'll, see." Adam kissed her head. He unconsciously held his mother's locket that was now around his neck.

She could tell that he didn't want to talk about what happened anymore and she didn't blame him. Confessing to what he had done had given Adam a kind of peace. Robert had murdered Adam's mother to make him feel abandoned. And even then it had taken Robert eight years to convince Adam to kill.

But Robert was gone and Adam was free now.

Soon to be imprisoned, but Adam's heart and soul were his own again.

Mara reached up and kissed him.

It was the first time since all of this happened.

Pulling away, both of them knew it would be their last for a while.

Adam lightly touched his forehead to hers. "Sleep?"

Mara nodded then closed her eyes.

And the two of them dreamed.

Other Books

The Riser Saga:
Riser

Reaper

Ripper

The Atlas Series:
Atlas

Grigori Returned

The Underworld

Riser Saga/Atlas Series Finale:
Atlas Rising

The Dream Diaries:
The Dream Diaries

The Dream Diaries: Blood Ties

Jeraline's Alley

Alexis Tappendorf Series:
Alexis Tappendorf and the Search for Beale's Treasure

Alexis Tappendorf and the Search for Atlantis

Love & Dark Series (with Hina McCord):
Vessel

First Born

Gutian Code

BIOGRAPHY

Becca fell in love with storytelling at an early age. The first book she read was The Lion, The Witch and The Wardrobe and she's been looking for the door to Narnia ever since! Becca is a passionate reader, consuming anything sci-fi or fantasy. Mix it in with YA and she is a fan for life. So it's no surprise that she writes in these genres as well. When Becca isn't writing, she loves to sew. From Mortal Instruments rune pillows, to elaborate Firefly/ Serenity bags, Becca loves to create!

.